All those dragons were creepy enough, but it seemed like every single one of the monsters turned its head, narrowed its eyes, and glared at Devon, Felix, and me as we crept past.

I shivered. Sometimes, I would have been happy not to see so well with my sight magic . . .

We made it to the opposite side of the greenlab, and I sidled up to the glass doors there and peered out into the hallway beyond. The lights were turned down low in this part of the mansion, creating more shadows than not. Just the way I liked it.

Since the coast was clear, I opened one of the glass doors and stepped out into the hallway—

I spotted a glint of metal out of the corner of my eye. Even as I turned toward it, a sword zoomed out of the shadows, heading straight for me.

The Mythos Academy Series
by JENNIFER ESTEP

Touch of Frost

Kiss of Frost

Dark Frost

Crimson Frost

Midnight Frost

Killer Frost

In e-book only

First Frost

Spartan Frost

The Black Blade Series

Cold Burn of Magic

Dark Heart of Magic

Bright Blaze of Magic

Bright Blaze of Magic

JENNIFER ESTEP

KENSINGTON PUBLISHING CORP.
www.kensingtonbooks.com

KENSINGTON BOOKS are published by

Kensington Publishing Corp.
119 West 40th Street
New York, NY 10018

All Kensington titles, imprints, and distributed lines are available at special quantity discounts for bulk purchases for sales promotions, premiums, fund-raising, educational, or institutional use.

Special book excerpts or customized printings can also be created to fit specific needs. For details, write or phone the office of the Kensington sales manager: Kensington Publishing Corp., 119 West 40th Street, New York, NY 10018, attn: Sales Department; phone 1-800-221-2647.

ISBN-13: 978-1-61773-828-9
ISBN-10: 1-61773-828-X

First Trade Paperback Printing: May 2016

10 9 8 7 6 5 4 3 2 1

Printed in the United States of America

First electronic edition: May 2016

ISBN-13: 978-1-61773-829-6
ISBN-10: 1-61773-829-8

As always, to my mom, my grandma, and Andre,
for all their love, help, support, and patience
with my books and everything else in life

ACKNOWLEDGMENTS

Any author will tell you that her book would not be possible without the hard work of many, many people. Here are some of the folks who helped bring Lila Merriweather and the world of Cloudburst Falls to life:

Thanks to my agent, Annelise Robey, for all her helpful advice.

Thanks to my editor, Alicia Condon, for her sharp editorial eye and thoughtful suggestions. They always make the book so much better.

Thanks to everyone at Kensington who worked on the project, and thanks to Alexandra Nicolajsen, Vida Engstrand, and Lauren Jernigan for all their promotional efforts. Thanks to Justine Willis as well.

And finally, thanks to all the readers out there. Entertaining you is why I write books, and it's always an honor and a privilege. I hope you have as much fun reading about Lila's adventures as I do writing them.

Happy reading!

Bright Blaze of Magic

CHAPTER ONE

"You are the worst thief I have ever seen."

Felix Morales frowned, stopped walking, and dropped the black duffel bag he was carrying on the ground. I winced at the *clank-clank* of the items inside the bag banging together.

"Why would you say that?" he asked.

"Oh, I don't know," I sniped. "Maybe the fact that you're tromping through the woods like you are trying to kill every single blade of grass under your feet. Not to mention hacking through the bushes with your sword like we're on a jungle safari. And then of course, there's the talking. There is *always* the talking. It's a wonder you don't pass out from lack of oxygen."

His eyes narrowed. "And what is wrong with having a little light conversation while we hike through the woods?"

"Light conversation? You've been talking nonstop ever since we left the mansion."

"So?"

I threw my hands up in the air. "So you actually have to *stop talking* and *be quiet* to be a thief! That's why!"

Felix gave me a mulish look and started to cross his arms over his chest—until he realized that he was still holding on to his sword, the one he'd been swinging around like a machete for the past twenty minutes. He glared at me, but he finally slid the weapon into the scabbard belted to his waist. Well, that would cut down on some of the noise. Now, if I just had some duct tape for his mouth. . . .

Felix stabbed his finger at the guy standing with us, who was busy setting his own black duffel bag onto the ground, although with far less noise than Felix had made. "And why aren't you lecturing *him* about being quiet?"

"Because Devon can actually walk through the woods without cracking every single branch he steps on."

Felix snorted. "You're just saying that because the two of you have been sneaking around the mansion sucking face for the last two weeks."

I tensed, still not used to having a relationship with a guy, much less talking about it with that guy's best friend. But Devon Sinclair stepped up and slung his arm around my shoulder, pulling me close.

"And it's been the best two weeks of my life," he said, grinning at me.

With his black hair, bronze skin, and dark, soulful eyes, Felix was undeniably cute, but Devon was the one who made my heart race like a tree troll hopping from one branch to another. The setting sun filtering in through the leaves brought out the rich honey highlights in Devon's chocolate-brown hair, even as it cast his handsome face in shadows. But it was his eyes that always hypnotized me—eyes that were the same deep, dark evergreen as the forest around us.

I laid my head on his muscled shoulder and leaned into him, letting the heat of his body soak into my own and his sharp, tangy pine scent seep deep down into my lungs. So far, being with Devon had been a wonderful dream, and sometimes I had to remind myself that we were really—finally—together.

Who would have thought it? Not me, Lila Merriweather, the girl who'd been living on the streets for four years before I'd gone to work for the Sinclair Family earlier this summer. And I'd never expected to fall for Devon Sinclair himself, the Family bruiser and the son of Claudia Sinclair, head of the entire Family.

I might be a great thief, but I wasn't so great when it came to people, preferring to pick their pockets than to make friends with them. But Devon had steadfastly ignored and overcome all my defenses, just by being the kind, caring, genuine, loyal guy he was. I hadn't done a single thing in my life to deserve him, but now that he was mine, I was going to care for and protect him as best I could. Technically, being Devon's bodyguard was one of my jobs within the Family, but he watched out for me just as much as I did for him.

Don't get me wrong. It wasn't like I'd gone *soft* or anything. I still picked plenty of pockets on the streets of Cloudburst Falls, West Virginia, and I wasn't above snatching phones, cameras, and other shiny things from people who could afford to lose them. After all, a girl had to keep in practice. But now I did most of my thieving for the greater good and with a little mob muscle behind me. Like my job tonight. One that Felix was jeopardizing with his constant chattering and tromping around.

Felix rolled his eyes. "Enough with the lovey-dovey stuff already," he groused, grabbing his duffel bag and hoisting it onto his shoulder again, making more *clank-clanks* ring out. "I thought we had places to break into and stuff to steal tonight."

Instead of letting me go, Devon wrapped both arms around me and pulled me even closer. "And you're just jealous that Deah's not here, or you would be doing the same thing with her."

Felix huffed. "Please. I would already be kissing my girl and telling her how beautiful she is—and that's *before* I took her for a moonlit stroll. Totally working my romantic A game from start to finish, which I intend to do the second we sneak into the compound and meet up with her. So, if you'll excuse me, my lady awaits."

He snapped up his hand in a cheeky salute, then whirled around and started stomping through the woods again, making almost as much noise as he had before. He might have put away his sword so that he wasn't hacking through the bushes anymore, but he started muttering instead. Felix wasn't completely happy unless his mouth was going a hundred words a minute, even if he was only talking to himself.

I sighed. "I don't know whether to strangle him or admire his confidence."

"Relax, Lila." Devon turned so that he was facing me, his hands dropping to my waist. "Felix will quiet down once we actually get close to the mansion. He knows how important this is. We all do."

I nodded. "You always know just what to say to make me feel better."

He grinned. "That's part of being a good boyfriend, right?"

I looped my arms around his neck. "The *best* boyfriend."

Devon stared at me, his green eyes glimmering like dark emeralds. My gaze locked with his, and my soulsight—my magic—kicked in, letting me look into the depths of his heart and feel all of his warm happiness flooding my chest as if it was my own emotion. In a way, it *was* my own emotion since I felt the exact same thing whenever I looked at Devon, whenever I heard his voice, whenever I made him laugh or smile or brightened his day in any way.

I stood on my tiptoes and pressed my lips to his. Devon's arms tightened around me, and he kissed me back, our lips coming together time and time again, until I felt as though we were spinning around and around in dizzying circles, even though we were standing still.

"Any time you two lovebirds are ready!" Felix called out, his voice loud enough to make the rockmunks on the forest floor scurry into their stone dens.

Devon and I broke apart, both of us breathing hard and holding on to each other.

"Unfortunately, duty calls," he murmured in a husky voice. "To be continued later?"

I grinned. "You'd better believe it."

Devon and I caught up with Felix, and the three of us headed deeper into the woods.

The summer sun had set while Devon and I had been kissing, and darkness was quickly creeping over the land. We didn't dare use a flashlight, and Devon and Felix fell back, letting me take the lead, since I could still see everything around me as clearly as if it were noon. Not only could I use my rare soulsight magic to look into people and feel what they were feeling, but I also had the much more common and mundane Talent of being able to see everything around me in crystal clarity, no matter how dark it was.

And the place we were going was definitely dark—the Draconi Family compound, home of Victor Draconi, the most powerful person in Cloudburst Falls, the sworn enemy of the Sinclair Family.

And the monster who'd murdered my mom.

The longer we hiked, the darker it got, and the quieter the three of us became. Even Felix stopped talking, dropped his hand to his sword, and scanned the trees around us, though he couldn't see through the thick fog that was slowly sliding down from the top of Cloudburst Mountain and invading the forests below.

Every once in a while, I could hear the faint rush of water in the distance from one of the many waterfalls that tumbled down the mountain. The resulting clouds of mist always cloaked the top of the rugged peak, even during the hottest part of the day, but at night, after the sun had set, the fog grew thicker and thicker and sank lower and lower on the mountain.

But the white clouds did little to hide the eyes that stared at us.

Sapphire blue, ruby red, emerald green. The colors were the same as all the jewels I'd stolen over the years, but these were the bright, glowing orbs of the monsters that called the mountain home—tree trolls, rockmunks, copper crushers, and the like. Some more dangerous than others, but there were plenty of monsters lurking in the trees with enough teeth and claws to make meals out of all three of us.

I didn't mind the cool clouds of mist, the watching monsters, or the soft, shimmering sheen of dew that covered everything. It made for better cover for us.

Because if we were caught, we'd be executed on the spot.

Twenty minutes later, we reached the edge of the trees, crouched down, and peered at the structure before us. Technically, it was a mansion, although the gleaming white stone and architecture made it look more like a castle. Tall, skinny, diamond-paned windows. White trellises with red roses winding up through the slats. Towers topped with red flags bearing the Draconi Family crest of a snarling gold dragon. Everything about the castle made it seem as though it had been dropped on top of the mountain right out of a fairy tale. But there were no happy endings here—just danger, despair, and misery.

Devon, Felix, and I had been sneaking over here every night for the past two weeks on our thieves' errand, and we fell into our usual routine of watching the guards patrolling the grounds. It was almost full dark now, and Devon and Felix were both wearing black cloaks to help them blend into the shadows. I sported my mom's long, sapphire-blue trench coat, made out of spidersilk, which also helped me melt into the growing blackness.

The Draconi guards were dressed in black boots, pants, and shirts, along with blood-red cloaks and matching feathered cavalier hats, making them look like extras from a *Three Musketeers* movie. But they were much more dangerous than that. All of the guards had their hands on the swords belted to their hips, looking for intruders, as well as keeping an eye out for any monsters that might be creeping up on them. Many an inattentive guard had been snatched by a copper crusher and dragged into the forest, unlucky enough to be the oversize, venomous snake's dinner date.

"Are we good?" Felix asked, checking his phone. "It's almost time for us to meet Deah. You know how she worries if we're even one minute late."

With good reason. If she was caught helping the enemy, Deah would be executed right along with us, despite the fact that she was Victor's daughter.

Instead of answering him, I started counting the guards along the perimeter. One, two, three. . . . It didn't take me long to realize that something was different tonight. Worry shot through me.

"Wait," I whispered. "There are more guards patrolling tonight."

Devon frowned and squinted at the compound. "How can you tell?"

"I can see them. Trust me. There are more guards."

"Can we still take our usual route into the mansion?" he asked in a tense voice, his hand dropping to the duffel bag sitting at his feet. "This is our last trip. If we can get in and out tonight, then we're done with this."

"Give me a second to work it out," I said.

Devon and Felix both fell silent, although they kept looking from me to the guards and back again. I focused on the guards, staring at first one, then another. It took me a minute to realize that Victor had only doubled the number of guards, pairing them up in teams of two. I wondered at the change and why he thought he needed so many men up here at the castle, instead of patrolling down on the Midway like usual. But Victor hadn't altered the guards' routes, which meant that we could still get into the mansion the same way as before.

"We're good," I said. "Text Deah and tell her that we're on our way in."

Felix nodded, his thumbs flying over the screen. A second later, his phone lit up with a message. "Deah says that the coast is clear on her end."

"Good," I said. "Follow me."

Keeping low, I left the woods behind and hopscotched my way across the lawn, hiding behind various trees and bushes and only moving when the guards' backs were turned. Devon and Felix followed along behind me, both of them being as quiet as possible and clutching the duffel bags to their chests to muffle any telltale *clank-clanks*.

Less than three minutes later, we were at one of the side patio doors. I reached up and gently turned the knob. Unlocked. How disappointing. It was no fun breaking into a mansion when your inside woman left a door unlocked for you.

But I opened the door and ushered Devon and Felix inside. I slipped in after them and locked the door behind me, just in case one of the guards decided to check it. Then I took the lead again, creeping from one hallway and staircase to the next.

The outside of the Draconi mansion might resemble a castle, but the furnishings inside were the real riches. Just about everything gleamed with bits of gold, from the chandeliers overhead to the gilt-edged mirrors on the walls to the trim on the tables and chairs. And Victor's snarling dragon crest was painted, carved, chiseled, embroidered, and stamped into practically everything, from the crown molding that ringed the ceilings, to the stained glass windows set into the walls, to the white flagstones underfoot.

All those dragons were creepy enough, but it seemed like every single one of the monsters turned its head, narrowed its eyes, and glared at Devon, Felix, and me as we crept past. I shivered. Sometimes, I would have been happy not to see so well with my sight magic.

We quickly made our way up some stairs to the Draconi greenlab. Once again, the glass doors were unlocked, and the three of us slipped inside and moved through the area, which was part chemistry lab, part greenhouse, where a variety of magical and other plants were grown and harvested. The long, sharp needles on the stitch-sting bushes quivered as we hurried past them, but we didn't get close enough for the evergreen plants to lash out and try to scratch us for disturbing them.

We made it to the opposite side of the greenlab, and I sidled up to the glass doors there and peered out into the hallway beyond. The lights were turned down low in this part of the mansion, creating more shadows than not. Just the way I liked it.

Since the coast was clear, I opened one of the glass doors and stepped out into the hallway—

I spotted a glint of metal out of the corner of my eye. Even as I turned toward it, a sword zoomed out of the shadows, heading straight for me.

CHAPTER TWO

The sword stopped an inch from my throat.

I froze, my eyes wide, my body tense, my hand curling around the hilt of my own sword, even though I knew that I wouldn't be fast enough to draw the weapon, much less defend myself with it, before I got skewered.

"You're late," a familiar voice growled.

Deah Draconi stepped out of the shadows, her sword still at my throat. I looked down at the weapon and the stars carved into the dull, ash-colored metal. A similar pattern adorned my own sword. Each of our weapons had been given to us by our respective mothers, and both were black blades, so named because the more blood you got on the blades, the blacker they became.

Deah was quite pretty with her golden hair and dark blue eyes the same color as my own—another sign of our Sterling Family blood, along with our black blades. She was wearing white shorts and sandals with a red T-shirt, but my gaze dropped to the gold cuff stamped with the Draconi dragon crest that gleamed on her right wrist. Deah might be helping us now, but part of me still wondered whose side she would choose in the end, when Victor finally tried to destroy all the other Families, starting with the Sinclairs.

"Why, hello, cousin," I drawled. "I didn't see you there.

You're getting better at sneaking around. I approve. We might make a thief out of you yet."

Deah rolled her eyes at my calling her *cousin*, but she dropped her sword from my throat. Neither one of us had known about our connection until a couple of weeks ago when it had come out during the Tournament of Blades, and we were both still getting used to the idea that we were family and trying to figure out what kind of relationship we wanted to have.

"Where's Seleste?" I asked in a kinder voice, referring to her mother and my aunt.

"Right here, darling," a lilting, almost sing-song voice called out.

Seleste Draconi rounded the corner and skipped down the hallway toward us. She was beautiful, with long blond hair that rippled around her shoulders like a river of gold, and a gauzy white dress that fluttered about her body like wisps of mist. She had this light, ethereal air to her, like the fairy queens in all those old tales that my mom used to read to me when I was a kid.

Seleste stopped in front of me, smiling wide, her dark blue eyes glowing as bright as any monster's. Even though she was looking right at me, I could tell that she wasn't really seeing me. Like the rest of the Sterling women, Seleste had sight magic, but her Talent let her see the future, which led to her doing and saying all sorts of strange things. Most people thought that she was crazy or made fun of her, but I'd grown to like her odd ways. Besides, Seleste and Deah were the only blood family that I had left now, and I was going to look out for them. That's what my mom would have wanted.

"Lila, darling!" Seleste said, taking my hands in hers. "Come walk with me!"

In addition to her sight magic, Seleste also had a strength Talent that let her pull me halfway down the hallway before I dug my sneakers into the carpet. Even then, she still managed to twirl me around, as though we were dancing, before I could stop her.

"Hello, Seleste," I said in a gentle voice. "It's good to see you too."

She tightened her grip on my hands, holding me in place with her strength magic. "I'm so glad you're here, darling. I need to talk to you."

Despite the fact that we were several feet away from Deah, Felix, and Devon, who were talking among themselves, Seleste still glanced around, as though she expected someone to be hiding in the shadows, listening to us. When she was satisfied that no one was eavesdropping, she leaned forward and gave me a dreamy smile, staring straight into my eyes, the magic in her own gaze burning brighter than before.

"Don't be afraid of the lightning," she whispered in an urgent voice. "It's your friend, just like the monsters are. Monsters are your friends. Never forget that."

Seleste had said some strange things to me over the past few weeks, especially during the Tournament of Blades when I was first getting to know her, but this was just plain *bizarre*. What lightning? And why did she think that monsters were my friends? They were just monsters. I paid their tolls, and they left me alone. Nothing more, nothing less.

Her message delivered, Seleste let go of my hands and stepped back. Then she gave me another dreamy smile, turned around, and skipped back down the hallway to the others.

"Seleste!" I hissed, wanting to ask her exactly what she meant. "Seleste!"

But she just waved goodbye to me and kept going, right on past Deah and the guys.

"Mom!" This time, Deah was the one who hissed at her. "Mom!"

"Don't worry, darling!" Seleste called out over her shoulder. "I'm going to bed right now! Promise! Have fun with your friends!"

A second later, she rounded the far end of the hallway and disappeared from sight.

I walked back to where the others were, all of us staring in the direction that Seleste had gone.

"Well," Devon said, breaking the silence. "She certainly was . . . cheerful."

"How has she been?" I asked.

Deah looked at me. "She's actually been doing a lot better these past two weeks. It's like seeing you at the tournament and then us working together has quieted her mind and made her sharper, clearer, more focused."

I nodded, still wondering about Seleste's strange warning. Lightning and monsters. Worry rippled through me. Whatever vision she'd seen of my future, it didn't seem to be a good one.

"Um, I hate to be whiny, but can we get on with things?" Felix asked, shifting on his feet and hoisting his duffel bag a little higher on his shoulder. "These things are heavy."

Deah stared at him, her eyes softening. "You know, I really like seeing you every night. Even if it is because of my dad and what he's planning to do."

Felix's face lit up. "I like seeing you too."

Then he grinned, stepped forward, and slung his free arm around her shoulders. "Have I told you how beautiful you look tonight—"

He started whispering to her as they walked down the hallway in front of us. Devon grinned and nudged me with his elbow. I rolled my eyes, but I was grinning too. I was glad that Felix and Deah had found happiness with each other, despite how dangerous it was for them to be together.

The four of us reached Victor's office, and Deah gestured at the double doors, which had two gold dragons for knobs. The snarling creatures looked like they were ready to come to life and bite off the fingers of anyone who tried to open them.

"Locked," she said. "Sorry, but I haven't been able to get a key yet. I tried to open it earlier with those lock picks you gave me, but I'm still not as good with them as you are."

"No worries," I said, smiling. "Finally, something fun for me to do."

Deah shook her head. "You are seriously strange, Merriweather."

My smile widened. "You have no idea, Draconi."

While the others kept watch, I reached up and removed two thin chopsticks that were stuck through my ponytail. The sticks were the same black as my hair, but a twist of the lacquered wood revealed the lock picks hidden inside. The tools felt as familiar to me as my own fingers, and I started humming a soft, happy tune as I bent over the lock and inserted the picks.

Over the past two weeks, I'd had a lot of practice on this particular lock, and it *snicked* open less than thirty seconds later. Still, we all tensed, knowing that we were stepping into the dragon's den—and that he could come and catch us at any moment.

I stuck the chopstick lock picks back into my ponytail, then took hold of the knobs. "Here we go," I whispered and opened the doors.

The four of us crept inside, and I shut and locked the doors behind us. Victor's office was as richly furnished as the rest of the mansion, but I ignored the glimmers of gold and went over to the wall behind his desk. An enormous dragon was carved into the white stone there, with flames curled all around it, as though it was continuously setting itself on fire.

I stopped a moment, staring at the fist-sized ruby that was the dragon's evil eye. I shivered. No matter how many times I snuck in here, I never got used to looking at this particular dragon—or having it stare right back at me. Or perhaps it was what was behind the carving that worried me so much.

But I forced my unease aside, stepped forward, and pressed on the ruby, which sank into the stone. A second later, the wall slid back, revealing a large, secret room—one that was filled with weapons.

An overhead light clicked on in the room, revealing the black blade swords, daggers, and other weapons that lined the shelves covering three walls. Each weapon was on a peg by itself and carefully labeled, with codes like *TT29*, *CC2*, and *RM55*—for all the tree trolls, copper crushers, and rockmunks that Victor had trapped and killed over the years.

Black blades were made out of bloodiron, a special metal that could absorb, store, and transfer magic from one person or monster to another. Victor had used these weapons to rip the monsters' magic out of them, so that he could harness it for his own evil plan to destroy all the other Families. I could feel the creatures' power pulsing through the blades, each one proof of Victor's cruelty and his delight in sickening slaughter. The cold burn of magic made me sick to my stomach.

"Let's move," I whispered. "I don't want to be in here one second longer than necessary."

Devon and Felix put their duffel bags down on the floor and unzipped them, revealing the swords, daggers, and other weapons inside. They grabbed the weapons and handed them to Deah and me, and the two of us switched out the real black blades with the fakes. We also labeled each weapon with a small sticker with Victor's code written on it.

We'd been breaking in here and doing this same thing every night for the last two weeks, slowly exchanging the magic-filled weapons with empty ones. We'd removed most of the black blades, but not all of them. I hated leaving a single sword behind for Victor to use, but he had a lot of Talents, and it was possible that he could sense magic the same way that I could. So we had to leave some of the real weapons here or he would realize what we'd done. Still, I made sure that we only left the blades that pulsed weakly with magic.

We worked quickly, and it only took us ten minutes to switch out the last of the weapons, although it seemed much longer than that. By the time we were done, Devon and Felix were both sweating beneath their long, black cloaks. Deah was too, despite her T-shirt and shorts. I wasn't sweating, but my stomach churned and churned at the cold chill of all the magic in the air and what Victor had done to get so much of it.

Devon and Felix zipped up the duffel bags with the real black blades and slung them over their shoulders. I pressed on the dragon's ruby eye again, and the wall slid back into place, hiding the secret room from sight.

"Well, I guess this is it," I said, trying to make my voice light. "No more late-night trips to raid Victor's secret weapons stash."

Nobody moved or spoke for a moment.

I looked at Deah. "Thank you again for helping us."

She nodded, but she stared at the floor instead of at me. Betraying her Family and her father was no easy thing, despite how evil Victor was.

I glanced at Devon and Felix, who both nodded. We'd discussed this for several days now, and it was finally time to ask Deah to do one more thing.

"Come with us," I said.

Her head snapped up, and she looked at me with wide eyes. "What?"

"You heard me. Come with us. Go pack a bag, get Seleste, and come with us. Right now."

She stared at me, and my soulsight kicked in, letting me feel all of her emotions. Electric shock. Sharp worry. Stomach-churning fear. For a moment, warm happiness mixed in with the other feelings, but it was quickly smothered by cold sorrow. I knew what her answer was going to be before she even opened her mouth.

She shook her head, her golden ponytail slapping against her shoulders. "I can't do that. You know I can't."

Felix stepped forward and grabbed her hand. "Please, Deah. You're not like the other Draconis. You don't belong here."

"But I *am* a Draconi." She glanced at me for a second. "At least, part of me is. But that doesn't matter. I can't go with you. My dad would flip out if he realized that Mom and I were gone. And you all know what he would do if he realized that we'd defected to the Sinclair Family."

We all winced. Victor would attack the Sinclairs with every guard he had in order to get them back. Deah's mimic magic and Seleste's visions were Talents that he didn't have and would never let slip through his fingers.

But Felix cared too much about Deah to give up so easily. "Please," he repeated. "Just come with us. We can figure out the rest later. Let's just get you and your mom out of here while we still have a chance."

Deah stared at him, and I saw and felt all the warm, soft love she had for him. She bit her lip and shifted on her feet, as if she were actually considering changing her mind and going with us—

One of the knobs *creaked*, and the double doors rattled in their frames.

We all froze.

Someone was trying to get into the office.

CHAPTER THREE

The doors rattled again, harder than before.

Devon, Felix, and Deah stared at the doors, but I darted forward, grabbed the back of Devon's and Felix's cloaks, and pulled them across the office.

"Hide! Hide! Hide!" I hissed, shoving them down behind a long red couch shot through with gold threads near the back of the room.

Devon and Felix dropped the duffel bags with the real black blades onto the floor. I winced at the loud *clank-clanks* of the weapons rattling around inside the bags, but the two of them quickly crouched down out of sight. There wasn't enough room for me to hide behind the couch too, so I sprinted over to the wet bar in the corner, dropping behind the gleaming wood. Then I peered around the end of the bar, looking at Deah, who remained frozen in the middle of the office, right in front of Victor's desk. She stared back at me, her hot, sweaty panic flooding my own body. Deah wasn't supposed to be in here any more than we were, but I stabbed my finger at the door.

"Open it!" I hissed again. "Remember that this is *your* mansion!"

Deah stared at me another second; then her mouth tightened, and she gave me a sharp nod, understanding what I was saying and what I wanted her to do. She drew in a deep breath, then squared her shoulders, marched over to the doors, turned the lock, and threw them open.

A guy wearing black cargo pants and a red T-shirt emblazoned with a gold dragon stumbled through the opening. His golden hair was a shade darker than Deah's, and his thick, strong body was all muscle. He would have been handsome, except for his brown eyes, which were cold and empty, just like those of all the dragon carvings in the mansion.

Blake Draconi, Deah's older brother, Victor's second-in-command, and the guy who'd helped murder my mom.

Blake straightened up and stared at his sister. "What are you doing in here? Especially with the doors locked behind you? You know that Dad doesn't like anyone being in his office when he's not around."

Deah chewed her lower lip, and I could almost see the wheels turning in her mind as she tried to come up with some explanation that wouldn't make Blake any more suspicious than he already was.

My hand dropped to my sword. If necessary, I would draw the weapon, leap to my feet, and defend Deah, but I decided to see how things played out. Devon, Felix, and I still needed to get out of here with the real black blades, and I'd rather sneak out undetected than have to fight my way through Blake and the rest of the Draconi guards.

But Deah had been dealing with Blake her whole life, and she knew exactly how to handle her half brother. She crossed her arms over her chest and gave him the same flat look that he was giving her. "First of all, the doors weren't locked."

"Yes, they were," he insisted. "I couldn't get them open no matter how hard I tried."

"Maybe they were just stuck," she replied in a cool, slightly mocking voice. "Or maybe you need to start hitting the weight room a little more often."

An embarrassed flush stained his cheeks a dark, mottled red. Blake had strength magic, so he should have easily been able to open the doors, something that Deah knew. His eyes narrowed at the insult, and he opened his mouth, but she cut him off.

"Besides, if the doors had really been locked, then how could I have gotten in here to start with?" she scoffed. "It's not like I'm a *thief* or anything."

I rolled my eyes. Now she was just being snarky.

"Well, why weren't the doors locked?" Blake snapped, still not ready to believe her.

Deah shrugged. "I don't know. Maybe Dad forgot to lock them before he went to meet with Nikolai Volkov. He left in a hurry, remember?"

Blake crossed his arms over his chest and gave her another suspicious stare. "But that still doesn't explain what *you're* doing in here."

"I put my mom to bed a few minutes ago, and I walked back this way to check that the greenlab was secure for the night. I noticed that one of the office doors was cracked open, so I came in here to make sure that everything was okay." She threw her arms out wide. "Which you can totally see it is."

Blake glared at her a few more seconds before his brown gaze flicked over the rest of the office. He looked in my direction, and I stayed absolutely still in the shadows behind the bar, hoping that Devon and Felix would do the same behind the couch.

Finally, Blake turned back toward the front of the office. He didn't even glance at the closed laptop, crystal paperweights, or gold fountain pens on the desk to make sure that nothing was missing or out of place. Instead, his gaze locked onto the dragon chiseled into the white stone wall behind Victor's desk. His eyes narrowed, and he stared and stared at the dragon, examining every single inch of the carving, looking for the smallest sign that it had been tampered with or disturbed in any way. Shock zipped through me.

He knew.

Blake knew about Victor's secret room and all the black blades hidden inside it. That was the only reason he would bother to stare so long and hard at the dragon carving. He was making sure that Deah hadn't discovered the room and the weapons, that nothing was going to derail his dad's plan to massacre all the other Families.

I shouldn't have been so shocked. As the Draconi bruiser, Blake was Victor's second-in-command, and I'd suspected that he might be helping Victor at least trap the monsters he'd killed. More than that, Blake was just as cruel as his father was, something he'd proven by helping Victor cut my mom to pieces. But I was surprised all the same. I wouldn't have thought that Victor would have told *anyone* what he was really up to, how he wanted to use his collection of black blades to give his guards extra boosts of magic so they could attack and kill all the other Families.

But he'd obviously told Blake, and I wondered why. Because Blake was his son and right-hand man? Or was there another, more sinister reason? Was Victor putting his plan into action sometime soon?

That terrifying thought made my hand clench tight around my sword, the five-pointed star carved into the hilt pressing against my skin like a cold brand.

Blake finally turned away from the dragon carving and secret room and faced Deah again. "Okay, so the door was open and you came in here to check on things. That still doesn't explain why you stayed in here so long."

Deah chewed her lip again, her gaze flicking around as she searched for another excuse. Blake's back was to me now, so I sidled forward so that she could see me again. Deah looked at me, and I pointed over to the shelves that took up one of the walls. She turned her head the tiniest bit, and her mouth flattened out as she realized what I was pointing at. She didn't like my idea, but she decided to go along with it.

"I was looking at my trophies," she said in a soft voice.

Blake snorted and stomped past her. He grabbed a solid gold cup, also stamped with the Draconi dragon crest, off one of the shelves and held it up.

"Oh, you mean *this* trophy? The one that Lila Merriweather let you win during the Tournament of Blades?" he sneered. "I told Dad that he should throw it out with the rest of the garbage, but he didn't listen to me."

Tears gleamed in Deah's eyes at his mean taunt, but she ruthlessly blinked them back, crossed her arms over her chest, and lifted her chin. "Well, at least I got further in the tournament than you did. Then again, I always do. Poppy Ito knocked you out of the competition in less than a minute this year." She laughed, but it was a harsh, mocking sound. "And she only has speed magic."

Blake's hand tightened around the trophy, and his arm lifted like he was going to rear back and throw the gold cup at Deah. But she held her ground and glared right back at him, daring him to do something stupid.

Blake studied her, and he slowly lowered the trophy to his side. He might have a strength Talent, but Deah's mimic magic made her the far better fighter and Blake knew that she would mop the floor with him. Plus, he must have realized how angry Victor would be if he messed up the office because he whipped around and shoved the gold cup back onto the shelf.

"Yeah, well, you're still not supposed to be in here," Blake growled. "So let's both leave before Dad finds us. I'm not getting in trouble because of you."

He gestured at Deah, who had no choice but to turn around and head for the double doors. She glanced at me out of the corner of her eye, and I flashed her a thumbs up, telling her that everything was okay. As long as Blake left with her, I could still get Devon, Felix, and myself out of the mansion and off the grounds without any of the guards spotting us or realizing that we'd ever been here.

Deah nodded back at me, relief filling her face.

A second later, she stepped out into the hallway, and Blake shut the doors behind the two of them. The lock *clicking* into place sounded as loud as a clap of thunder in the absolute quiet of the office, but I welcomed the noise because it meant that we were safe.

For now.

I waited several seconds to make sure that Blake wasn't coming back in here, then slowly got to my feet. Behind the couch, Devon and Felix did the same, both of them clutching their swords in their hands.

"That was close," Devon muttered.

"Yeah," Felix chimed in. "Too close."

"Too close is right. Now, come on," I whispered, heading toward the glass door on the far side of the office. "Let's get out of here while we still can."

Devon and Felix grabbed the two duffel bags full of black blades, and we slipped out of the glass door and onto a balcony before sneaking down some stone steps and back across the yard. We made it to the woods without any of the Draconi guards spotting us, and we all sighed with relief as the trees, shadows, and growing clouds of mist swallowed us up.

It took us almost an hour to hike through the forest back over to the Sinclair Family compound, and I was happy to see the mansion loom up out of the darkness before us. Unlike the white, airy elegance of the Draconi castle, the Sinclair mansion was made out of black, blocky stone that looked as if it had been chiseled out of the mountain itself. The mansion rose up seven stories in places, with towers that soared even higher into the night sky, each one topped with a black flag bearing the Sinclair Family crest—a hand holding a sword aloft, all of it outlined in white. The same symbol was stamped into the silver cuffs that Devon, Felix, and I wore on our right wrists.

"Home, sweet home," Felix said in a relieved voice.

"Absolutely," Devon agreed, hefting his bag of weapons a little higher on his shoulder. "I'm glad this mission is over. Aren't you, Lila?"

But it wasn't over. Not for me. I still had more stealing to do tonight. But I smiled at him, glad that the shadows hid how fake the expression really was.

"Yep. Now, come on. The others will be waiting for us."

Instead of striding straight across the lawn to the front entrance, we hunkered down in the bushes until the Sinclair guards' backs were turned. Our guards were dressed the same way that the Draconis had been—black boots, pants, and shirts—the only difference was that the Sinclairs wore black cavalier hats topped with white feathers, along with the same black cloaks that Devon and Felix still sported. The white feathers made it easy for us to spot and duck around the guards. Then we crossed the lawn, crept up some stone steps to a balcony, and stopped in front of a series of glass doors.

I tried one of the knobs, but it, too, was unlocked, just like the ones at the Draconi mansion. I sighed with disappointment, but I opened the door and the three of us stepped inside an enormous library that soared three stories high in this part of the mansion.

A white stone fireplace took up most of one wall, while ebony shelves covered another. White stone balconies wrapped around the two upper levels of the library, revealing more ebony bookcases, before giving way to the pointed ceiling, which featured black and white panes of stained glass. Through the glass, I could see the full moon and a sky studded with stars, all of which cast a dim, silvery light that frosted the tops of the books on the upper levels.

"You're late," a voice called out.

Devon, Felix, and I looked over at a woman sitting behind an antique ebony desk in front of the doors. She had the same green eyes as Devon, but her hair was a rich auburn. She wore a sleek white pantsuit, and a wide silver cuff flashed on her right wrist.

"Sorry," I drawled. "We ran into a little problem at the Draconi mansion."

Claudia Sinclair laid her silver reading glasses down on top of the desk, worry flashing in her eyes. "What sort of problem?"

I shrugged. "Blake almost caught us in Victor's office."

She hissed out a breath between her teeth, but I grinned.

"Notice that I said *almost*. Don't worry. Blake didn't even realize that we were there, and none of the guards spotted us either. We got in and out, and no one was the wiser, especially not Victor."

"And Deah and Seleste?" she asked, her voice still full of worry.

"They're okay too. So relax. Everything's fine, and my plan went off without a hitch, just like I told you it would."

Claudia gave me a sharp, suspicious look, but the tension in her beautiful face slowly eased as she studied Devon, Felix, and me in turn and realized that we really were okay.

"See? I told you everything would be okay. You worry *way* too much, Claud," a deep, masculine voice chimed in.

Claudia swiveled around in her chair so that she was facing a tall, muscular man who was sprawled across a white velvet settee by the fireplace. Unlike Claudia, who looked as professional as could be in her pantsuit, the man wore a gray Hawaiian shirt patterned with large, neon-blue parrots, along with white linen pants and white flip-flops. A white straw hat was perched on the settee beside him.

The man leaned forward and grabbed a small sandwich off a sterling silver tray on the table in front of him. The overhead light from the crystal chandelier made his ebony skin gleam, along with the silver threads in his black hair.

My gaze locked on to the food. My nose twitched and my stomach rumbled in anticipation. "Are those mini bacon cheeseburgers?"

Mo Kaminsky, my friend, my fence, and the Family broker, grinned at me. "Don't you know it. Fresh from the kitchen." He waved his hand over the tray of food, making a diamond signet ring flash on his hand. "Come and get 'em, kid. I saved some just for you."

Typical Mo, looking out for me. Mo had been good friends with my mom, and he'd watched out for me in so many ways after she died, from giving me jobs to letting me hang out in his pawnshop to even setting me up with the Sinclair Family. For a long time, he'd been the only friend I had, and he meant so much to me.

Mo didn't have to tell me twice about the food. I went over, grabbed one of the cheeseburgers, and popped it into my mouth. Like everything else the kitchen pixies made, it was utterly divine. A buttery roll, grilled meat, fresh veggies, cheddar cheese, a dollop of mayonnaise, and best of all, crunchy pieces of salty, smoky bacon. Mmm. Bacon. Best food *ever*.

I polished off that cheeseburger, grabbed another one, and downed it as well. I thought about swiping a couple more and sticking them in my pockets for later, but Oscar would complain about having to clean food stains out my clothes again. So I contented myself with just eating them here. Mo toasted me with his own mini cheeseburger, then chowed down on it.

Devon and Felix carefully set the two black duffel bags down on the floor. The distinctive *clank-clanks* of metal sliding together rang out through the library, and Claudia tilted her head to the side, interest and appreciation sparking in her gaze.

"You got the last of the black blades?" she asked.

"Of course we did," I said, swallowing the last of my cheeseburger. "You are talking to Lila Merriweather, thief extraordinaire, you know."

I gave an elaborate flourish with my hand and bowed low, sweeping my long blue coat out to one side, as though I were curtsying before a queen. In a way, I was, since Claudia was the head of the entire Sinclair Family and just as powerful as any queen.

She sighed at my showing off, but Mo grinned again and held out his fist. I bumped him back, then grabbed another mini cheeseburger. Stealing stuff always made me extra hungry.

Claudia sighed again, louder and deeper this time, but she also nodded, silently telling me *good job*. I nodded back at her and polished off the rest of my cheeseburger.

Devon unzipped his duffel bag and pulled out a few of the black blades to show his mom, then zipped up the bag again and slung it over his shoulder. "You want us to put the weapons down in the training room and lock them away with all the others?"

Claudia nodded. "Of course."

Once we'd started stealing the weapons from Victor, we had to do *something* with them, since black blades were far too valuable to just leave lying around the mansion. Just by themselves, the weapons would fetch a pretty penny on the black market. But the real problem was all the magic that filled the weapons—power that we couldn't get rid of, not without stabbing ourselves with the swords and daggers and injecting all that stolen monster magic into our own bodies.

That was something that none of us wanted to do. We didn't know how we might react to the monster magic—or how addicted to the power we might become. Like Katia Volkov, a girl who'd also trapped and killed monsters in order to take their magic and use it for her own twisted ends. Given all the risks, Claudia had decided that locking away the weapons in the training room was the safest option right now.

Devon nodded back at his mom. Felix grabbed the second bag, and the two of them headed toward the library doors.

"I'll catch up with you guys later," I called out.

The guys waved back at me and left the library. I waited until the double doors had swung shut behind them before I turned back to Claudia and Mo.

Claudia sighed for a third time, realizing that I had some bad news. "What is it now?"

"When Blake came into Victor's office tonight, he looked right at the wall where the secret room is."

Mo frowned. "You think Blake knows about the black blades and what Victor wants to do with them."

I nodded. "Blake barely glanced at the rest of the office, but he kept staring and staring at that dragon carving like it was the most important thing in the entire mansion. He was making sure that Deah hadn't messed with the carving and opened up the secret room. Blake has to know what Victor's planning. It's the only thing that makes sense. He wouldn't have even looked at the wall otherwise."

Claudia picked up her reading glasses and started tapping them on top of her desk. "If Blake knows about the weapons, then Victor is probably going to strike soon.

You're sure you left enough black blades behind to fool him into thinking that they're all still there and full of magic?"

I shrugged. "I think so, but I don't know for sure. I just don't know if Victor can sense magic like I can, if it feels cold to him the same way it does to me. Hopefully, he'll be too busy thinking about how he's going to use the black blades to focus on how they actually look and feel."

The weapons we'd left behind at the Draconi mansion weren't black blades, so they weren't made out of bloodiron and they couldn't absorb, store, or transfer magic from one person or monster to the next. Not even close. They were just plain old swords and daggers, junk weapons mostly, that mortals and magicks had hocked at Mo's pawnshop, the Razzle Dazzle. Devon, Felix, and I had spray-painted all of the fake weapons a dull, ashy gray to hide the nicks and scratches on them and make them look like black blades. The swords and daggers might not be the real things, but they were still weapons that Victor could give to his guards, weapons that could be used against us and the other Families. After all, a regular sword could kill you as easily as a magic-filled one.

Claudia stopped tapping her glasses on the desk and set them aside. Then she raised her hands to her face and massaged her temples, as though they were suddenly aching. "You did your job, Lila. There's nothing else we can do now but try to figure out when Victor is going to attack and which Family he might target first."

Instead of answering her, I wandered over to the shelves along the wall and started looking at the photos, figurines, and other knickknacks perched there. My gaze locked on to a photo of my mom, Serena Sterling, with her sister, my aunt Seleste. The two of them could have been twins, except for my mom's black hair and Seleste's golden locks, just like me and Deah and our own hair coloring. I only hoped that Deah and I would stay together through the coming fight with Victor, and not let him tear us apart the way he had our moms years ago.

"Now that he's brought Blake in on his plan, when do you think Victor will attack?" Mo asked.

Claudia dropped her hands from her temples and started drumming her fingers on top of the desk. "If I had to guess, I would say after the dinner for all the Families tomorrow night. No doubt Victor will come to the dinner, talk about how he wants peace, and do his best to soothe everyone's fears. Then he'll wait a couple days or maybe even weeks until our guard is down and stab us all in the back the second he has the chance. That's what I would expect him to do. Either way, we've taken away most of his weapons, so we've at least weakened him."

She was right. By switching out the black blades for fakes, we had taken away some of Victor's power and thwarted part of his plan to attack the other Families. But her words didn't make me feel any better, and worry still pinched her face, along with Mo's and my own.

Because we all knew how much magic Victor had himself and just how determined he was to destroy all of us.

CHAPTER FOUR

Now that my first thieving mission of the night was finished, I left the library and went up to my bedroom to get ready for the second one.

The Sinclair mansion wasn't quite as richly furnished as the Draconi castle, but plenty of fine things still adorned the rooms, including antique furniture, silver bookends, and crystal chandeliers that had been turned down low for the night. It was after ten now and the mansion was quiet, except for a few pixies fluttering through the hallways, doing their last chores before going to bed. I nodded to the pixies that I passed and headed up to my bedroom.

When I opened the door, the twangy sounds of country music assaulted my ears. I sighed. I'd hoped that Oscar, the pixie who took care of me, would have already gone to bed by now, but it looked like he'd waited up for me. So I shut the door behind me, walked past the black leather couch and matching recliners in front of the TV mounted to the wall, and went over to a long table that was near the French patio doors. A rundown, ramshackle ebony trailer sat on the table, along with a carpet of real grass that led over to a corral and a rickety barn, also made out of ebony.

A six-inch-tall man with translucent wings attached to his back was perched on top of one of the corral fence posts, chewing on a long blade of grass. He wore black cowboy boots with shiny silver tips, along with faded black jeans with holes in the knees and a pale blue T-shirt that had seen better, cleaner days. A black cowboy hat was tipped back on his head, and he was clutching a tiny can of honeybeer in his right hand. Out in the grassy corral, a small green tortoise was slowly lumbering over to a pile of shredded lettuce.

"I thought you'd be back sooner," Oscar said, his voice even twangier than his country playlist.

"It took us a little longer than usual to get out of the Draconi mansion, but we made it back with the weapons, so it's all good."

Out in the grass, Tiny, the tortoise, turned his head and studied me with his black eyes. When he realized that I didn't have any strawberries to add to his pile of lettuce, he let out a reproachful snort, stuck his beak into the long, green strips, and started chowing down on them like a cow eating hay in a field. The whole scene made me feel like I was staring down at a doll-size, Western dude ranch, instead of a table in my bedroom.

Oscar stood up on the fence post, twitched his wings, and rose into the air in front of me, hovering there like an oversize bee. He tipped back his cowboy hat a little more, revealing his sandy hair, and gave me a critical once-over with his violet eyes. Some of the tension leaked out of his face when he realized that I really was okay.

Technically, pixies were monsters, just like the tree trolls and copper crushers that lurked in the forests, but I always thought of them as miniature humans. They were the housekeepers of the world, offering their cooking, cleaning, and other skills in exchange for a safe place to stay and protection from larger mortals, magicks, and monsters. I hadn't been here all that long, but I already considered Oscar and Tiny to be two of my best friends, and I was going to protect them just like I was going to look out for the rest of the Sinclairs.

That sobering thought reminded me that I needed to get on with my second thieving mission of the night. So I scratched Tiny's head and gently tipped Oscar's cowboy hat back down low on his forehead.

"You two boys have fun," I drawled. "I'm going to go hang out with Devon for a while. Don't wait up for me."

Oscar snorted and pushed his hat back up to where it was supposed to be. "Ah, young love. Enjoy it, cupcake."

He saluted me with his can of honeybeer, then flew over and landed on the front porch of his trailer. Oscar finished off his honeybeer, burped, and tossed the can down onto the grass, where it *clink-clink-clinked* against several others that were already there. Then he disappeared inside his trailer, shutting the screen and front doors behind him.

I waited a few seconds until Oscar had cranked up his country music even louder and I was sure that he wasn't going to come back out and check on me again. Tiny was completely focused on his lettuce, and he ignored me too. So I went over, opened one of the glass doors, and slipped out onto the stone balcony.

I breathed in, enjoying the cool, mist-filled air, and took a moment to admire the scenery. The Sinclair mansion was near the top of the mountain, offering a spectacular view of the rocky ridges and lush forests that ran all the way down to the valley far, far below. The sharp, sticky tang of the pines and other evergreen trees mixed with the clouds of mist from the waterfalls, creating a pleasant, woodsy perfume. The moon and stars were as full and bright as before, giving everything a soft, silvery tint, and the fireflies had come out for the night, flashing their yellow lights and signaling back and forth to each other.

But the fireflies' quick glows were nothing compared to the dazzling neon lights of the Midway. Nestled in the center of the valley, the Midway—the commercial heart of Cloudburst Falls—looked like a giant Ferris wheel that had been laid flat on its side in the middle of the mountains. Every part of the Midway pulsed, sparked, and shimmered with blue, red, green, white, and other dazzling lights, as did the various shopping squares that branched off the main circular area, as though they were the Ferris wheel's carts.

I could have put my elbows down, leaned against the stone ledge, and kept right on watching the flashing lights and the fireflies, but I still had work to do tonight, so I turned away from the view and peered up at the part of the mansion looming above me.

I tilted my head to the side, listening. Sure enough, several steady *thwack-thwack-thwacks* sounded, telling me that Devon had finished putting away the weapons in the training room and was on one of the roofs, working out with the boxing bags attached to the scaffolding up there. Normally, I would have taken hold of the closest drainpipe, climbed up to the roof, and joined him, but I had a different destination in mind right now.

So I reached into one of my coat pockets and pulled out a pair of gloves made out of ironmesh, a thin, but protective metal. I tugged the gloves onto my hands, still listening all the while, but Devon kept up his steady assault on the boxing bags, and I felt safe enough to get on with the rest of my mission for the night.

Instead of climbing up, I took hold of the drainpipe and stepped out into the night air, plummeting down, down, down like a shooting star streaking out of the sky. I always enjoyed the sensation of free-falling, of the air rushing over my face and tangling my hair, the wind whistling in my ears, my long coat flapping against my legs. Although tonight I resisted the urge to laugh for fear that Devon might hear me and come investigate.

Just before my gray sneakers hit the ground, I gripped the drainpipe much tighter, slowing my descent and making a bit of silvery smoke waft up from my gloves. The black stone drainpipe was as smooth and slick as glass from years of being exposed to the elements, and it would have bruised and bloodied my hands if I hadn't been wearing my ironmesh gloves to protect my palms.

The second my sneakers touched the grass, I crouched down in the shadows, looking left and right, but none of the guards had spotted me and they continued with their normal patrols.

I waited until the guards were all turned away from me, then left the shadows behind and sidled along the perimeter of the mansion, stopping when I came to a wide window that was set just above ground level. I tried the window, which pushed inward, since it, too, was unlocked. I sighed. I was getting tired of people making this so *easy* for me, but I slid through the window, dropping down into a room inside the mansion. Sure, I could have just used the stairs and snuck down here from my bedroom, but where was the fun in that?

I straightened up, staring out over the thick mats that covered most of the floor and a glass partition that separated the sparring area from several rows of seats. This was the training room where the guards came to hone their skills, although the doors were locked and the lights were off, given how late it was. But the moon and starlight streaming in through the window was more than enough to let me see the sturdy metal grates that covered one of the walls—and the weapons hanging behind them.

The training room also doubled as the Sinclair armory,

and this was where Devon and Felix had brought all the black blades that we'd stolen from Victor tonight, putting them behind the grates for safekeeping.

But the weapons weren't going to be locked up for long, since I was going to steal them again right now.

I moved past the glass partition, crossed the mats, and stopped in front of the last row of weapons, the ones that pulsed with magic, the ones that Devon and Felix had just brought in here less than an hour ago. A heavy padlock secured the grate and it was actually locked. Of course it was. Devon would never be so careless as to leave the weapons unprotected.

Finally, a small challenge. Grinning, I slid my chopstick lock picks out of my hair, bent over, and went to work on the padlock. It *snicked* open less than a minute later, and I unhooked it from the grate and slid it into one of my coat pockets. I opened the grate, wincing at the faint *creak* it made, then reached inside to grab the first sword—

"You've gotten awfully good at picking that lock," a voice called out behind me.

I tensed, then hissed out a breath and turned around. "Really? Because I think I'm losing my touch. I keep letting people sneak up on me tonight. First Deah and now you."

The overhead lights snapped on, revealing Claudia Sinclair standing by the double doors, the training room's only other entrance, besides the window that I'd shimmied through.

"Oh, Serena showed me a few of her tricks," Claudia said, locking the doors behind her so that we wouldn't be discovered. "Besides, I knew that you'd come down here as soon as possible to move the weapons. It's the same thing your mother would have done."

She smiled, her green eyes soft and warm with memories. Claudia and my mom had been best friends back when they were about my age, and Claudia still missed her just as much as I did.

"Well, are you just going to stand there, or are you going to help me move the weapons?" I asked. "This was your idea, after all."

Claudia arched her eyebrows at my snarky tone, but she stepped forward and helped me strip the swords and daggers off the pegs on the wall. I placed the real black blades into the same two duffel bags that Devon and Felix had used to carry them down here, since the guys had left the bags behind after they'd finished hanging up the weapons. Then Claudia moved behind the rows of seats and dragged out two more bags of weapons that she'd hidden back there sometime earlier today. More fakes from Mo's pawnshop spray-painted to look like black blades.

We switched out all the magic-filled weapons for the fake ones; then I closed the grate, locked the padlock over it again, and stepped back, scanning everything with a critical eye.

"How does it look to you?" Claudia asked, knowing that my sight magic let me examine every little detail.

"Exactly the same as before. No one will know the difference. They haven't noticed so far, have they? Not even Devon and Felix, and they've been bringing weapons down here for the last two weeks."

She shook her head. "No, they haven't noticed. But it's a necessary precaution."

It had been Claudia's idea to switch out the weapons again and hide them somewhere else. A lot of people and pixies lived and worked in the Sinclair mansion, and folks were constantly roaming through the halls. With all the tension between the Families these days, it wasn't out of the realm of possibility to think that someone could be a spy for Victor or had seen Devon, Felix, and me carrying bags of weapons around the mansion. So Claudia had wanted a little extra insurance that the black blades would be safe.

That's why I snuck into the training room every time we came back from the Draconi compound and took the weapons we'd stolen to another hiding spot. I was actually storing the weapons in a couple of different places, along with some other supplies. Victor would strike out against the other Families soon, and I was going to be ready to protect my friends and myself when he did.

"Are you ready for the next step?" Claudia asked.

I nodded, braced myself, and held out my hand. "Hit me with your best shot."

She rolled her eyes at my flip response, but she took my hand in her own. Claudia stared at me, making sure that I was really ready.

And then she blasted me with her magic.

Most magic fell into three categories—strength, speed, and senses. People who could lift cars with their bare hands, or move faster than I could blink, or hear a quarter hit the floor from a hundred feet away. But there were also other people like Claudia who had more unique Talents. People in the other Families called Claudia the Ice Queen, since she was always so calm, cool, and in control. But in her case, the nickname was literally true as well, since she had the power to freeze people with a mere touch of her hand.

Just like she was doing to me right now.

Claudia kept her gaze steady on mine even as her magic washed over me, the chilly wave of her power zipping up my hand and arm.

But it was nothing compared to the cold that exploded inside my own body.

In addition to my soulsight, I had another very special, very rare Talent—transference magic, the ability to absorb any magic directed against me. Whenever someone tried to knock me out with their strength or trip me with their speed, my own transference power flared to life, and I felt the cold burn of the other person's magic running through my body, as if I had ice in my veins instead of blood. Not only that, but I could actually *use* that magic in different ways, like making myself stronger or quicker or even healing a horrible stab wound that someone had inflicted on me.

In a way, I supposed that I was just like Victor Draconi. He used black blades to rip magic out of monsters, while I used my Talent to steal power from other people. The thought made me frown, but I focused on Claudia.

Her frosty power blasted over me in intense waves, making me wince, but almost immediately it congealed into an even stronger cold, one that roared through my body like an icy fire. Oh, magic affected—and hurt—me just like it did everyone else, but thanks to my transference power, magic almost always made me stronger too. And I would need all the extra strength I could get to carry the heavy bags of weapons over to my hiding spot.

Not even Claudia knew where I was keeping the weapons, and she said that she didn't want to know. I supposed that it was better this way, although part of me hated lying to Devon, Felix, Oscar, and Mo. But I'd rather have them be safe and angry at me than dead, and that's exactly what would happen if Victor ever got his hands on all the magic-filled blades.

After about a minute of dousing me with her power, Claudia dropped her hand from mine and stepped back. "Is that enough?"

She stared down at my hand, which had turned a dark blue—almost black, really—from frostbite. But even as she looked at my hand, the blue started to fade as my body quickly absorbed all her magic. In a few seconds, my skin was its normal color again. I flexed my fingers, then curled my hand into a fist, enjoying the sudden surge of strength.

"I'm good," I said. "You gave me enough strength to haul the weapons out of the mansion and then some. That's all I need."

She nodded. "I'll leave you to it then."

Claudia went over and unlocked the training room doors. She started to open one of them to slip outside, but she stopped and glanced back over her shoulder at me.

"Good luck," she said.

I arched my eyebrows. "You keep telling me that, but luck has nothing to do with it. It's all part of our plan, remember?"

"I know, but it still doesn't hurt to say it. Besides, Serena always used to wish me luck whenever I was doing something important for the Family. I like upholding her tradition." Claudia gave me a soft, sad smile. "And I think that we'll need all the luck we can get before this battle with Victor is over."

She smiled at me again, but her expression was even more troubled than before, and she quickly dropped her gaze from mine, turned off the lights, and slipped out of the training room.

I shivered, but not from the cold magic coursing through my body.

No, this time, I shivered because her words were likely all too true.

I grabbed the two duffel bags full of weapons, went back over to the window that I'd slid through before, and hefted the bags up and out of it, before crawling through the window myself and back out onto the mansion lawn. Then I closed the window behind me, shouldered the heavy bags, clutching them both against my chest to avoid any telltale *clank-clanks*, and crept through the shadows, avoiding the guards until I was able to slip into the woods that surrounded the mansion.

While I'd been in the training room, thick, heavy rain clouds had slid in front of the moon and stars, obscuring their silvery light and making it even darker than before. But my sight magic let me easily navigate through the trees to my ultimate destination—the Sinclair Family cemetery.

I stepped out of the trees and into a large clearing. No guards were stationed this deep in the woods, but I still glanced around, making sure that I was alone. And I was, except for a few tree trolls that peered at me from their nests in the treetops, their green eyes burning like electrified emeralds in the darkness. A few of them *cheep-cheeped*, chiding me for disturbing their sleep, but I'd make it up to them later.

A black, wrought-iron fence ringed the cemetery itself, and I dropped the two duffel bags by the fence before pushing through the gate and walking to the very back of the cemetery.

I stopped in front of a black tombstone with a five-pointed star carved into the top, along with the name Serena Sterling. I stepped forward and laid my hand on the tombstone, which was cool and damp with mist. Claudia had shown me my mom's grave several weeks ago, when I'd first joined the Sinclair Family, and I'd been coming here ever since. Even though my mom had been dead for four years now, just seeing her tombstone made me feel a little closer to her, like she was still with me in spirit, like she was watching over me from wherever she was. Coming out here and having these quiet moments didn't keep me from missing her, but they made my heartache over her loss just a little easier to bear.

I ran my hand over the star carved into her tombstone, the same symbol that was etched into the hilt of my—

her—sword. The motion made a star-shaped sapphire ring on my finger gleam, the gem shimmering like a dark blue tear that was about to drop from my hand and splatter against the tombstone. My mom's engagement ring, the last present my dad had given her before he'd died.

I could have stayed here longer—much longer—just thinking about my mom and how much I missed her, but I still had work to do. So I drew in a breath, then let it out, turned around, and walked back through the gate.

I grabbed the two bags of weapons from where I'd left them in the grass and headed over to a large blood persimmon tree that leaned over the cemetery, right above my mom's tombstone. I slung the two bags across my chest, making sure that I wouldn't lose them, then took hold of the trunk and started climbing.

I always enjoyed climbing, whether it was snaking up a tree so I could get a better view of my surroundings, scurrying up the drainpipe on my balcony to go see Devon at the mansion, or scaling the outside of some brownstone in town in order to get on the roof so I could sneak inside and see what all I could steal. But the two bags of weapons were heavy and awkward and made this particular climb more difficult than normal. I couldn't have managed it at all, if not for the extra boost of strength that Claudia had given me in the training room.

That extra magic burned out of my body just as I reached the spot in the tree that I wanted. I leaned back against the trunk, wiped the sweat off my forehead, and caught my breath. Then I carefully removed the two bags from across my chest, making sure that I had a good grip on them, and shimmied up a little higher in the tree, getting into position.

At my chest level, two thick branches split off from the main trunk, dipping down before rising up and out and snaking skyward again. Together, the branches formed a perfect, sturdy crook for me to nestle the bags in. For extra insurance, I drew out a long length of spidersilk rope from one of my coat pockets, looped it around both bags several times, and tied them down to the branches. This way, I didn't have to worry about the bags falling out of the tree or some troll getting curious about what might be inside them, jumping up and down on the branches, and knocking the bags down to the ground.

Of course, a treetop in the woods wasn't the most secure place, but the weapons would be okay here for a day or two until I could take them to my other, better hiding spot. It was the same procedure I'd used with all the other black blades we'd stolen from Victor, sneaking them away from the mansion and over to my final hiding spot a few at a time, and it had worked like a charm so far.

Besides, it wasn't like I could get into a car and drive down to the city. Not this late at night. At least, not without attracting the attention of the guards on duty. They might not spot me creeping through the shadows, but a car was another matter. The guards would wonder where I was going and what I was doing, which was exactly what I wanted to avoid. So it was better to leave the weapons out here in the woods where there was little chance that anyone would find them.

Once the two bags were secured to the branches, I climbed down the blood persimmon. The trolls in the neighboring trees were still watching me, their green eyes full of curiosity, and a couple of them *cheep-cheeped* at me again. So I reached into my coat pockets and drew out several bars of dark chocolate. Many folks were afraid of monsters, but not me. My mom had taught me that most monsters were actually pretty easy to get along with, if you knew what toll to pay to get them to leave you alone. In the tree trolls' case, dark chocolate was the preferred bribe of choice.

So I held the candy bars up where all the trolls could see them, then laid the chocolate down on a flat rock off to one side of the clearing.

"Sorry if I kept y'all up past your bedtimes," I said. "So here's a treat to make up for it."

The trolls' eyes brightened with sly satisfaction and they *cheep-cheeped* again, but it was a far happier sound than before. I grinned, knowing that they would climb down from their nests and snatch the chocolate bars the second I was gone.

I started to leave the clearing, but my gaze went over to my mom's tombstone at the back of the cemetery. My grin faded, and the old, familiar pain of her loss flooded my chest again, like a copper crusher coiled around my heart, squeezing, squeezing tight.

"Good night, Mom," I called out in a soft voice.

I waited, but of course there was no response. No voice, no whispered words, not even the whistle of the wind in the trees. I blinked back a few tears, then sighed, stuck my hands in the pockets of her spidersilk coat, and trudged back to the mansion for the night.

CHAPTER FIVE

The next morning, I got up, got dressed, and went down to the dining hall as usual, as though I hadn't spent most of the previous night skulking through the shadows and stealing things that didn't belong to me.

Nothing that I hadn't done before.

The dining hall was one of the largest rooms in the mansion, the place where everyone gathered to meet, eat, and more. Long tables that could seat dozens of people each crouched on top of black-and-white Persian rugs, while floor-to-ceiling windows lined the back wall, offering a lovely view of the landscaped grounds and the deep, dark woods beyond.

I'd gotten here a little later than normal, so everyone was well into their breakfasts. My stomach growled, reminding me that I hadn't eaten anything since the mini cheeseburgers in the library last night, so I went over to the buffet tables that lined one of the walls and fixed myself a heaping plate of blackberry pancakes, cheesy scrambled eggs, grilled hash browns, and of course, bacon—lots and lots of bacon.

I crunched down on one of the crispy strips, enjoying the smoky applewood flavor, then grabbed a tall glass of orange juice and headed over to the table where Devon and Felix were sitting with Mo. Oscar was at another table, and he waved at me before turning back to his pixie friends.

Felix and Mo were both talking a hundred words a minute to each other, so I slid into the seat next to Devon.

He leaned over and bumped his shoulder against mine. "I missed you on the roof last night."

"Sorry," I said. "But once I got back to my room, I took a shower and went to bed. I guess all that sneaking around made me more tired than I'd realized."

Devon nodded, accepting my explanation, although his eyes sharpened just a bit. I focused on my breakfast instead of looking at him. Devon was supersmart and it wouldn't take much for him to realize what I'd really been up to last night. I'd have to be more careful about lying to him. I didn't like keeping him or the others in the dark about my moving the black blades out of the mansion, but Claudia wanted it this way, and she was the head of the Family. So I'd follow her orders—for now.

Devon's suspicion quickly melted away, and he grinned at me. I grinned back at him, and we both focused on our food, since we couldn't get a word in edgewise with Felix and Mo both talking as fast as they possibly could. I polished off one plate of food, went back over to the buffet, and got another plate. This time, with even more bacon. Mmm. Bacon. It really was the perfect food.

"So what do you think, kid?" Mo asked, waving his hand over several paint swatches that he'd laid out on the table. "Cerulean blue or smoke gray?"

I sat down with my fresh plate of food. "You're repainting the Razzle Dazzle? Again? Why? You just painted it a few weeks ago. Seafoam green, if I remember."

Mo tipped his white straw hat back on his head. "I read this article that muted colors, like blues and grays, soothe people. And you know when people are calm, they—"

"Spend more money," I said in unison with him.

He winked at me. "You got it, kid."

I couldn't help but laugh. Mo had a bit of an obsession with interior decorating. He was always painting, cleaning, arranging, and rearranging the merchandise at his pawnshop in hopes of luring more customers inside and then getting them to buy more stuff while they were there.

He nudged the paint swatches a little closer to me. "So which color do you like?"

Before I could answer him, Claudia strolled into the dining hall, followed by two men. The older man had snow-white hair and was wearing a black tweed suit. William Reginald, the Family butler, responsible for overseeing the mansion and everyone inside it. The other man had wavy black hair and bronze skin and sported a far more casual look with his black polo shirt and khakis. Angelo Morales, Felix's dad and the Family chemist, who grew and harvested the stitch-sting bushes and other magical plants in the greenlab.

At first, I thought the three of them were just here for breakfast, like everyone else. Then I noticed the hard set of Claudia's lips and the worry that darkened her eyes. Devon noticed it too.

"Is something wrong?" I asked.

He shook his head. "Not that she's told me."

Claudia strolled into the middle of the dining hall and stopped, clasping her hands in front of her. Slowly, everyone quieted down and turned to face her. Claudia looked out over the pixies, guards, and other workers who made up the Sinclair Family. She stared at me for a second, but her gaze darted past mine before I could use my soulsight to see what she was really feeling.

"I just wanted to remind everyone that tonight is the dinner for all the Families," she called out. "As usual, several of you will be attending the actual dinner itself, along with me and the other senior members of the Family, while the rest of the pixies, guards, and workers will either remain here or man their usual stations down on the Midway. Given all the recent tensions with the other Families, I want everyone to be especially sharp and on guard tonight. Is that understood?"

Everyone nodded back at her, their faces suddenly serious.

Claudia scanned the crowd again. "Good. That is all. Enjoy the rest of your breakfast."

She nodded to everyone, then turned on her heel and left the dining hall. Reginald and Angelo stayed behind, both of them going over to talk to the pixies, guards, and workers about their duties for the day. Mo got up and went over to the other two men. Slowly, everyone else turned back around and focused on their food and conversations again.

"What was that about?" Felix asked.

Devon shrugged. "You know the dinner for the Families is always a tense time. She's probably just worried about that. After all, things didn't go so well at the last dinner."

"You mean Grant kidnapping and almost killing you and Lila?" Felix snorted. "Yeah, I'd say that *didn't go so well* is a total understatement. But Grant got turned into lochness food, thanks to Lila, so at least you don't have to worry about him tonight."

Grant Sanderson had been the Sinclair Family broker, but he'd wanted more magic and more power within the Family, and he'd tried to kill Devon and me to get it. I'd turned the tables on Grant instead, and he was the one who'd ended up dead, just like Felix had said.

Devon shrugged again. "According to my mom, there's always something to worry about during the dinner."

Felix shook his head. "Well, you would think that your

mom would relax a little, now that we have all of Victor's black blades."

"*Most* of Victor's black blades," I corrected. "We had to leave some behind, remember?"

Felix rolled his eyes. "Yeah, yeah, I was there too, remember? But what could he possibly do with the few weapons we left behind?"

"I don't know," I muttered. "I just don't know."

But Claudia was obviously worried about it, and so was I.

Despite Claudia's warning, the morning passed by quietly. Devon helped his mom with some Family business, while Felix and I went down to the training room. Felix had healing magic, and he was definitely more of a flirt than a fighter, but he was determined to improve his skills, something I was helping him with.

The two of us sparred for a couple of hours, then got lunch together in the dining hall before going our separate ways for the rest of the day. Felix headed up to the greenlab to help his dad harvest some stitch-sting bushes. Me? I went to my room and took a nap, trying to catch up on some of the sleep that I'd missed last night when I'd been skulking through the woods. All this thieving was wearing me out.

At six o'clock that evening, I was back in the library, wearing a black pantsuit that was almost a mirror image of Claudia's, although I'd opted for a pair of black sneakers, instead of the stilettoes she wore. Devon, Felix, Angelo, and Reginald all sported black suits and shirts as well. So did Mo, although he'd paired his suit jacket with a black Hawaiian shirt patterned with white hibiscus flowers. The same splashy pattern also adorned his shiny wingtips.

My jacket was unbuttoned, revealing my black camisole

underneath, but I was far more interested in the wide, black leather belt cinched around my waist. Three stars were hooked to the belt, but they were far more than the pretty decorations they appeared to be. Several quarters were also tucked into one of the hidden slots in the belt, and I ran my fingers all the way around the leather, making sure that everything was secure.

Devon reached over and grabbed my hand. "You've checked and rechecked your belt and your quarters three times now. All your supplies are right where they're supposed to be."

"I know," I muttered. "And I'd be checking and rechecking my sword if it wasn't up in my room. I really want to take a weapon tonight."

He grinned and squeezed my hand. "And you know that no one is allowed to have any weapons at the dinner. Be glad you can get away with wearing those three throwing stars on your belt."

I squeezed his hand back, then buttoned up my jacket, hiding the belt and throwing stars from sight. "I know, but I still wish I had a sword. Or a dagger. Or something else really sharp and pointy."

"Don't worry," he said. "Everything will be fine, and the other Families will be on their best behavior tonight, including Victor, Blake, and the rest of the Draconis."

He was probably right, but I still couldn't help but worry all the same. Even if tonight's dinner went peacefully, Victor didn't plan on keeping those black blades locked away in his secret room forever. He'd stockpiled all those weapons and all that magic with the sole purpose of destroying the other Families. And now that he'd told Blake his plan, it was only a matter of time before Victor attacked us.

But I kept my worries to myself. If I'd voiced them,

Devon would have tried to reassure me. He would have said that we'd stolen almost all of the black blades and that Victor couldn't hurt us with them now.

But that wasn't true. Not really. Because Victor didn't need black blades and stolen monster magic to kill us.

Not when he'd so easily murdered my mom.

Serena Sterling had been one of the best fighters around. She was smart, strong, and had survived more battles and monster attacks than anyone I'd ever known. When I was younger, I'd thought my mom was invincible, and that nothing could ever really hurt her. But Victor had stormed into our apartment that hot summer day four years ago and killed her in a matter of minutes.

I'd always wondered how he'd done that, since I'd only seen the horrible, bloody aftermath and not the actual attack itself. Victor was rumored to have many, many Talents, and I'd lain awake countless nights, trying to figure out exactly what magic he could have used to get the drop on my mom, what power he had that had let him so easily cut her to pieces, without getting so much as a scratch on himself in return. Or maybe it had taken the combination of his magic and Blake's strength to overpower her. I doubted that I'd ever know for sure, and part of me didn't really want to.

Because my mom had been the best fighter I'd known, and if Victor could kill her, then he could do the exact same thing to me and my friends, black blades or not.

Devon grabbed my hand again. "Are you okay? You look like you're about to be sick."

I threaded my fingers through his and forced myself to plaster a smile on my face. "Never better," I muttered. "Never better."

CHAPTER SIX

We left the library, went outside, and got into a black SUV with the white Sinclair hand-and-sword crest emblazoned on the doors. Devon drove, while I sat in the front passenger seat, and Felix and Mo chatted in the back. Claudia, Angelo, and Reginald were in another vehicle in front of ours, along with a couple of guards.

The vehicles wound down the curvy mountain roads, and thirty minutes later we were cruising through the town of Cloudburst Falls. It was almost seven o'clock now, but people still filled the streets on this hot July evening, taking photos, buying hats and matching T-shirts, and chowing down on burgers, fries, nachos, and other treats from the food carts that lined the sidewalks.

Normally, I would have enjoyed watching all the tourist rubes, but that strange tension I'd felt back at the mansion just wouldn't leave me. My sight magic didn't let me see the future, not like Seleste's Talent did, but I couldn't help but feel something bad was about to happen. Or maybe that was just because I'd spent the last two weeks stealing weapons from the most dangerous man in town. During the last four years, I'd avoided the Families—and especially stealing from them—as much as possible. But now, I'd swiped the very thing that Victor prized above all—his magic-filled black blades—and I was afraid it was going to come back around and bite me, like a monster I'd gotten a little too close to.

Sometime very, very soon.

Devon pulled into a parking lot off the Midway that was reserved for the Families, but it was already full of cars and there weren't any empty spaces. The surrounding streets were also full of vans, buses, and other tour-group vehicles, and he had to drive five blocks over before he found an empty spot on one of the quieter side streets.

"Come on," Devon said, getting out of the car. "We're on the opposite side of the Midway from the restaurant. We'll have to hurry to catch up with the others."

Felix and Mo took the lead, both of them still talking about Mo repainting the Razzle Dazzle and arguing about which colors were more soothing, but Devon stepped up beside me and held out his hand. I smiled and laced my fingers through his, enjoying the warmth of his skin against mine. Together, we followed our friends.

We cut through a couple of alleys and stepped out into the Midway, which was even more crowded than the surrounding streets and shopping squares. Loud, upbeat music blasted out of the restaurants, candy shops, and other businesses that made up the enormous outer circle of the Midway, with still more music blaring from the carts selling popcorn, cotton candy, T-shirts, and sunglasses that were spaced along the cobblestone paths winding from one side of the area to the other. The scents of funnel cakes, corn dogs, and other deep-fried treats filled the air, and neon lights flashed on practically everything, all of them in the shapes of swords, monsters, and other magic-themed objects. Despite their modern goods, almost all of the businesses had old-timey-sounding names like Courtly Chocolate Creations and Princely Pizzeria. It was an odd mix of contemporary and renaissance faire, with a whole lot of cheap and tacky thrown in for good measure.

We slowly maneuvered through the crush of people, made it over to one of the cobblestone paths, and wound our way through the large park that took up the center of the Midway. Fountains bubbled up into the air, with kids laughing, shrieking, and running through the cool, arching sprays of water while their parents looked on from their perches on nearby benches. The heat of the day had finally broken, but the air was still as thick and sticky as one of the caramel apples you could buy from the food carts.

But I looked past the running kids, tired parents, and busy vendors at the other people in the park—the guards.

The Families had long ago divided up the Midway like the sections of a pie, and every Family's guards patrolled their respective area. It was easy to tell the tourists with their matching, neon-colored T-shirts and baseball hats from the guards, who were dressed in black boots and pants, along with cloaks and feathered cavalier hats that boasted their Family's colors. Of course, the tourist rubes thought that the guards, their old-fashioned clothes, and the swords and daggers belted to their hips were all just part of the fun, and many of the rubes stopped to snap photos of the men and women who were patrolling through the park. What the tourists didn't realize was that the guards and swords were more than just cheesy decorations. The guards all took their jobs very, very seriously, watching out for everything from shoplifters to pickpockets to monsters who might wander out of the shadows and slither a little too close to the crowds.

I grew especially tense as we moved through the Draconi section of the park and started seeing men and women wearing red cloaks and hats, along with gold cuffs stamped with that dragon crest. Of course the Draconi guards knew that our black suits and shirts marked us as Sinclairs, and they all turned to follow our movements as we walked through their territory.

The guards didn't make a move to attack, but they all glared at us and dropped their hands to the hilts of their swords. My own fingers twitched, itching to feel the security of my own sword strapped to my side. Beside me, Devon gripped my hand a little tighter, as tense as I was. Even Felix and Mo stopped talking and picked up their pace, wanting to get through this section of the park as quickly as possible.

Still, the deeper we moved into Draconi territory, the more something bothered me, something about the guards. I don't know exactly why or when I started counting the ones we passed, but I did. One, two, three. . . . Just like up at the Draconi mansion last night, it didn't take me long to figure out what was different.

There weren't nearly as many Draconi guards patrolling here tonight as there usually were.

With their blood-red cloaks and feathered hats, the guards were easy to pick out of the crowd. Given how many tourists were out on the Midway, I would have expected at least three dozen guards to be patrolling, if not more, but I only spotted a handful of them. I scanned the food carts, the bubbling fountains, and the grassy areas beyond, but I didn't spot any other Draconis. Weird.

Last night, Victor had had too many guards up at the Draconi mansion, and now there weren't enough down here on the Midway where they were truly needed. What was he up to? Maybe he thought that doubling the guards at the mansion would keep all of his black blades safe and secure inside his secret room until he was ready to use them. Of course, that wasn't the case, but still, I wondered why he'd changed the guard rotations so much.

"Something wrong?" Devon asked.

I shook my head. "Still wishing I had my sword, that's all."

"Don't worry. In a couple of hours, we'll be back at the

mansion, and this dinner will be nothing but an awkward memory."

"Yeah, you're right." I forced myself to smile at him.

Devon grinned back at me, then turned to keep an eye on the Draconi guards as we hurried past them.

A minute later, we finally left their territory behind. Devon, Felix, and Mo all relaxed and started talking back and forth to each other, but I remained quiet, still scanning everything and everyone around us, and still feeling like something was seriously wrong.

Fifteen minutes later, we made it to the far side of the Midway, walked down another cobblestone path, and entered one of the shopping squares. A single building made out of gray stone took up the back of the square, with a neon sign spelling out the words The White Orchid in beautiful, flowing script. An orchid also burned at the end of the sign, slowly lighting up one white petal at a time as though it were blossoming over and over again. The Salazars had hosted the last dinner for the Families several weeks ago, and now it was the Ito Family's turn. Devon, Felix, Mo, and I hurried over and entered the restaurant, which had been closed to the public for the night.

The White Orchid was as beautiful and elegant as its name suggested, with shimmering silver cloths and white candles covering all the tables, as well as the booths that lined two of the walls. Fountains made out of gray stone gurgled in all four corners of the room, each one surrounded by potted orchids of all shapes and sizes, but all in hues of white, from the palest, purest snow white to a rich cream to a silvery shade that almost looked blue under the lights.

Mixed in with the orchids were crystal vases filled with large, fragrant clusters of purple wisteria—the Ito Family crest. Still more orchids and wisteria were nestled in alcoves and nooks carved into the walls, as well as lining the mirrored shelves behind the bar that ran along the back wall of the restaurant.

A large round table covered with a neutral white cloth perched in the center of the restaurant. That's where the heads of the Families would sit, eat, and talk when the dinner started. Smaller tables were evenly spaced around that center one, with booths hugging the walls on either side and padded stools running along the bar in the back. Soft, soothing music that sounded like a mix of rain, wind, and chimes hummed in the background, and the wisteria clusters perfumed the air, along with sweet notes of vanilla from the lit candles.

We'd arrived a bit late and the restaurant was already packed, with folks milling around and talking to each other, including Claudia, Angelo, Reginald, and the Sinclair guards. Mo waved and went over to join them, but Devon, Felix, and I hung back, scanning the crowd.

Everyone wore a black suit, and the color of the shirts and ties represented which Family the wearers belonged to. Black for the Sinclairs, purple for the Itos, dark green for the Volkovs, and so on. I didn't spot any red shirts and ties in the mix, though, and no one was wearing a gold dragon cuff. None of the Draconis were here yet.

My worry kicked up another notch. I'd been hoping that the Draconis would already be here so I could discreetly check on Deah. She'd texted me late last night saying she was fine, and Felix had said he'd gotten a similar text from her this morning too. But that had been hours ago, and I wanted to see for myself that she was really okay—

"Finally! There you are! I thought you guys were *never* going to get here," a voice called out behind us.

We turned to find a slender, petite girl with black hair and dark eyes grinning at us. She wore a black pantsuit with a purple shirt, and she'd braided a purple ribbon through her hair. A silver cuff stamped with wisteria flowers glimmered on her right wrist.

"Hey, Poppy," I said, grinning back at her.

I hugged her, and so did Devon and Felix. Even though Poppy Ito belonged to another Family, she was still a good friend, and the four of us started talking about the latest superhero movie that Poppy and I had dragged the guys to see last week. Poppy and I were both action-movie junkies, but instead of being totally into our conversation the way she usually was, she kept checking her watch, a worried expression on her pretty face.

Devon noticed it too. "Something wrong?"

"My dad's getting angry," Poppy said. "The Draconis were supposed to be here an hour early so that my dad and Victor could talk about a new treaty, but Victor hasn't shown up yet. He didn't even call or text my dad and tell him that he was going to be late. So rude."

Once again, that worry bubbled up in the pit of my stomach, but I forced it aside. "Well, you know Victor. He and Blake think the world revolves around them. He's probably just not considerate enough to call and tell your dad that he was going to be late."

Poppy shrugged. "Either way, my dad is angry about it. I should go check on him. I'll see you guys later, okay?"

We murmured our goodbyes, and Poppy headed over to her father, Hiroshi Ito. Poppy was training to become her Family's broker, and all of the Itos nodded respectfully as she passed them. Poppy was as well regarded in her Family as Devon was in ours.

I looked at Devon. "Has Victor ever done that to Claudia? Set up a meeting and then been late with no explanation?"

He shook his head. "Victor and my mom don't meet—*ever*. The only contact they have is at these Family dinners.

That's the one time and place they get together in the same room to talk business. The rest of the time, Victor is happy to pretend that my mom doesn't exist, and she does the same thing to him."

I frowned. Instead of reassuring me, his words bothered me even more, although I couldn't put my finger on exactly why.

Devon, Felix, and I moved deeper into the restaurant, saying hello to the members of the other Families that we knew, like Julio Salazar, a guy our age that I'd beaten during the Tournament of Blades a few weeks ago. Julio joked that he wanted a rematch next year. I grinned and told him to bring it on. Julio grinned back at me, then went over to talk to Poppy.

Hiroshi Ito pinged a fork against his water glass. The crowd quieted down, and he welcomed everyone to the dinner. I glanced at a clock on the wall. It was almost seven-thirty now and the Draconis still hadn't shown up, even though everyone was supposed to have been here by seven.

But Hiroshi pinged his fork again, and tuxedo-clad waiters emerged from the double doors at the back of the restaurant, carrying trays filled with fresh fruits and vegetables, chicken skewers, and other appetizers. Looked like the dinner was going to start without the Draconis. Weird. What was Victor up to? Was arriving late some sort of power trip on his part? Something he was doing just because he could? I didn't know, and it bothered me.

Apparently, it bothered Claudia too. She sidled over to me and raised her water glass up to her lips, as though she didn't want anyone to realize that she was talking to me.

"Are you sure that Blake didn't spot you leaving the Draconi mansion last night?" she murmured. "That he didn't realize you'd stolen Victor's weapons?"

"He didn't see us. I'm sure of it. Why?"

She shook her head, but her gaze locked with mine and her sharp worry pricked my chest. She was afraid that we hadn't gotten away as cleanly as I'd thought and that Blake and Victor had realized what we'd done.

But there was nothing either one of us could do about that right now, so Claudia moved on to mix and mingle with the heads of the other Families. Devon and Felix were talking with Poppy and Julio, while Mo, Angelo, and Reginald were chatting with Roberto Salazar, the head of the Salazar Family. Everything was normal; everything was fine.

The waiters circulated with the food, which looked and smelled delicious, especially the bacon-wrapped pineapple chunks, but I didn't eat a single bite. I couldn't, not with the way my stomach was churning. And something else was bothering me too, something about the restaurant. I frowned. No, not the restaurant, but the temperature inside.

I felt . . . *cold*.

I froze, my gaze flicking around the room. It might be a hot July night outside, but the air conditioning was going full blast, cooling the inside of the restaurant to a pleasant temperature. But I felt colder than that, cold enough to shiver, despite my long-sleeved pantsuit. And I realized that it wasn't just the air-conditioning—there was a frigid chill in the air that only meant one thing.

Someone here was using magic.

My gaze flicked around the room again, trying to figure out who was using magic and what they were doing with it. Normally, someone had to actually use their magic on me in some physical way—hit me, punch me, trip me, whatever—before my own transference power flared to life and let me absorb their magic. But if someone's magic was strong enough, I could feel that familiar chill of power all by itself.

Just like I was right now.

So who here had that much magic? I looked over all the folks in the restaurant, but everyone was laughing, talking, eating, and drinking, and I didn't see anyone doing anything suspicious, much less something that involved actual magic.

Oh, sure, a Salazar guard in the corner was juggling bottles of water, using his speed magic to make the bottles spin impossibly fast, but he was just showing off. So was the Ito guard in another corner who was bench-pressing another guard up over his head. Since the Draconis weren't here, it seemed everyone was determined to relax and have a good time.

So I turned around in a slow circle, scanning everyone again, still searching for the source of the magic. If I could just pinpoint which person it was coming from, then I could reassure myself that someone was just goofing around and there was no serious threat here.

But I couldn't do that.

Because the magic wasn't coming from one person—it was moving all around the restaurant, getting closer and closer all the while, like a net slowly tightening over a bunch of trapped tree trolls. And I suddenly realized exactly why the Draconis were late, why there had been so few guards on the Midway tonight, where they were right now, and what they were doing.

I whipped around toward the front of the restaurant and opened my mouth to shout a warning, even though I knew I was going to be too slow to stop what was about to happen. Sure enough, a second later, the front doors burst open and men and women wearing blood-red cloaks stormed inside the restaurant.

And each one of them was carrying a black blade.

CHAPTER SEVEN

The Draconi guards ran into the room, quickly spreading out into a solid line, a barricade at the front of the restaurant to keep anyone from leaving.

People let out shocked gasps and scrambled back. More than one person dropped his hand to his side, reaching for the sword that wasn't there. But the Draconi guards raised their weapons and everyone else froze, realizing they couldn't take on the Draconis and win without weapons of their own.

I cursed. I should have known that Victor would do something like this. That he would wait until the heads of the Families, including Claudia, were all gathered together in one place so that he could take them all out at the same time. He'd had to do things this way. Devon had told me as much, when he'd said that Claudia was only in the same room with Victor during the Family dinners. He'd want to kill her first, and this was his best chance to do that.

I looked at Claudia, who was standing on the opposite side of the restaurant with Mo, Angelo, and Reginald flanking her. She narrowed her eyes at me, then deliberately flicked her gaze to the right, where Devon was standing about thirty feet away from her. I nodded back, knowing what she wanted. I would do whatever it took to protect Devon and make sure he lived through this. Claudia nodded back at me, some of the tension in her face easing.

The Draconi guards moved deeper into the restaurant, with one stopping every few feet, until they had everyone surrounded. Once the room was completely under their control, the guards by the front doors stepped aside so that three more people could enter the restaurant—Victor, Blake, and Deah.

Victor and Blake swept into the restaurant as if they owned it, with Blake in particular swaggering like everything had already gone his way.

Deah crept in behind her father and brother, her head down, her shoulders slumped. She shot Felix a quick glance that was full of sorrow, worry, and misery. Felix glanced down at his phone, then back at her, his eyebrows knitting together in confusion. She must not have texted or called him about what was happening. I wondered why she hadn't tried to warn him and the rest of us.

Victor and Blake strode out into the middle of the restaurant, but Deah stayed back against the wall, her hand curled around the hilt of the sword belted to her waist, staring at the Draconi guards instead of the other folks in the restaurant, as if she knew that her own Family members were the greatest danger to her.

When she realized that the guards were ignoring her, Deah glanced around the restaurant, and her eyes finally met mine. Her worry, fear, guilt, and dread punched me in the chest one after another, but I pushed her tense emotions aside and tipped my head at the guard closest to me, discreetly pointing at the sword in his hand.

Deah frowned, but then she realized what I was asking and gave me a short, sharp nod. So our plan had worked, and the guards were carrying the weapons that had been stored in Victor's secret room. That meant that some of the guards were clutching real, magic-filled black blades, the source of the cold power that I'd sensed earlier and could still feel. But most of them were just holding regular old swords and daggers, which meant we still had a chance to fight back and get out of here alive.

I nodded back at Deah, then focused on Victor, since he was the one in charge. Even I had to admit that he was a handsome man, with a lean, trim figure and thick, wavy, golden hair that was brushed back from his forehead. His eyes were golden too, but instead of being warm and welcoming, they reminded me of coins that had been left outside in a blizzard—completely, utterly cold.

I knew better than anyone else that the eyes were truly the windows to the soul and that despite his handsome exterior, Victor was as black and rotten as they came on the inside, with the darkest heart I'd ever seen.

Victor was the only Draconi who wasn't carrying a weapon. Then again, he didn't need to; a cold chill of magic continually blasted off his body. Victor's own magic was greater than that of any of the black blades in the restaurant, and it made goosebumps rise on my skin in a way that the other stolen magic didn't. Maybe that was because I knew how horribly he'd tortured other people to get so much magic and so many Talents.

White stars winked on and off in my field of vision, and for a moment, the image of my mom's broken, bloody body filled my mind. Her arms and legs bent at awkward angles, the deep, vicious stab wounds in her chest, all the horrible cuts and gashes and slashes that marred her skin, her mouth frozen open in one last helpless scream. . . .

I blinked and blinked, forcing away the white stars and the horrible memories they brought along with them. Now was not the time to let my soulsight magic throw me back into the past and make me relive my mom's murder. Not if I wanted to survive this and help my friends do the same.

"Good," Victor said in a deep, silky voice, clear menace rumbling through each and every one of his words. "I'm so glad that we aren't late to the party."

He waved his hand and all the Draconis snapped up their weapons to an attention stance, including Blake and Deah. Blake realized that I was staring at him and he sneered back at me. My hands curled into fists. When the fighting started, he'd come after me sooner or later. Good. Let him come. I'd show him that I didn't need a weapon to take him down.

Hiroshi Ito stepped to the front of the crowd. "Victor!" he barked out. "What is the meaning of this?"

Victor gave him a cold look. "The meaning is that from this night on, there's only going to be one Family in Cloudburst Falls—the Draconi Family." He looked out over the crowd, his gaze flicking from one face to another. "I'm giving everyone in this room a choice. Join my Family, become a Draconi, and swear your allegiance to me right here and now."

"Or what?" Hiroshi barked again.

Victor gave him another cold look, as if the answer was obvious. "Or die."

Even though everyone knew he was going to say something like that, shocked gasps still rang out, and excited, worried chatter rippled through the crowd. I ignored it all and looked around, glancing at first one Draconi, then another, trying to sense exactly which guards had real black blades and which ones didn't.

One, two, three . . . I counted a dozen guards with black blades, which was the same number of magic-filled weapons I'd left in Victor's secret room. So he hadn't discovered that the weapons were fakes after all. Deah had told me as much with her earlier nod, but it was still good to confirm it for myself. All we had to do was get out of the restaurant and make it back to the Sinclair mansion, and we'd be safe.

Easier said than done, though. But I started looking at all the doors and windows, planning the best and quickest way to get my friends to safety. We could smash through the windows, but that would take precious time and leave us exposed to the Draconi guards. The swinging double doors on the back wall of the restaurant that led into the kitchen were our best bet. Only a few guards were stationed in front of them, and there had to be a rear exit out of the kitchen.

But Hiroshi wasn't about to be cowed so easily by Victor, especially not in one of his own restaurants. "You really think your guards can kill all of us?" he asked. "My Family will fight you to the death before ever we join you."

All around the room, the other Itos muttered their agreement, including Poppy, who now stood next to her father, her eyes narrowed and her hands clenched into fists, ready to fight alongside the rest of her Family.

"I don't *think* my guards can do anything," Victor said, a mocking note creeping into his voice. "I *know* they can. You see, I've known that this day was coming for a long time now, and I've planned accordingly."

He swept his hand out to the side, gesturing at all his guards. "That's why I've outfitted every single one of my guards with a black blade that's filled with magic. Strength, speed, enhanced senses . . . it's all there, all taken from monsters, with each blade matched to a specific guard to best take advantage of my men's natural Talents, to increase their strength and speed until no one can stand against them."

More shocked gasps rang out as people realized that Victor wasn't joking—and just how many monsters he had murdered in order to amass that much magic. But the gasps quickly died down into an eerie, charged silence, as everyone understood just how much trouble we were really in—and how easily the Draconis could use that stolen monster magic to kill every single person in the restaurant.

"So you see, it would be far better to swear your loyalty to me now," Victor purred, satisfaction rippling through his words. "Or I will order my guards to cut you all to pieces."

That eerie silence descended over the restaurant again, more tense than ever before, and everyone started looking back and forth between Victor, the Draconi guards, and their own Family members, debating what to do. No one wanted to bow down to Victor, but they didn't want to get slaughtered either, especially when they knew that they didn't have a fighting chance.

"How about a demonstration then?" Victor called out. "Just to assure you all how serious I really am."

No one answered him, so he turned and gestured for one of his guards to step forward into the center of the restaurant where everyone could see him. I didn't recognize the guard, but he wasn't important right now. Getting my hands on a weapon was.

So I sidled forward, creeping up on the Draconi guard closest to me. But he noticed the movement out of the corner of his eye, and he turned and glowered at me, brandishing his sword in a clear warning to stand still or else. So I stood still. Now wasn't the time to make a move, but soon—very, very soon.

"Go ahead," Victor told the guard. "Stab yourself in the heart with the blade black. Take the magic in it for yourself, and show everyone how strong you can truly be."

The guard stared at Victor, then down at the sword in his hand. I looked at the weapon—*really* looked at it with my sight magic. To the casual observer, it was a genuine black blade, right down to its dull, ash-gray color. But I could see the sword in supersharp detail, and I could tell that the ashy color wasn't from any natural bloodiron, but rather from the paint that had been sprayed on the surface.

So the guard had one of the fake weapons. I almost felt sorry for the guy. He didn't know what he was about to do to himself, but there was no way I could stop him. Not with Victor and all the other Draconis here. Even if I'd shouted a warning to the man, I doubted he would have believed me. Not with the head of his Family urging him on.

"Go on," Victor ordered. "Do it. Stab yourself. Now. Or I'll have Blake do it for you."

Blake stepped up and gave the guard an evil grin, swinging his own sword back and forth in warning. I looked at his weapon too, but it was as fake as the guard's.

The guard swallowed and nervous sweat beaded on his forehead, but he had no choice but to do as his boss commanded. So he slowly changed his grip and turned the point of his sword around, so that it was facing in toward his own chest.

"Go on," Victor said. "Stab yourself. *Now*."

The guard nodded at no one in particular, then sucked in a breath, lifted the sword, and plunged the tip into his own chest, close to his heart. Blood arced through the air, spattering onto one of the white tablecloths. The guard screamed in pain and doubled over. Horrified gasps rippled through the crowd, but no one dared step forward to try to help him.

It was too late for that anyway.

I'd only seen one other person stab herself with a black blade in order to absorb the magic stored in the weapon. When Katia Volkov had plunged two daggers into her own body, she'd screamed and doubled over in pain too, just like this guard. But after a few seconds, Katia had straightened right back up and yanked the daggers out of her chest. The black blades—and the bloodiron they were made out of—had transferred the monster magic from the daggers into Katia's body, and they had also sealed up her wounds, making it seem as though she had never stabbed herself in the first place.

But that didn't happen with this guard.

Since his sword wasn't made out of bloodiron, it didn't contain any magic, and the wound the man had just inflicted on himself was very, very real—and very, very fatal. Blood poured out of the deep stab wound, and the man screamed again and collapsed in a heap at Victor's feet, clutching at the sword that was still stuck in his chest.

Silence descended over the restaurant again. Blood kept oozing out of the man's chest, and his screams quickly faded to hoarse rasps, before his head lolled to one side and his body went slack altogether.

Dead—the guard was dead.

Killed by plunging a fake black blade into his own chest. Victor might have ordered him to do it, but guilt still burned in my heart at the part I'd played in the man's death, even though I couldn't have saved him.

Victor's mouth dropped open and he stared down at the dead guard in disbelief, trying to figure out what had gone so wrong with his perfect plan.

A low laugh sounded, and everyone's heads snapped around, as they wondered who would be laughing at a time like this.

The answer? Claudia.

She strode forward and the crowd parted to let her through. She skirted guards and tables, moving through the restaurant until she was standing in the middle of the open space behind the dead guard and directly opposite Victor.

He looked at her, then down at the dead man on the floor. His mouth flattened out into a harsh line.

"What did you do?" he growled.

Claudia laughed again. "Why, I didn't *do* anything, Victor," she said in a voice that was as icy as his was angry. "You're the one who was stupid enough to give your guards fake black blades. Not me."

His golden eyes narrowed with understanding. "You switched out the blades. Somehow, you found out about them. You broke into my office and swapped the real weapons for fakes."

Claudia nodded. "Now you're catching on."

She stared Victor down for another moment, then deliberately turned her back to him, as if she no longer considered him a threat, and walked over to Hiroshi Ito.

Claudia turned back around so that she was facing Victor again, then looked at Hiroshi. "It seems as though Victor and his Family aren't as strong as they think they are. What do you say that we finally do something about them?"

Hiroshi nodded, knowing what she was really asking—that he unite with her and the Sinclairs against Victor and the rest of the Draconis.

"Agreed," he said. "Victor has held sway over us for far too long."

"I'm with you too." Roberto Salazar stepped up beside the two of them, adding his Family's support.

"Well, I am not," another voice piped up. "I want no part of this nonsense and neither does anyone in my Family."

Everyone turned to look at Nikolai Volkov, who backed up so that he was standing against one wall of the restaurant. His guards moved to follow him, and it was clear that they wouldn't take part in any fight—either to help the Draconis or the other Families.

Victor glared at Nikolai. "Don't be so stupid as to think that you can go back on our deal now. Not after our meeting last night. You want the other Families wiped out as badly as I do. You knew exactly what was going to happen here tonight, and you agreed to help me and my men."

Nikolai shrugged. "And you promised me black blades for my guards when you don't even have them for your own. The deal is off, as far as I'm concerned."

"I'll kill you for this," Victor hissed.

Nikolai laughed. "Good luck with that."

Nikolai jerked his head, and he and his guards started easing toward the back of the restaurant, away from the line of Draconi guards still blocking the front doors. Claudia, Hiroshi, and Roberto stood their ground, with their guards moving to flank them and form a united front.

Victor looked back and forth from Nikolai to Claudia and the heads of the other Families. After a second, his face twisted into a cruel, ugly expression, and cold, cold hate flared to life in his eyes, chilling me to the bone. His original plan might not have worked, but he'd come too far to back down now. He waved his hand at his guards, then stabbed his finger across the restaurant at all of his enemies.

"Attack!" Victor yelled. "Kill them! Kill them all!"

CHAPTER EIGHT

For a moment, everyone remained frozen in place, shocked by his harsh, brutal command.

"Attack!" Victor roared again. "Kill them all! Every last person who stands against me!"

At his continued urging, the Draconi guards yelled, snapped up their weapons, and charged forward into the crowd of people. None of them tried to turn their black blades on themselves, though. They'd already seen what a deadly disaster that had turned out to be for one of their own.

The Draconi guard who'd been watching me whipped around and raised his sword high, intending to bring it down on top of my head. But I was quicker than he was and I stepped up and punched him in the throat, making him gasp for air and stagger back. His weapon slid from his grasp and tumbled to the floor, and I darted forward and snatched it up before he could grab it again.

The cold burn of magic flooded my veins the second I touched the sword.

So this guard had a real black blade, although I had no idea what kind of magic it might contain. Strength from a copper crusher, most likely, or perhaps speed from a tree troll. But I wasn't about to stab myself with the sword to find out. I wasn't that desperate—yet.

Besides, just holding the weapon was enough to get my own transference power to kick in, and I felt myself growing stronger and stronger the longer I held the sword, almost as if the mere touch of my hand on the black blade was enough to pull the magic stored inside the bloodiron into my own body. Maybe it was, with my transference Talent.

But I didn't have time to figure it out. In an instant, the tense quiet of the restaurant exploded into one loud, enormous fight. Tables and chairs flipped over, platters of food crashed to the floor, and glasses shattered as people dropped their drinks and stampeded every which way, trying to escape the Draconi guards and their slashing swords. Screams, shouts, and shrieks filled the air, along with blood.

So much blood.

Even though most of their weapons weren't real black blades, the Draconi guards still had swords and daggers, and they pressed their advantage, cutting into every single person they could reach. Two of them realized that I'd disarmed one of their friends, and they engaged me, swinging their swords back and forth.

Left, right, left, left, right.

Thanks to the extra strength running through my veins, I parried their blows with ease, crashing my sword into theirs time and time again, then whipped around and unleashed my own attacks on them.

Right, left, right, right, left.

I cut one guard across the stomach, making him scream and stagger back, then whirled around and drove my sword through the chest of the second man. He collapsed when I pulled the weapon free from his body.

I turned around, looking for the next guard to battle. The Draconis had most people pinned up against the booths and walls, but there were a few folks who were fighting back, even though they had nothing to defend themselves with but their bare hands.

Like Devon.

He ducked one guard's sword, stepped up, and plowed his fist into another man's face, breaking his nose. That second guard yelped in pain, and Devon smoothly plucked the man's sword out of his hand before whipping around and slicing it across the man's stomach. That guard dropped to the floor screaming, and Devon whirled around, searching the restaurant.

His green eyes locked with mine, and his sharp worry flooded my chest, along with his rock-hard strength and determination to get me and the rest of the Sinclairs out of here. When he realized that I was okay and that I had a weapon, some of his worry eased, and his head swiveled around, searching for the rest of our friends.

His gaze moved on to Claudia, who was hunkered down behind a table, hurling glasses at the Draconis that were creeping up on her. Angelo was flanking her, also throwing glasses, while Mo and Reginald had grabbed the chairs from the table and were holding them out in front of them like makeshift shields, trying to keep the Draconis and their swords at bay.

Devon hesitated, torn between helping me and his mom, but he was closer to Claudia and the others than I was. Besides, I could take care of myself, and Claudia was the head of the Sinclairs. Devon needed to get her to safety—now.

"Go!" I yelled, waving at him. "Get Claudia!"

I don't know if he heard me over the continued screams and shouts, but he saw me waving. Devon nodded, then pivoted to face another guard coming up on his left. He pushed that man down and started to run over to his mom, but two more guards stepped up to block his path.

I started to shove my way through the crowd so I could

help him, but a guard fell down a few feet away from me, letting out a loud cry and drawing my attention. For a second, I thought that the guard had just tripped over the debris littering the floor, but then I realized that Felix had pushed him down, trying to get to Deah, who was still standing along the wall, staring out at the scene before her as if she couldn't believe what was happening. That Victor, Blake, and the rest of the Draconis were actually attacking all the other Families and doing their best to kill everyone in the restaurant.

I wasn't the only one who noticed that Deah wasn't fighting alongside the guards like she was supposed to.

"What are you doing?" Blake yelled at his sister, even as he stabbed a Salazar guard in the chest. "This is the moment we've been waiting for! Kill them! Kill them all!"

Deah stared at him, then back out at all the fighting. After a moment, she shook her head, lowered her sword, and stepped back.

Blake's mouth gaped open, surprised that she wasn't as eager to hurt everyone as he was, but his brown eyes narrowed and his lips twisted into a snarl.

"Well, if you're not with us, then you're against us!" he screamed, raising his sword and charging at her.

Deah's eyes widened, shocked that Blake was actually attacking her, his own sister. But he was, and if she didn't do something to stop him, he was going to kill her.

I headed in that direction, but there were too many people, tables, and chairs in between us, and there was no way I could reach Deah in time. I'd lost my mom to Blake, and now I was going to lose my cousin too.

"Deah!" Felix yelled. "Deah, look out!"

At the last second, he broke free of the crowd, surged forward, and rammed his shoulder into Blake's as hard as he could. Despite Blake's strength magic, the unexpected blow sent him plowing into one of the booths, but he bounced off and quickly regained his balance. Blake whipped around and glared at Felix with murder in his eyes.

"You!" he yelled. "I'm going to kill you for that!"

"Blake! No!" Deah screamed, but it was no use.

Felix scrambled backward, managing to put a table between the two of them, but Blake slammed his sword down on top of the table, using his strength magic to crack it right down the middle. He snarled, waded through the two broken halves, and charged at Felix again.

Felix didn't have a weapon, and his Talent was for healing, not fighting, but he stood his ground and raised his fists, just like I'd taught him to.

But it wasn't going to help him. Not against Blake, his sword, and his strength magic.

"Run, Felix! Run!" I yelled, but my voice was lost in the screams, shrieks, and shouts of the fight.

Blake lashed out with his sword. Felix dodged the blow, but his foot slipped in a puddle of water, and this time he was the one who slammed up against one of the booths. His legs went out from under him and he sat down hard in the padded seat. He landed awkwardly and started struggling, trying to get out of the booth and back up onto his feet. But he was moving slow—way too slow—and Blake was already surging forward for another strike.

Felix was trapped and there was nothing I could do to help him. Still, I kept shoving people out of my way, trying to get to him. Across the restaurant, I spotted Devon doing the same thing, realizing that Blake was about to kill Felix. But neither one of us was going to be able to save our friend.

But we didn't have to.

At the last second, Deah stepped in front of Felix and snapped up her sword so that it *clanged* against Blake's. The sound seemed as loud as a clap of thunder in the restaurant, although it was quickly drowned out by all the continued fighting.

Blake stood there, his sword locked with Deah's, glaring down at his sister. "I knew it!" he hissed. "I knew that you liked him! Traitor! You little traitor!"

Instead of answering, Deah shoved him away. Behind her, Felix finally managed to get to his feet and stumble out of the booth. He staggered forward and stopped so that he was standing right beside Deah.

Blake roared and charged forward again, bringing his sword up over his head and then down at Deah, trying to kill her with that one, powerful blow. But Deah raised her own sword and blocked his blow again.

"I'm not going to let you hurt anyone else!" she screamed.

She whipped her sword out in a quick counterstrike, although it wasn't nearly as vicious as her brother's attack had been. Blake dodged her blow and came right back at her, attacking her with all the skill and strength magic he had. But Deah was the far better fighter, and she parried his blows with ease, using her mimic magic to copy and counter every single one of his moves, even as her face grew harder and tighter with each of Blake's charges.

Her own brother was trying to kill her and it was breaking her heart, one *clash* of their swords at a time. Deah whirled around and her eyes locked with mine, just for a moment. The red-hot needles of her pain and anguish stabbed me in the gut, just as Blake was trying to do to her with his sword.

Once again, I started to head over to help her, but a man screamed, the sound louder and sharper with fear than all the others. I whipped around just in time to see Claudia clamp her hands around the wrists of the Draconi guard that was attacking her. As soon as her skin came into contact with his, Claudia blasted the guard with her magic, and his hands immediately turned a dark blue from the force of her cold touch Talent. The guard screamed again and wrenched his wrists out of her grasp, although his own frostbitten hands flopped uselessly by his sides, his sword painfully frozen to his own fingers.

Claudia turned to freeze another guard who had been creeping up on her, but that man quickly backed away from her, as did all the other Draconis.

Except for Victor.

He'd been hanging back during the fight, letting his guards do his dirty, bloody work for him, but now he stepped up so that he was standing directly in front of Claudia. The way they were facing off reminded me of an old spaghetti western that Poppy and I had watched a few weeks ago.

"You think you've won?" Victor snarled. "You haven't won *anything*. I'll get my weapons back. And by the time I'm done with you, you'll wish that you and everyone else in your pathetic Family was dead."

Claudia's hands curled into fists. "I will *never* give you those weapons," she spat out. "I'll die first."

Victor's hands tightened into fists as well. "Something that I will be happy to help you with."

The guards standing between them realized that they were in the line of fire, and they scrambled out of the way. Claudia and Victor didn't move, though, each one glaring at the other, even though the fight still raged in the rest of the restaurant.

I looked for my friends. Deah and Felix were still battling Blake, and Mo, Angelo, and Reginald were standing back-to-back-to-back, punching, kicking, and lashing out at the guards who surrounded them. Devon was fighting two more guards, trying to reach Claudia again, now that he realized she was about to go toe-to-toe with Victor.

But I was closer to them than Devon was now, and it

was up to me to help Claudia battle Victor. *Good.* My hand tightened around the hilt of my stolen sword and another surge of strength flowed from the black blade into my body. I'd waited a long time to make Victor pay for what he'd done to my mom, and this was finally my chance.

But I was too late.

Even as I headed toward them, Claudia surged forward to touch and freeze him with her power the same way she had the guard. But Victor casually waved his hand, as if he wasn't worried about her magic at all.

And that's when the lightning started.

At first, I thought that I was just imagining the white lightning that was crackling on Victor's fingertips. But the sudden, intense chill of magic flooding the restaurant told me the lightning was very, very real—and very, very deadly.

Claudia stopped short, her eyes widening as she stared at the lightning flashing on Victor's hand. She couldn't get close enough to freeze him with her magic, not without getting electrocuted herself, and Victor knew it. He let out a low, satisfied chuckle.

Then he reared back and threw his lightning magic at her.

Crackling white streaks of magic erupted from Victor's palm, zipped through the room, and slammed straight into Claudia's chest, knocking her back. She hit a table and dropped to the floor. She didn't move after that, and I couldn't tell if she was just unconscious or dead.

My heart twisted and a scream rose in my throat. Claudia couldn't be dead. She just *couldn't* be. Not like this. Not like my mom. Not at Victor's hand.

"Mom!" Devon screamed, his voice rising above the crashes, clangs, and bangs of the fight. "Mom!"

He started shoving people aside, more desperate to get to Claudia than ever before, but it was no use.

Victor snapped his fingers at the guards that were flanking him. "Bring her and all the other Sinclair leaders!" he called out in a loud voice.

Two of the guards hustled forward, grabbed Claudia, picked her up, and carried her out of the restaurant. Meanwhile, more guards split off from the people they'd been attacking and quickly cornered Mo, Angelo, and Reginald up against one of the walls.

This time, I was the one who screamed and started shoving people out of my way. "Mo!" I yelled. "Mo!"

Even with the extra strength still flowing through my body, I wasn't any more successful than Devon had been, and it only took the guards a few seconds to surround Mo, along with Angelo and Reginald. The Draconis put their swords up against my friends' throats and forced them to the front of the restaurant.

"Lila!" Mo yelled back at me, struggling against the guards as they strong-armed him outside. "Get out of here, kid! Run! Now!"

His black eyes locked with mine and his white-hot rage erupted in my chest, even as his worry and fear for me squeezed my heart tight.

I started forward again, but a guard stepped up and brandished his sword, blocking my path and making me pull up short.

"Mo!" I screamed again. "Mo!"

But he was already gone, and so were Angelo and Reginald.

I was dimly aware of Felix screaming for his dad just like Devon and I were still yelling for Claudia and Mo. I looked past the guard in front of me at Victor, who turned and glanced over at Blake and Deah. They'd stopped fighting each other during Victor's lightning blast, and the shock on both of their faces told me that neither one had realized what their father could *really* do with his magic.

Don't be afraid of the lightning. Seleste's voice whispered in my mind. But how could I not be? Especially since Blake and Deah had been just as surprised by it as I had?

Victor looked at Deah, his golden eyes cold and hard in his handsome face. "I always knew you were a traitor, just like your worthless mother."

Tears shimmered in Deah's eyes, but she blinked them back and stepped in front of Felix, ready to protect him in case her own father blasted her with his lightning.

Victor scoffed, then waved his hand at Blake. "Take your sister alive, but kill the rest of the Sinclairs."

His order delivered, Victor turned and strode out of the restaurant, leaving Blake and the rest of his guards to finish the bloody battle he'd started.

CHAPTER NINE

Blake looked at the Draconi guards. "You heard him!" he yelled. "Kill them all!"

With a collective roar, the guards charged forward again, swinging their swords even more viciously than before, determined to follow Victor's command to cut down every single person still inside the restaurant.

Blake turned back to Deah, ready to finish the fight he'd started, but I shoved past the guard in front of me, dodged a couple more, and sprinted across the restaurant to them. Blake saw me coming out of the corner of his eye, but I was faster, and I raised my sword and slammed the hilt against the side of his head before he could attack me. He dropped to the floor.

"Let's go!" I yelled at Deah and Felix. "Now! Follow me!"

Felix stepped up, but Deah hesitated, looking down at Blake, who was already groaning and getting back up onto his hands and knees.

"There's nothing left for you here!" I yelled at her. "He'll kill you if you stay! Now come on!"

Felix grabbed Deah's hand and she finally let him drag her away from Blake, who was reaching out for the edge of the closest booth to pull himself back up onto his feet.

I whirled around, searching for Devon. He was pinned

up against a wall, facing down four guards at once. Devon parried two of the guards' swords, then whipped around to the other two. The four men looked at each other, getting ready to attack all at once, knowing that he couldn't defend against all of them at the same time.

But Devon realized what they were up to, and he stared at the two guards closest to him. "*Stop!*" he yelled, a cold crack of magic in his voice.

Those two guards immediately froze, their weapons held high overhead at awkward angles as though they were statues. The guards grunted and snarled, their muscles bulging as they tried to finish their strikes and bring their swords down, but they couldn't move an inch thanks to Devon's compulsion magic, the powerful, secret Talent that let him control other people.

While those two guards were frozen in place, Devon stepped up and punched them both in the face, knocking them to the ground. He started to reach for one of their swords, so that he would have two weapons, but the other two guards who weren't being compelled surged forward and pinned him against the wall again. One of the men snapped up his sword, preparing to drive it through Devon's chest.

"Devon!" I screamed, racing in that direction. "Devon!"

The two guards whipped around at my screams, and I barreled into both of them, knocking all three of us down to the floor. The guards cursed, but I lashed out with my sword, cutting into their arms and legs, until they screamed with pain and rolled away from me. I scrambled up to find Devon heading for the front of the restaurant, where Blake had gotten back up onto his own feet.

I reached out and latched on to Devon's arm. The stolen magic still running through my veins made me strong enough to pull him back.

"It's too late!" I yelled. "Your mom is gone. So are Mo and the others. We have to get out of here. We can't save them if we're dead!"

Blake focused on Devon and me, and Felix and Deah standing behind us. He grinned, his eyes just as cold as Victor's had been, and stabbed his sword at us.

"Kill them!' he yelled. "Now!"

The guards surged forward again. Devon raised his sword, ready to fight them, but I grabbed his arm and yanked him back, putting myself between him and the Draconis, just the way a good bodyguard would. This was what Claudia had hired me to do, and I would protect Devon until my dying breath.

Even though I wanted to stand and fight as much as he did, this was a battle that we just couldn't win. Sure, we'd taken out a few of the Draconi guards, but they still outnumbered us at least three to one, and we simply didn't have enough weapons and men to take them on and win, no matter how good our fighting might be. We had to get out of here—now.

"Move!" I yelled at my friends. "Out the back! Go! Go! Go!"

Felix grabbed Deah's hand again, and the two of them sprinted for the rear of the restaurant. Devon and I held off the two guards that charged at us, disarming and knocking them down, then turned and hurried after our friends.

By this point, most folks had given up trying to fight the Draconis and were running away, either by stampeding toward the back of the restaurant like we were or scrambling out of the windows that they'd broken out. Devon and I moved as fast as we could through the debris, swinging our swords at any Draconi who tried to stop us. My eyes cut left and right, but I didn't see Poppy or Hiroshi Ito anywhere. Hopefully, their guards had gotten them to safety. Roberto Salazar and Nikolai Volkov had vanished as well. Now we needed to do the same.

We ran past the bar and I shoved through a pair of double doors that led into the kitchen. The workers were all long gone, having darted out the back as soon as the fighting had started in the front of the restaurant. We sprinted past counters piled high with half-chopped vegetables, sinks filled with dirty dishes, and stoves with pans of food still bubbling away on the hot burners. Felix and Deah were already standing next to an open door at the very back of the restaurant. Everyone else had rushed past them; we were the last people still in the kitchen.

"This way!" Felix yelled, waving at us. "Hurry!"

He and Deah turned and disappeared through the door. Devon went through next, with me right behind him. Together, the four of us raced out into the night.

I sprinted through the open door and almost tripped on a couple of loose soda cans rolling around in the alley behind the restaurant. But I righted myself, whipped around, and sprinted back over to the door.

"Lila!" Devon shouted. "What are you doing? Come on! We have to get out of here!"

"Just a second!" I yelled back.

I slammed the door shut, then looked around for something to barricade it with. A small dumpster was sitting next to the door, so I ran around behind it, dug my sneakers into the asphalt, and started pushing. The metal container didn't want to move, not even with the extra strength still coursing through my body, so I let go, took a couple of steps back, and got a running start, putting my shoulder down into the dumpster like a football player making a tackle.

Screech.

Screech-screech.

Screech-screech-screech.

Slowly, very, very slowly, the dumpster rolled forward one inch, then two, then three. Devon realized what I was trying to do, and he raced over and added his strength to mine. Together, we managed to push the metal container in front of the door.

And not a moment too soon.

Bang.

Bang-bang.

Bang-bang-bang.

Someone—Blake most likely—was ramming his shoulder into the door over and over again, trying to bust it open from the other side. The wood groaned and started to splinter, and I knew that it wouldn't be long before he used his strength magic to break through it and shove the dumpster out of the way.

Devon grabbed my hand and pulled me away from the door. Together, we sprinted to the end of the alley where Felix and Deah were waiting for us.

I looked around. The White Orchid was located on the edge of the tourist section of town, where the shopping squares full of businesses gave way to more industrial areas. Still, I knew exactly where we were—and the only thing that might save us now.

"This way!" I yelled. "Follow me! Run!"

I set off down the street, with the others following along behind me like we were all a pack of joggers. Only this wasn't a casual run. It was a race—one that would determine whether we lived or died.

Bang!

It sounded like Blake had already gotten through the alley door, and we weren't even at the end of the block yet. I risked a quick glance over my shoulder. Sure enough, Blake ran out into the street a second later, flanked by several Draconi guards. He must have heard the swishing sound of our footsteps because he whirled around and looked in our direction.

"Get the cars!" he yelled. "Cut them off and chase them down!"

Some of the guards headed in the other direction to follow his orders, but Blake sprinted after us, with close to a dozen guards trailing along behind him. If they caught up to us, we were dead.

I looked over at Devon, who was running along beside me, his strides long, smooth, and easy. Deah was also running well, but Felix had already started to lag behind, sweat pouring down his face. We still had about a mile to go, and I knew that he wouldn't be able to make it that far before Blake and the other guards caught up with us.

Devon glanced back at Felix, then over at me, his face creasing with worry as he realized the same thing I did.

"Tell us all . . . to run," I said between gasps of air. "It's the only way . . . we're going to make it."

Devon nodded. I grabbed Deah's arm and made her stop, and Felix staggered up beside us. Then all three of us looked at Devon.

He drew in a deep breath, then stared me in the eyes. "*Run!*" he screamed in the loudest voice he could.

Devon's compulsion magic immediately wrapped around my body, making it feel as though I was a puppet and someone else was pulling my strings. Beside me, Deah and Felix also jerked upright, their fingers twitching, their bodies going into spasms, and their feet and legs churning of their own accord. With one thought, we all started running again.

Deah and Felix had no choice but to run as Devon had commanded, but my transference magic quickly overcame his compulsion, until his power was mine to use however I wanted. And right now, I wanted to get us as far away from the Draconis as fast as possible.

So the four of us ran and ran and ran . . . pulling away from Blake and his guards, although they continued to yell and chase after us. Devon's magic made it easier for us to run, but his compulsion power didn't help with anything else. It was still a hot night and sweat soaked my body, streaming down into and stinging my eyes, and the air was so humid that it was like trying to breathe in warm soup. But I didn't dare break stride, not even to take a second to rest. I'd rather be hot, sweaty, and miserable than dead. Beside me, the others gasped, wheezed, and panted for air as well, but we all kept running.

We rounded a corner and a bridge loomed up in the distance, arching over this section of the Bloodiron River. I used to be wary of the bridge, and especially of the lochness monster that lived underneath it, but not anymore. The lochness was going to save us, just the way it had Devon and me once before.

"We just have to get across the bridge!" I yelled to the others. "Blake won't be able to follow us, and we can disappear into the alleys!"

Deah looked confused, but Devon and Felix both nodded, some of the tension easing in their red, sweaty faces.

We ran on. Devon's compulsion magic weakened and finally faded away altogether in the others, who began to slow down. I could have kept right on running, with the magic and strength still pumping through my veins, but I eased my pace to match theirs. We needed to stick together no matter what.

The bridge loomed up before us and I risked another glance over my shoulder. Blake and his guards had closed the gap again and were much closer than before. Blake had his phone clutched up against his ear as he ran, barking orders at whoever was on the other end, but I wasn't worried. Once we reached the bridge we'd be safe—

Headlights flared to life in the distance.

I squinted against the harsh, unexpected glare. An SUV had turned onto the street on the far side of the bridge and was closing in fast on the span. The vehicle's headlights clearly illuminated us, like four deer out on the road late at night, before it swerved to the side and stopped, blocking off the far end of the bridge. My heart sank as I spotted the symbol emblazoned on the SUV's doors—a snarling dragon crest.

The vehicle ahead of us belonged to the Draconis. Blake was still coming up behind us, and now he'd cut off our escape route on the other side of the bridge.

Trapped.

We were trapped.

CHAPTER TEN

The others spotted the SUV at the same time I did, and we all skidded to a stop right before we would have stepped onto the lochness bridge.

Deah blinked. "That's a Draconi car."

"We're cut off," Devon said in a tense voice.

"Now what?" Felix asked. "Because Blake and his guards will be here in a minute, and we can't fight them all off."

Devon squared his shoulders and turned to face Blake and the oncoming guards. "You guys run. If you hurry, you can get away from the bridge, duck into one of the alleys that we just passed, and sprint out the far end. I'll stay behind and hold them off as long as I can. It's my job as the Family bruiser. Besides, I'm the one that Blake really wants. You heard what Victor said about capturing all the Sinclair leaders. I'm the only one he doesn't have yet."

His mouth tightened into a grim slash and he raised his sword and stepped forward, calmly facing Blake and the approaching guards.

But I wasn't about to let Devon sacrifice himself for us. Not when I knew that Blake would probably kill him, despite Victor's orders, just for making Blake chase us. So I whirled around and around, trying to figure some way out of this mess. I'd thought that once we'd gotten across the lochness bridge, we'd be safe, but Blake had cut off our escape route by sending that SUV to the opposite side. And despite what Devon said, we couldn't go back, not now, not with Blake and his men getting closer and closer by the second.

Desperate, my head snapped left and right, my gaze scanning the surrounding buildings, searching for a ladder or a fire escape or even a drainpipe that we might climb up to at least get off the street and give me a few more moments to think.

But there was nothing. No ladders, no fire escapes, no drainpipes. Just the rundown warehouses and the bridge and the dark, glimmering surface of the river below where the lochness made its home—

The river.

My head whipped around again. The lochness had saved Devon and me once before when we'd been on the bridge because I had paid its toll. I wondered if the creature would do the same thing if we actually went down to the water where it lived.

Monsters are your friends. Never forget that. Seleste's voice whispered in my mind. That was the prophecy, the warning, the message she'd given me last night. I just hoped that her words were true. That the lochness really was my friend and that I wasn't about to get eaten, along with my friends.

Only one way to find out.

"This way!" I hissed. "Down the riverbank!"

"What?" Deah hissed back at me. "Are you crazy? A lochness lives under this bridge! It'll drag us into the river and drown us before it eats us. And that's if we're *lucky*."

"Trust me. This is our only option. Now let's go."

Still holding on to my stolen sword, I raced over to the bridge, using my free hand to shove up my black suit jacket and dig into one of the hidden slots on my belt. I didn't have time to sprint out to the stone marked with three Xs in the center of the bridge where you were supposed to leave your tribute, but I was hoping that the lochness wouldn't be too picky about where I put the coins, as long as it got paid. So I grabbed all the quarters I had in my belt and slapped them down on the stone column at this end of the bridge. Then I sprinted back toward my friends.

"This way! Follow me! Hurry!"

A wide swath of grass ran alongside the bridge before gently sloping down and running all the way to the water's edge. It would have been a pretty picnic spot, but none of the locals ever stayed close to this part of the river for long, knowing that it was the lochness's territory. Several black-and-white monster warning signs were also planted in the grass to keep the tourist rubes away. DON'T FEED THE LOCHNESS.

But I sprinted past the warning signs and scrambled down the bank anyway, hoping that I hadn't just made it that much easier for the creature to snatch us up with its long, black tentacles. All the while, I kept listening, hoping to hear the *scrape-scrape-scrape* of coins sliding off the stone column above as the lochness accepted my tribute.

But try as I might, I couldn't hear anything over the rapid thump of my heart, the slap of my sneakers on the grass, and my friends' harsh, ragged breathing. I'd just have to risk it.

We reached the bottom of the riverbank and stopped. A wide stone ledge ran along the edge of the grass, almost like a boardwalk, separating it from the water. The moon and stars were shining brightly tonight, making the rippling surface of the river gleam like a sheet of polished silver. The air was even more humid down here than it had been up on the street, and the entire area smelled wet and fishy. I stared out at the water, using my sight magic, but I didn't see anything lurking in the dark depths.

"Now what are you going to do?" a snide voice called out. "Go for a swim?"

The four of us whirled around.

Blake and his guards stood at the top of the riverbank, swords clutched in their hands. I raised my own stolen sword, ready to defend myself and my friends. But instead of charging down the slope after us, Blake snorted and actually sheathed his weapon.

"You are without a doubt the four stupidest people *ever*." He stabbed his finger at the closest warning sign. "Don't you know that this is a lochness bridge?"

I didn't say anything, and neither did any of the others.

He laughed and shook his head. "I don't even have to come down there to kill you. The lochness will do it for me. All I have to do is wait."

All around him, the guards snickered and sheathed their own swords. Across the bridge, Draconi guards got out of the SUV, spreading out until they had lined the opposite side of the river. All of them sneered down at us as well, just like Blake was doing.

I tensed, but I still didn't move or say anything, and neither did my friends.

Blake and the guards all focused on the river, expecting the lochness—or at least its long, black tentacles—to shoot up out of the water, grab us, and drag us down, down, down to the bottom of the river, never to be seen or heard from again.

But nothing happened. No tentacles, no sprays of water, nothing.

A minute passed, then two, then three.

And still, nothing happened.

I took deep breaths, trying to calm my racing heart and frayed nerves, listening for the faintest splash that would tell me the lochness was about to strike, but I didn't hear anything. No splashes, no slaps of water, nothing.

Beside me, Devon, Felix, and Deah all kept glancing at the river, with Devon and Deah clutching their swords tightly, ready to lash out with the weapons if the monster did attack us.

And still, nothing happened.

The Draconi guards started muttering and shifting on their feet, wondering what was taking so long. Blake scowled. Apparently, the lochness wasn't killing us fast enough for his liking.

"Fine," he muttered. "I'll just come down there and finish you off myself."

Blake unsheathed his sword, twirled it around in his hand, and left the street behind. I wondered if he might go over to the bridge to leave some money for the lochness like I had, but he ignored the stone column where I'd left my quarters. I sucked in a breath, my heart lifting with sudden hope.

He hadn't paid the toll.

Sure enough, Blake had only taken a single step down onto the grassy riverbank when the *clink-clink-clink* of coins sounded, as the lochness finally accepted my tribute.

"Duck!" I yelled at my friends.

The four of us had barely crouched down on the stone ledge before a long, black tentacle shot up out of the river, spraying water everywhere. The tentacle undulated back and forth over our heads, like a copper crusher about to strike.

And then it did.

The tentacle zipped forward, heading straight for the cluster of men still up on the street. Blake's eyes widened and he managed to avoid the tentacle, but the guard standing next to him wasn't so lucky. The tentacle wrapped around the man and hoisted him high in the air before snapping him back and forth, and back and forth, almost as if the lochness was waving a flag, declaring that this was its territory and no one else's. Then the tentacle tossed the guard aside, as easily as I could throw one of the stars hooked to my belt. The guard slammed into the side of the stone bridge, then plummeted down into the river below.

The guard screamed all the way down, and water spewed up like a geyser as he plunged below the surface of the river. The water bubbled up all around that spot, frothing and foaming like rapids, but the man didn't reappear, not even for an instant, and I knew that the lochness had him.

The smart thing would have been to retreat, but Blake was too angry and too determined to get us.

"Kill them!" he roared, whipping up his sword and starting down the riverbank.

He hadn't taken three steps before more tentacles started shooting out of the water, one right after another, this time attacking the Draconi guards on both sides of the river, making them scream, shout, and lash out with their swords.

But the lochness was quicker and much, much stronger than any human, and its tentacles whipped back and forth, easily dodging all of the guards' frantic, clumsy blows. We were still between the monster and the guards, right in the danger zone. One of the tentacles clipped Devon, spinning him around, and I had to lunge forward and grab him before he toppled backward into the river. The lochness wasn't attacking us, but we still needed to get out here before the creature accidentally knocked us into the river and drowned us.

Since we couldn't climb up the riverbank where Blake and the guards were, there was only one other place to go.

"We have to get out of the way!" I yelled. "Get under the bridge! Go! Go! Go!"

Deah and Felix both looked at me like I was crazy and

was going to get them killed after all. Maybe I was, but I'd rather be eaten by the lochness than let Blake capture me. So I got to my feet and darted toward the bridge, and the others fell into step behind me.

The ledge ran all the way under the bridge, and the stone curved up, like the inside of a pipe, before becoming part of the bridge itself. The span blocked out all the moon and starlight above, making it almost pitch-black down here. I could still see just fine, but the others couldn't, and Devon stumbled into me, almost knocking me off the ledge and down into the water. I grabbed his hand and pushed his shoulder up against the curving stone wall.

"Grab Felix, and tell him to get Deah!" I yelled. "Press yourselves up against the side!"

Devon nodded and did as I asked. With one hand, he reached out and touched Felix, so that Felix would know where he was. Then, Devon wrapped his arm around me, shielding me with his body and pulling us both up as close to the wall as he could get. On his other side, Felix did the same thing with Deah.

By this point, it seemed as though the entire river was boiling at our feet, the water frothing and foaming like a science experiment volcano that was about to explode. Wave after wave of water dashed against us, soaking us from head to toe. Despite the day's heat, the river was cold enough to make me shiver and I had to press my teeth together to keep them from chattering.

Despite the constant cascades of water, I peered over my shoulder, looking back toward the river. The others didn't have my sight magic, so they didn't see the pair of enormous eyes that glowed a bright, vivid, sapphire blue out in the center of the water, or how the lochness lashed out again and again at the Draconi guards with its thick, strong tentacles.

But I could see it all as clear as day, and it chilled me far more than the water did, even though the lochness was only protecting us as I'd asked it to. Maybe Seleste was right. Maybe I'd paid enough tolls for the lochness to think of me as a sort of pet, the way I did it. Or maybe the monster really was my friend, for whatever reason.

The lochness's attack seemed to go on forever, although it couldn't have lasted much longer than a couple of minutes. But the Draconi guards must have finally retreated out of the monster's reach because the tentacles slid beneath the surface of the water, and the river slowly calmed until the current was as soft and steady as before.

Under the bridge, in the blackness, the four of us remained still and frozen, barely daring to breathe, much less move.

Finally, I heard the steady *thud-thud-thud-thud* of boots smacking against stone, as though someone were pacing back and forth along the street above us.

"They have to be dead." Blake's voice drifted down to me. "No one could have survived that. Not down there so close to the river. The other cars have come. Let's get out of here before that, that *thing* decides to attack us again."

The remaining guards quickly chimed in with their own murmurs of agreement, wanting to get away from the bridge and the lochness as fast as possible. More footsteps slapped against the street, and car doors slammed shut one after another. A few seconds later, the *crunch-crunch-crunch* of tires sounded, and several vehicles drove away, the rumbles of their engines fading to nothingness.

Slowly, the four of us relaxed, although we still didn't move from our spots under the bridge.

Behind me, Devon shifted.

"What's wrong?" I asked.

"Something's digging into my back," he muttered.

"Mine too," Felix chimed in. "Do you think it's safe for us to move now?"

I stared out over the river, but I didn't see the lochness's tentacles or its blue eyes. "I think it's gone . . . for now. Besides, we can't stay here all night."

I stepped away from Devon, and he pushed away from the wall. Beside him, Deah and Felix did the same thing. Devon and I had managed to hang on to our stolen swords, Deah still had her own weapon, and we all raised them back up, ready for another attack, while Felix fished his phone out of his pants pocket. It still worked and he used the screen as a flashlight and held it up to the wall.

Coins had been driven deep into the stone, all of them in neat rows, stretching from the bottom of the wall all the way up to the top and then across the underside of the bridge over our heads. Quarters, mostly, with some nickels and dimes mixed in. But no pennies. I guess the lochness preferred the way the silver shined, since all the coins gleamed as though they had just been polished.

At first, I didn't see any order to the rows, but then I realized that symbols had been scratched beside some of them—vines, flowers, trees, and more, many of them looking like Family crests—almost as if the lochness had used the coins like a kid with a piece of chalk.

"The lochness," I whispered, pointing to the symbols. "It looks like it actually keeps track of who pays its toll."

The others squinted, but they didn't have my sight magic, so they couldn't see the faint marks, not even with the light from Felix's phone. But the longer I looked at the symbols, the more I noticed that one kept appearing over and over again—a five-pointed star.

The Sterling Family crest.

It was scratched on the wall in several places, as well as on the underside of the bridge. One, two, three . . . I lost count of the number of stars, but it looked like my mom and I had given the lochness more coins and had paid its toll more times than anyone else. Maybe that was why it had helped me again tonight. My mom had always told me to pay the tolls so the monsters would leave me alone, but I'd never considered that there could be something more to it than that.

"There has to be thousands of dollars' worth of coins here," Deah whispered.

I thought about telling the others about all the stars on the bridge, but I didn't know what to make of the symbols, or how I felt about them right now, so I decided to keep it to myself. Besides, what really mattered was that the monster had protected us from Blake and the Draconi guards, so I was going to consider all the coins money well spent.

"Come on," I said. "I'm all out of quarters, so let's get out of here before the lochness decides that it wants more tribute tonight."

The others nodded, and Felix used the light from his phone to guide them out from under the bridge and toward the riverbank so they could climb back up to the street. But I lagged behind my friends, staring out over the river again. I didn't see anything, so I turned to catch up with the others.

A long, black tentacle hovered in the air right in front of me.

I froze, not knowing what to do. I couldn't get around the tentacle, and the others were too busy climbing the riverbank to realize what was happening. Besides, they couldn't have saved me from the lochness anyway.

The tentacle slowly moved back and forth through the air, almost as if it were a person gesturing for me to come closer. I eased forward one step, then two, then three, until I was less than three feet away from the lochness.

The tentacle kept waving back and forth, creeping a little closer to me with every passing second. I stood absolutely still, not wanting to do anything to upset it. Finally, the tentacle reached out and touched my shoulder, almost as if it was giving me a pat and making sure that I was okay. Then it retreated and started waving back and forth in the air in front of me again, waiting for me to make the next move.

I hesitated, then stepped forward, reached out, and gingerly ran my fingers over the tentacle. It was cool and wet, but not unpleasantly so, and the lochness's skin was much smoother than I'd expected, almost like damp velvet. My attention seemed to please the creature, and the tentacle leaned in to my touch, like a dog wanting me to keep on scratching its ear. So that's what I did.

The river started rippling again, but the motion was calming rather than threatening, and I actually found myself enjoying the steady rush of water slapping against the shore—

"Lila!" Devon called out. "Are you okay? I can't see you under the bridge."

At the sound of his voice, the tentacle waved at me a final time, then sank down below the surface of the river. I tiptoed over to the edge of the ledge and peered down. Two bright, sapphire-blue eyes stared up at me through the water. My gaze locked with the lochness's and the creature's emotions flooded my chest. Sly satisfaction at protecting me and my friends from Blake and the Draconis. Calm respect for the way I always paid its toll. And most of all, aching loneliness that was slowly being overcome by warm happiness and pride that it was finally communicating with me. Maybe monsters needed friends too, as crazy as that sounded.

"Lila?" Devon called again.

I blinked, breaking eye contact and shaking off the creature's emotions. "Yeah, I'm fine," I called out. "I'm coming up right now."

I hesitated, then waved goodbye to the lochness before stepping out from under the bridge and hurrying after my friends.

CHAPTER ELEVEN

I scrambled up the riverbank to where Devon, Felix, and Deah were waiting at the top.

"Now what?" Deah muttered, swinging her sword at the grass like she wanted to hack through every single blade of it.

"We have to get back to the mansion," Devon said.

Felix pulled his phone away from his ear. "I've called the main line three times now, but no one's answering. I also tried some of the guards, but no one's picking up." Concern filled his face. "Do you think the Draconis attacked the mansion too?"

Devon shook his head. "I don't know. Surely, by now, everyone at the mansion knows what happened. But the fact that they're not answering their phones . . ."

His voice trailed off, but we all knew what he was thinking. That Victor could have easily sent some of his guards to attack the mansion at the same time we were all gathered at the White Orchid. It would have been the perfect way to wipe out all the Sinclairs at once. That's exactly what I would have done, especially since the Sinclair mansion was just a short hike through the woods from the Draconi compound. That was probably the reason why all those extra guards had been at the Draconi mansion last night. So they would be in position and close enough to attack the Sinclairs tonight.

A cold fist of fear and dread wrapped around my heart. Oscar and Tiny had stayed behind at the mansion. If the Draconis had indeed attacked, the pixie and the tortoise could already be captured—or worse.

"Devon's right," I said, trying to ignore my worry. "We have to go back to the mansion to see what's happened to everyone." I paused. "And that's not the only reason we have to go back."

"What do you mean?" Felix asked.

"We have to get the black blades—the real ones," I said. "They're the only leverage and the only bargaining chip we have right now."

Understanding sparked in Devon's eyes. "You think that Victor would be willing to trade my mom and the other Sinclairs for the black blades?"

I shrugged. "You heard him threaten Claudia when he realized the weapons were fakes. Victor wants those black blades and the magic that's inside them more than anything else. If he'd had them tonight, he could have killed us and taken over all the Families. Maybe he thinks that if he gets them back, he can still do it. It's worth a shot, anyway, and it's the only chance we have."

"Lila's right," Deah chimed in. "My dad will do anything to get those weapons back, and he'll . . . hurt your mom to try to get her to tell him where they are." Her lips pressed together into a tight line. "I've seen him do it to other people."

Devon's jaw clenched, and it took him a moment to force out his next words. "You mean he'll torture her and the other Sinclairs."

Deah winced, then slowly nodded.

The thought of Claudia being tortured, the thought of Mo being tortured, made hot, sour bile rise in my throat, but I swallowed it down and forced myself to stay calm and think about what we needed to do next—get to the Sinclair mansion.

Devon scrubbed his hands over his face, as if the simple motion could erase all the horrors of the last hour. If only it could, we all would have been doing it. Felix kept scrolling through his contacts, dialing every single Sinclair's number, but no one answered him. Deah started whacking at the grass with her sword again.

I was as scared and worried for the Sinclairs, especially Claudia and Mo, as everyone else. I kept waiting for one of my friends to move, to speak, to step up and take charge, but they were all too numb with shock and grief right now. Up to me then.

"Well, we can't do anything from here," I said. "So first things first. Devon, you still have the keys to the SUV, right?"

He nodded, dug in his pants pocket, and pulled out the keys.

"Good. Let's go back to the SUV then. Maybe we'll get lucky and the Draconis haven't found it yet."

"And if they have?" Felix asked.

"Then we'll find some other way to get back up to the mansion. Now come on. The longer we just stand here, the longer Victor has Claudia, Mo, and the others."

That cold, hard fact finally cut through some of my friends' shock, horror, and fear, and they followed me as I turned and hurried away from the lochness bridge.

It didn't take us long to hike back to the tourist section in the center of town. Even though it was after nine o'clock now, throngs of people still flowed up and down the sidewalks and moved in and out of the shops and restaurants, so it was easy for us to disappear into the crowd. We got a few odd looks, but no one stopped to question us, even though we were all still soaking wet and

Devon, Deah, and I were carrying swords. As we walked, Felix dialed the Sinclair mansion and all the guards again and again. Still no response. He tried Poppy Ito and Julio Salazar as well, but they didn't pick up either.

Finally, we reached the street where Devon had parked the SUV when we'd first come down into town earlier tonight. I made the others hang back while I peered around the corner, looking up and down the street and using my sight magic to stare into all the shadows, making sure this wasn't some trap set by Blake and the rest of the Draconis. But this area wasn't one of the main drags, and all the other cars that had been parked here earlier were gone. It was deserted except for the four of us.

I nodded at the others, and we jogged down the street. Devon used his key fob to pop open the doors, and we slid into the SUV. He cranked the engine, threw the vehicle into gear, and pulled away from the curb.

Devon drove, with Felix in the front, still calling and calling the mansion, but still with no response. I sat in the back with Deah, who stared out the window, her face blank.

"How are you holding up?" I asked. "I know tonight has been hard. Especially for you."

"Why? Because my dad called me a traitor and my brother tried to kill me? Why would I be upset about that?" She let out a bitter laugh, but she didn't turn to look at me. "Even after you showed me that room full of weapons, I still didn't want to believe what my dad and Blake were up to, but you were right. All the two of them care about is destroying the other Families."

"What happened tonight?" Devon asked. "Before the Draconis stormed into the restaurant?"

"Dad called everyone into the dining hall at the Draconi mansion and told us about his plan to attack the other

Families at the restaurant, and Blake started passing out the fake black blades to all the guards."

Deah glanced down at her own sword, which was propped up in the floorboard at her feet. The glow from a nearby streetlamp made the three stars carved into the hilt gleam.

"That's your regular sword," I said. "They didn't give you one of the fake weapons?"

She shook her head, making her damp blond hair flap against her shoulders. "Of course not. My dad could tell that I was horrified by his plan. I argued with him and Blake, tried to convince them not to go through with it, tried to tell them that it was cold-blooded murder, but they wouldn't listen to me. They *never* listen to me."

Felix finished his latest unanswered call and glanced over his shoulder at her. "Then what happened?"

"Dad took my phone away so I couldn't warn anyone about the attack." She hesitated. "He also had a couple of guards lock my mom in her room and stay behind with her. Just in case I got any ideas about fighting back and trying to stop him."

"So he threatened Seleste and blackmailed you into going along with them," Felix said.

Deah nodded. "They forced me into an SUV, and we drove down to the restaurant. But when we got there, I noticed that not all of the guards had come with us. I wondered why, but no one was even talking to me at that point. And now that Felix can't reach anyone at your mansion . . ."

She bit her lip and looked at Devon in the rearview mirror. "I think . . . I think my dad sent the rest of the guards to the Sinclair mansion." Tears gleamed in her eyes, and her voice dropped to a hoarse, ragged whisper. "I'm sorry. So sorry. For everything."

Devon glanced back at her and gave her a sharp nod. "It's okay. I understand. If it had been my mom in danger, I would have done the same thing."

Deah blinked away her tears and nodded back. "Thank you. But I should have stood up to my dad. I should have found some way to get my mom out of there, or at least warned you guys about what was happening."

"It's not your fault," I said. "It was an impossible choice."

"And I made the wrong one. What did I accomplish by going along with them? *Nothing*," she spat out the word. "Because innocent people still died, and my mom is still up at the Draconi mansion, and who knows what my dad and Blake will do to her now that I've basically defected from the Family."

Her dark blue gaze dropped to the gold cuff on her wrist. We passed another streetlamp, and the glow highlighted the snarling dragon crest stamped into the metal, making it look as though the monster were about to leap off the cuff and sink its teeth into her. Deah's mouth twisted with anger and disgust, and she yanked it off. She rolled down the window, as if she was going to hurl the cuff outside, but I reached out and grabbed her hand.

"Don't you dare do that," I said.

"Why not?" she muttered.

"Are you kidding me? That cuff is solid gold. It's worth a *fortune*," I drawled, trying to lighten the mood and cheer her up, if only for a few seconds.

For a moment, a ghost of a smile flashed across her face, but it quickly vanished. Deah hesitated, then rolled up the window. She stared at her Draconi cuff again, but instead of putting it back on her wrist, she slid it into her pocket before finally looking at me. Our eyes locked and I felt all of her deep, bitter, aching regret about everything that had happened tonight, along with her sharp worry for her mom.

Deah looked at me for another second before turning and staring out the window again. I opened my mouth to keep talking, but I thought better of it and clamped my lips shut. If I'd just been through what she had, I would have wanted some peace and quiet too. But I did reach over and place my hand on top of hers, letting her know I was here for her. After a second, Deah curled her fingers into mine.

And we stayed like that for the rest of the ride, drawing what strength, comfort, and support we could from each other, knowing that this horrible night was far, far from over.

Devon carefully steered up the curvy roads, his hands tensing around the wheel every time we passed another car. But none of the other vehicles had the Draconi crest painted on the doors, so he was able to drive all the way up the mountain with no problems.

Thirty minutes later, he pulled the car into a parking lot that led to a scenic overlook of a waterfall that was about a mile away from the Sinclair mansion. The area was deserted, since it was after ten now, but we all knew that it was risky to just drive up to the mansion, expecting everything to be fine. Blake might think that the lochness had drowned us, but if I were him, I would still have posted guards at the mansion just in case we weren't dead and decided to go back there.

Devon parked the SUV underneath a couple of weeping willows, trying to hide it in the trees' long green tendrils and the shadows they cast. Then the four of us got out of the car.

Devon, Deah, and I drew our weapons, but I frowned

at the stolen sword in my hand. I hadn't noticed it until right now, but the black blade didn't feel cold to the touch anymore. In fact, I couldn't feel any magic pulsing through the bloodiron at all. Weird. And all the stolen magic had burned out of my body as well.

"What's wrong?" Devon asked.

"This sword was one of the real black blades," I said, swinging it back and forth. "But it doesn't have any magic in it anymore."

"But how is that possible?" Felix asked. "You didn't stab yourself with it. Isn't that the only way to get magic out of a black blade?"

Deah tilted her head to the side, studying me and the sword. "Maybe not. Maybe Lila used up all the magic without having to stab herself."

"What do you mean?" I asked.

"Your transference Talent lets you absorb and use any magic that you come into contact with, right?"

"Yeah . . ."

She shrugged. "So you've been holding on to that sword for more than an hour now. Maybe that's all you needed to do to tap into the magic that was stored inside it."

Even though I'd had a similar thought back at the restaurant, I still looked at the sword, unease slithering down my spine. Up until a couple of weeks ago, I'd thought that my transference Talent and the magic I stole with it only made me stronger. But when Katia Volkov had stabbed me, I'd discovered that I could also use the power I absorbed from others to heal myself. And now, I'd somehow sucked all the magic out of a black blade without even trying.

I'd always thought I understood exactly how my power worked and everything I could do with it, but now I was wondering if there was more to my transference Talent than I'd realized, the same way I'd wondered about paying the lochness toll at the bridge and what it might really mean to the creature. But I pushed my thoughts aside. Right now, I needed to focus on getting to the mansion and finding out what had happened there. Not this strange new ability I might or might not have.

I looked at the others. "We all know that things at the mansion are probably going to be bad. So just follow me, and stay as quiet as possible. Okay?"

My friends nodded back. I took the lead, and we left the parking lot behind and plunged into the forest.

The moon and stars were still shining in the night sky, but the thick canopy of leaves blocked out most of their light, and the way the branches arched up and merged together overhead made it seem like we were trudging through a dark cave instead of the middle of the woods. The clouds of mist from the waterfalls were particularly thick tonight, obscuring the landscape even further, but I welcomed the white blanket that cloaked everything, including us. If there were any Draconi guards in the woods tonight, they'd have a hard time spotting us.

We moved through the trees as quickly as possible, but we hadn't gone far before I realized how absolutely quiet it was. No rockmunks scuttled through the underbrush, no tree trolls hopped from one branch to another, no bugs or birds of any sort darted through the air. Nothing moved or stirred, not even the wind.

It was quiet—too quiet.

The sort of too quiet that usually meant death.

My heart clenched, dreading what we were going to find at the mansion.

But we hadn't even reached the grounds before we came across the first body.

It was a Sinclair guard, wearing a black cloak and matching cavalier hat. He was sprawled across the ground, clutching at an ugly stab wound in his stomach with one hand, his sword hanging slack in his other hand. I didn't have to use my sight magic to see the blood that coated his body and blackened the leaves all around him.

"That's Charlie," Devon whispered in a sad voice. "He worked for the Family for more than ten years. He was a good guy."

We all stared at the body. Devon sighed, then leaned down and gently closed Charlie's open, sightless eyes. He straightened back up and his gaze locked with mine, all of his soul-crushing grief, stomach-churning fear, and sharp worry filling my heart as though they were my own emotions.

They definitely were tonight.

The closer we crept to the mansion, the more bodies we found, Sinclair and Draconi alike. My stomach knotted up. I wondered who had won in the end, if the Sinclairs had pushed Victor's guards back or if the Draconis had wiped them out.

We were about to find out.

Finally, we reached the edge of the woods that ringed the mansion. Still being as quiet as possible, we crept forward, hunkered down behind some bushes, and peered around the branches.

No guards patrolled the outside of the mansion, although more bodies littered the lawn, both Sinclairs and Draconis. The coppery stench of blood filled the air, and flies and mosquitoes buzzed over the bodies in thick, grotesque black clouds. Beyond the lawn, lights blazed in practically every room in the mansion, but no one moved back and forth past the windows, and I didn't hear any yells, shouts, or screams. Whatever had happened here, it was already over.

That cold fist of fear wrapped around my heart again as I worried about Oscar and Tiny. They'd both been in the mansion when we'd left, along with dozens of other people and pixies.

If Oscar and Tiny were hurt . . . if they'd been captured . . . if they'd been *killed* . . .

Tears pricked my eyes, but I forced myself to blink them back. If anything had happened to the pixie and the tortoise, I would never, ever forgive myself.

Because this was all my fault.

I should have realized that Victor wouldn't wait forever to use those black blades and that the Family dinner was the perfect time for him to strike. Stealing the weapons hadn't been enough, and I should have found a way to stop him completely. Now, people were dead—people I knew, respected, and cared about.

More tears welled up in my eyes, but I blinked them back as well. I couldn't change what had happened; all I could do now was press forward and do my absolute best to make sure that the rest of my friends stayed safe.

"Now what?" Felix said. "I don't see any signs of life, and nobody is answering their phone. I've tried every single person I can think of, and no one's picked up."

"Now we go into the mansion and see if anyone's left," I said. "Maybe some folks were able to hide before the Draconis found them. Then we get the black blades, get out of here, and figure out what our next move is. Follow me."

I headed toward the mansion, and the others fell in line behind me. Our footsteps didn't make so much as a whisper in the grass as we crept closer and closer to the mansion. Felix stopped to grab a sword from a dead guard, and I used my magic to look ahead, to stare in through the windows and get a better sense of what might have happened inside—and especially to see if there were any survivors.

But no one moved into my line of sight, and the mansion seemed completely empty and deserted.

We reached one of the side doors. I didn't even bother trying the knob, since all the glass in the door had been busted out, probably by someone slamming a sword through it. I looked at my friends, and they all nodded back at me. I stepped through the shattered glass, with them still following along behind me, all of our swords raised and ready.

The inside of the mansion was a disaster area. Glass had been smashed out of windows, locked doors had been broken down, tables, lamps, and chairs had been knocked over. It seemed as though every single piece of furniture had either been upended or shoved over onto its side, and then stomped on for good measure. Pillows were scattered everywhere, along with books, paperweights, and crystal candlesticks that had broken apart into jagged chunks when they'd hit the floor.

But the worst part was the bodies.

They were *everywhere*, crowded together right in front of the doors and windows, sprawled in the middle of the hallways, slumped over the stairs. Some of them were even pinned in place with swords up against the walls, looking more like dolls than real people. And blood covered *everything*, from the white marble floors to the few paintings still hanging crookedly on the walls to even the crystal chandeliers that dangled down from the ceilings.

The sight of the bodies was horrific enough to freeze us all in place, but I signaled to the others that we needed to keep moving. They nodded back, and still being quiet, the four of us tiptoed down the hallway and headed toward the dining hall. I was hoping that some folks might still be alive in here, but it was just as big a mess as everything else was.

Broken tables and chairs littered the area, along with

trampled platters of food. Puddles of water, lemonade, iced tea, and more covered the marble floor from where folks had dropped their drinks and the glasses had shattered. But the weirdest thing of all were the knives and forks stuck into the tables, walls, and even the ceiling, as if people had gotten so desperate for weapons that they'd started chucking silverware at their attackers.

Dinner must have been under way when the attack had started because the majority of the bodies were clustered in here. Guards, workers, even pixies, their tiny, crumpled bodies looking like small, sad butterflies compared to the larger humans. I'd hoped that we'd find some of the Sinclairs still alive, but it didn't look as though anyone had survived the attack.

Tears burned my eyes like acid, and I had to swallow down the screams and bile rising in my throat. This was . . . this was . . . *horrible.* One of the worst things I'd ever seen, right up there with the aftermath of my mom's murder. But what made this truly heartbreaking was that I'd had a chance to stop it, and I'd failed miserably.

My mom would have been so disappointed in me.

Beside me, Felix sniffled and wiped away the tears streaming down his face. So did Deah. But Devon was as stone-faced as I was, although his grief, disgust, heartbreak, and rage made his green eyes burn as bright as stars in his face. His emotions matched my own perfectly.

As I looked out over the blood and bodies, I focused on the white-hot rage burning in my own heart, more intense than any magic I'd ever felt. In that moment, I made a silent vow to myself. Victor Draconi was more of a monster than any creature that lurked in the shadow-filled alleys of Cloudburst Falls, and he was going to pay for what he'd done to my friends, my Family.

Whatever it took.

"Come on," Devon whispered in a rough, ragged voice.

"There's nothing we can do for them. Let's check the rest of the house and see if there are any survivors."

He whipped around and quickly strode out of the dining hall, as if he had to get out of the room before he broke down and just started screaming. Yeah, me too.

Felix, Deah, and I followed him. Together, the four of us checked every single room, every hallway, every broom closet, pantry, and cubbyhole where someone might have holed up during the attack. But we didn't find anyone, not so much as a single pixie, so we moved up to the next level and then up and up through the rest of the mansion.

Almost all of the bodies were on the first floor, so the destruction wasn't nearly as bad on the upper levels. But it was still easy to tell that the Draconi guards had been through here because of all the things they'd stolen.

Silver bookends, crystal keepsake boxes, wooden carvings. All of them were gone, and the Draconis had even used their swords and daggers to pry sapphires, rubies, and diamonds out of other expensive knickknacks. I spotted one gray stone statue of a Fenrir wolf that used to have amethysts for eyes, although the sockets were empty now. The creature almost seemed to be snarling, as if it wanted to track down and bite the person who'd stolen its eyes. I knew the feeling.

The more I looked around, the tighter my hand curled around my stolen sword, and the more white-hot rage surged through my body. It wasn't bad enough that the Draconis had killed so many people tonight. Oh, no. They'd had to destroy the mansion and take everything that belonged to the Sinclairs too.

It wasn't right—it just wasn't *right*.

I might be a thief, but at least when I stole something, I didn't hurt the person it belonged to, and I didn't wreck the rest of their possessions just for fun. This . . . this level of gleeful cruelty *disgusted* me.

In that moment, I wanted to destroy every single Draconi the same way that they'd destroyed the mansion and all the people inside. Cut and stab and hack and slash until there was nothing left of the Draconi Family. No guards, no workers, no castle, not so much as a single paperweight with that stupid dragon crest on it.

We moved on. Still, the longer we searched, and the more rooms and floors we went through, the more a teeny, tiny bit of hope sparked to life in my heart. Because I didn't see Oscar or Tiny anywhere among the bodies. Maybe Oscar had realized what was happening, that the Draconis were attacking, and had managed to get himself and his pet tortoise outside the mansion to safety. That was my hope anyway.

I didn't want to think about the alternative.

Finally, we reached my bedroom. The door had been busted open, just like all the others, and the wood was splintered right down the middle like a tree that had been struck by lightning. So the Draconi guards had been in here too. Of course they had. I drew in a breath and slowly let it out, steeling myself for the destruction—and the two small bodies—that might be waiting inside.

Devon put a hand on my shoulder, his face somber. He knew how worried I was about Oscar and Tiny. I reached up and squeezed his hand with my own. Then I faced the door, slowly eased the part of it that was still clinging to the frame open with the point of my sword, and stepped inside.

My room didn't have nearly as much damage as some of the others. Mainly because I didn't have anything that was worth stealing. Someone had rifled through my closet and tossed my clothes all over the floor, along with my ratty sneakers. They'd also ripped into the couch cushions and had even dragged the comforter, pillows, and mattress off my bed and cut them all open, so that piles of white, fluffy stuffing covered the floor like snow drifts.

But my gaze quickly moved past the debris and locked on to Oscar's trailer.

The ramshackle pixie house, corral, barn, and surrounding fences had all been knocked off their table, and splintered pieces of ebony littered the floor, as though someone had stomped on the wooden structures over and over again in order to smash them into as many pieces as possible.

Blake, I thought darkly. He was the one who'd done this. I was sure of it. He must have driven up to the Sinclair mansion after he'd left us at the lochness bridge. Blake would have come to my room looking for me, just to make sure that I wasn't still alive and up here hiding. While he was here, he would have delighted in destroying Oscar's pixie house and the rest of my things just because he could. Something else that he and Victor were going to pay for.

But I pushed my anger aside and scanned the room again, looking for the two most important things.

"Oscar?" I called out. "It's Lila. Are you in here?"

No answer, and nothing moved or stirred in the debris. I went over to the patio doors, which had had the glass busted out of them, stepped outside onto the stone balcony, and tried again.

"Oscar?" I called out again. "If you can hear me, please come out."

Still, no answer.

My heart dropped, my stomach clenched, and more tears gathered in my eyes, but I blinked them away and trudged back into my room. Given their small size, pixies were very good at hiding, and I had no easy way of finding Oscar. All I could do now was hope that he and Tiny were somewhere safe.

Devon and Felix looked at me, asking me the same silent question, but I shook my head. Their faces tightened and sympathy flashed in their eyes. They knew how much I cared about the pixie and his tortoise, how much I valued Oscar's friendship and Tiny's too, even if the tortoise couldn't actually talk.

I wandered around the room, kicking my way through my trampled clothes and causing the mattress stuffing to fly up into the air like snowflakes before slowly drifting down again. Devon and Felix stared out over the destruction, their faces still sad, but Deah looked much more thoughtful as she glanced from one side of the room to the other.

"Okay," she said. "So where did you stash your sword and all your other important stuff?"

I arched my eyebrows at her. "And what makes you think I would do something like that?"

She snorted. "Because you're not running from one side of the room to the other, ranting and raving about how the guards either destroyed or took all your stuff. That means the things you *really* care about are probably still here, hidden away somewhere. Once a thief, always a thief, right?"

"Funny you should say that. I *might* have tucked a few things away here and there before we left the mansion tonight. Just in case things didn't go so well at the dinner."

Deah winced at my careless words. Yeah, me too. The images of all the blood, bodies, and destruction at the White Orchid and here in the mansion flashed through my mind, making me even more heartsick.

I jerked my head. "Here. I'll show you."

I passed my stolen sword over to Devon, then went over to the corner of the bedroom, where a small plastic

Karma Girl trash can was sitting upright and in its usual place against the wall. It was just about the only thing in here that hadn't been torn apart, knocked over, or stomped to pieces. I tossed out the crumpled tissues, empty candy bar wrappers, and other actual trash inside, reached down into the bottom of the can, and drew out a clear plastic bag. My black, chopstick lock picks were nestled inside, along with my ironmesh gloves, and I held them up where my friends could see them.

"Nobody ever thinks to look in the trash for anything good," I said.

The faintest hint of a smile flashed across Devon's face. "A thief would."

I nodded back at him. "This thief definitely would."

I left the gloves in the bag, although I fished the chopsticks out of the plastic and stuck them through my ponytail like usual. Then I stepped into the adjoining bathroom, which was just as messy as the bedroom. Bottles of shampoo, conditioner, lotion, shower gel, and more had been opened up and poured all over the floor, creating a gloppy, sticky mess. The towels and washcloths had been pulled out of the bathroom closet and thrown down onto the floor as well, so that the goop there would soak into them. Someone had even ripped my bathrobe off the hanger on the back of the bathroom door, tossed it down, and stomped all over it, leaving dirty black footprints behind all over the fluffy white fabric.

I stepped on a couple of towels, trying not to get any more slime on my sneakers than necessary, and grabbed the robe off the floor. Then I reached down into a hidden pocket on the inside of the robe and pulled out a piece of sapphire-blue fabric about the size of my palm.

"And no one usually thinks to look in pockets either," I said, dropping the ruined robe back down onto the floor.

I carefully unfolded the sapphire fabric layer by layer, then gently shook it out. Despite how tightly the fabric had been packed down, it quickly sprang back into its original shape—a long trench coat.

"Spidersilk," Deah said in an approving voice. "I forgot that it always retains its shape, no matter how you wad it up or how small you fold it."

"Yep." I shrugged into the coat and smoothed some more of the wrinkles out of it before sticking the plastic bag with the ironmesh gloves into one of the pockets. "And now for the most important thing."

"Your mom's sword," Devon said.

I nodded and climbed up onto the bathroom counter. A metal vent was located above the mirror, high on the wall. I reached for one of the screws, which was so loose that it was about to fall right out of the vent frame. I frowned. I thought I'd tightened that back up before I'd left for the dinner—

The vent burst open, making me shriek in surprise and almost lose my balance on the counter. But before I could stagger away from the vent, something silver flashed, and a sword no bigger than a needle zoomed out of the darkness and pressed into my nose. I froze.

"Stop right there, or I'll stick you full of copper crusher venom," a low, angry voice growled.

I squinted, staring past the tip of my nose, and realized that two pairs of eyes were glaring at me from the dark depths of the vent—one pair an intense violet and the other a midnight black.

"Oscar! Tiny!" I sighed with relief. "You guys are okay!"

Oscar squinted back at me. "Lila? Is that really you?"

"Of course it's me. I showed you where I was putting my sword before I left. Remember?"

The pixie let out a tense breath and lowered his sword. Then he zipped out of the vent, flew over, and hugged my neck as tight as he could.

"It was . . . it was *awful*," Oscar whispered in a ragged tone, his voice even twangier than normal. "Just about everyone was in the dining hall eating dinner, but I decided to feed Tiny before I went down to eat myself. The Draconis must have snuck up on the perimeter guards and taken them out first because there was no warning. The Draconis just busted into the mansion and started killing people. I heard the shouts and screams, but by the time I grabbed my sword and flew downstairs, it was already too late. Most of the guards were already dead, and the Draconis were rounding up the survivors, forcing them outside, and making them get into trucks and vans. But they didn't see me, so I came up here to get Tiny and hide while they searched the rest of the mansion."

The pixie's small body trembled against my neck, and I reached up and gently patted his back, careful not to crush his wings, which were twitching in grief, anger, and agitation.

"It's okay," I whispered. "I'm here, and you and Tiny are safe now."

Oscar hugged my neck again, and he stayed perched on my shoulder while I reached up and lifted Tiny out of the air conditioning vent. I put the tortoise in one of the front pockets of my coat, so that he could stick his head up and see what was happening. Then I reached back into the vent and grabbed the final thing hidden inside—my mom's black blade.

The second my fingers touched the bloodiron, I felt just a little bit better, like I hadn't lost almost everything I cared about tonight.

I wasn't sure why.

Because things were still terrible, horrible, awful. This

was one of the worst nights of my life, second only to the one following my mom's murder. Victor had captured Claudia, Mo, Angelo, and Reginald. The rest of the Sinclairs were either captured or dead as well. And if my friends and I weren't careful, we'd end up just like everyone else.

But as I stared down at the five-pointed star carved into the sword's hilt, I felt as if my mom was standing right next to me, whispering to me about all the things I needed to do next. Get the black blades. Take my friends someplace safe. Strike a bargain with the Draconis to get back Claudia, Mo, and the others. And figure out a way to finally end Victor's reign of terror once and for all.

And that was exactly what I was going to do—or die trying.

"Lila?" Devon asked. "Are you okay?"

"No," I said, buckling the sword's scabbard to my belt and hopping down off the counter. "Not even close. But I will be. And so will everyone we have left. I promise you that."

CHAPTER TWELVE

I grabbed a few more things from my room that we might need; then we went back down to the dining hall. Devon, Felix, Deah, and I stood in the doorway, with Oscar riding on my shoulder and Tiny nestled in my coat pocket, and stared out at the sickening, senseless slaughter before us.

"I will never forget this," Felix said in a sad voice.

"You don't forget," Deah said, her tone harsh, her dark blue eyes blazing with grief, rage, and determination. "You *remember.* You use that anger, that pain, that grief, and you fight back with it, with everything you've got."

She reached down and yanked the gold Draconi cuff out of her pocket. Deah's fingers tightened around it, as if she were thinking about hurling it away from her as far and hard as she could. But in the end, she simply tossed it down at her feet, disgusted by the sight of it and everything it stood for. The *tink-tink-tink* of the cuff rattling around and around on the floor was as loud as a clap of thunder in the absolute quiet of the mansion—

"Over here!" someone called out. "I heard something!"

Deah's eyes widened. "That's Blake! He's here!"

We all froze. Sure enough, the *slap-slap-slap-slap* of footsteps sounded in the distance. More than one set, all hurrying this way. After they'd taken the prisoners away, Blake and the Draconi guards must have doubled back to make sure that there were no survivors—or to capture anyone who might come to the mansion looking for safety after the fight at the restaurant.

We didn't dare go back out the door and into the hallway, so I waved at the others and pointed over at the windows that lined the wall. Oscar zipped off my shoulder and flew over to the windows, peering out them.

"It's clear this way," he called out in a low voice. "Let's go!"

We hurried over to the windows, trying to make as little noise as possible as we waded through the broken dishes and smashed food on the floor. Like most of the others in the mansion, these windows had been shattered during the initial attack, so it was easy for us to climb out the jagged panes and drop down five feet to the soft grass below.

I scanned the landscape around us, but the Draconis weren't on this side of the mansion yet and we had a clear shot from the lawn all the way over to the trees. From there, we could disappear into the forest and head back to the SUV that we'd stashed down at the scenic overlook.

But instead of moving forward, Devon let out a soft curse.

"What's wrong?" Felix whispered.

"We didn't go down to the training room to get the black blades," Devon said, his mouth twisting with disgust. "We can't leave here without them."

I winced. "Yeah, about that . . ."

Devon, Felix, and Deah turned to look at me, with Oscar hovering in midair beside them.

"We don't have to go down to the training room because the weapons aren't there," I said, shifting on my feet. "Not the real, magic-filled black blades anyway."

Devon's eyes narrowed. "You stole the weapons, didn't you?"

I shrugged. "More like moved them to a safer location."

He kept staring at me, his mind churning as he put all the facts together. "That's what you were doing last night. Instead of sleeping in your room, you were breaking into the training room, switching out the black blades for another set of fakes, and hiding the real weapons somewhere else." His eyes narrowed a little more. "My mom helped you, didn't she?"

I blinked, surprised that he had guessed that. "How did you know?"

A ghost of a smile flashed across his face. "Because she wouldn't have wanted to risk Victor ever getting his hands on those black blades again, and who better to hide something that important than a thief? I bet she told you to take them someplace where only you would know where they were."

"Yeah. Are you angry about that?"

His smile widened. "Are you kidding? I think it's bloody brilliant."

I grinned back at him. "Good. Then let's go get them."

We sprinted across the lawn and stopped inside the tree line to look back at the mansion. Through the windows, I could see Blake moving from room to room, along with more Draconi guards, their red cloaks rippling around their shoulders like all the blood that stained the inside of the mansion. I'd thought that we'd at least put a dent in their numbers at the restaurant and then at the lochness bridge, but it looked as if Blake had just as many guards with him as before. Maybe even more.

"How many men does Victor have?" Felix muttered.

"You don't want to know," Deah replied.

"Too many for us to take on by ourselves," Devon said. "Come on. Let's go find the weapons and get out of here before Blake decides to start searching the forest."

He held his hand out, indicating that I should lead the way. Oscar fluttered over and slid into my coat pocket next to Tiny, while the others fell in step behind me. I led my friends through the woods and over to the Sinclair Family cemetery.

"This is it?" Felix asked, peering into the darkness. "This is where you hid the weapons?"

"Yep."

I headed over to the blood persimmon tree at the back of the cemetery, took hold of the trunk, and started climbing up it.

"I should have known," Felix muttered. "You like to climb more than a tree troll does."

I grinned and kept on going. It took me less than a minute to reach the crook where I'd hidden the two duffel bags last night. I used one of the throwing stars attached to my belt to slice through the ropes that anchored the two bags to the tree. Then I grabbed the bags and tossed them down to the ground, wincing at all the *clank-clanks* the weapons made, but it couldn't be helped and speed was the most important thing right now. Devon scooped up one bag, while Felix snagged the other. I shimmied down the tree and took the lead again.

We hiked through the woods, making sure to stay deep in the trees and well away from the mansion, where Blake and the Draconis were still searching for survivors. But they didn't spot us, and we made it back down to the scenic overlook with no problem. No one had bothered our SUV, so we loaded the weapons into the back and got inside the vehicle.

Devon cranked the engine, but he didn't make a move to actually put the vehicle in gear and drive down the mountain.

"What's wrong?" Oscar asked.

The pixie was still nestled in my coat pocket, along with

Tiny. From the faint rumbles that vibrated against my chest, it sounded as if the tortoise had actually gone to sleep. Well, I was glad that somebody was getting some rest.

"I . . . I don't know where to go," Devon admitted, his forehead creasing with worry. "We can't stay at the mansion, and we can't just get a hotel room down on the Midway. Victor probably has people watching all the hotels, even the cheap ones on the outskirts of town. One of the Draconis is sure to spot us the second we show our faces anywhere in town."

He scrubbed his hands over his face again, the same way he'd done at the lochness bridge. Felix had a stricken expression on his face as well, while Deah chewed her lower lip in worry.

"I know where to go," I said.

Devon looked over at me. "Where?"

"Someplace safe," I said. "Someplace that Blake wouldn't be caught dead in, and someplace that Victor and the other Draconis will never even think to look for us."

Thirty minutes later, we were back down in Cloudburst Falls, sitting in the SUV, which I'd told Devon to park behind a dumpster in an alley that was only a couple of streets over from the lochness bridge.

"Are you sure we should park here?" Devon asked, peering out the windshield at the other dumpsters and trash cans that lined the alley walls. "This is awfully close to the warehouses that the Draconis own in this part of town."

I shrugged. "We've done our best to hide the SUV. If they find the car, then they find it. But they won't find *us*, no matter how hard they look. Not where we're going. Now come on."

Devon still looked doubtful. So did Felix, Deah, and

even Oscar, still riding in my coat pocket, but my friends trusted me enough to get out of the vehicle. Devon and Felix each grabbed one of the bags of black blades, and we left the alley.

It was after midnight now and the streets were dark and deserted. Then again, we weren't in the nice, tourist part of town anymore. Far from it. Instead of the busy restaurants, food carts, and souvenir shops of the Midway, row houses, deserted storefronts, and abandoned warehouses stretched out as far as even I could see. Streetlamps were spaced down the block, but most of them only flickered with weak light, if they worked at all. The street itself was full of potholes, the sidewalks were cracked, and bags of trash were heaped at the corners. The sharp, pungent scents of greasy burgers, sticky soda, and other rancid food made my nose twitch with disgust, as did the black swarms of flies, mosquitoes, and other bugs buzzing around the bags.

We were the only people out on the street, but we were far from alone, given all the monsters prowling around.

They slithered right up to the ends of the alleys as we hurried past, peering at us with their jewel-colored eyes, debating whether or not we would make a good meal. Devon, Felix, and Deah pressed together in a tight knot in the middle of the sidewalk, their knuckles whitening around their swords as they picked up their pace, but I stared right back at the creatures that were watching us, even though it was so dark that all I could really see of them were their glowing eyes.

Monsters are your friends. Never forget that. Seleste's voice whispered in my mind.

I wondered what she'd glimpsed of the future that had made her say those exact words to me. Had she been trying to tell me that the lochness would save us from Blake tonight? Or was there more to her message? Some hidden meaning that I wasn't understanding? Or were her words as simple as they seemed? That I paid the tolls and that the monsters respected me for it. I didn't know, but I wasn't afraid of the monsters anymore, not even the ones watching us right now.

Oh, the monsters could still spring out of the shadows, attack, kill, and devour me and my friends. I wasn't so foolish as to think they would suddenly become tame and lovable and let me pet their furry and scaly heads like they were cute, wiggly puppies just because I gave them a few quarters and some candy bars. They were still *monsters*, after all. They had all those sharp teeth, talons, and claws for a reason, and they had to eat just like the rest of us did. But I wasn't afraid of them anymore.

Seeing them . . . it almost felt like . . . *home.*

Ever since I'd started working for the Sinclairs earlier this summer, I'd been counting down the days until Victor was defeated and I could finally leave town and all the ugly memories here behind. But now, I wasn't so sure I wanted to go. The mountains, the monsters, the magic, even the bad memories . . . it was all part of Cloudburst Falls.

It was all part of *me.*

Just as it had been part of my mom before me. Serena had worked for the Sinclairs, and she'd dealt with the monsters, paying the tolls and respecting the creatures, their quirks, and their territories. She had been happy to do it, to follow the old ways and traditions, and she'd taught me to do the same. More than that, she'd instilled her love of all the rituals in me as well. I liked carrying around quarters and chocolate bars and knowing that I could communicate with the monsters in a way that other people couldn't or simply didn't take the time to. It was my mom's legacy to me, and I couldn't have left it behind even if I'd wanted to—and I didn't want to anymore.

Sure, my mom had been murdered here, and I'd spent four years hiding and just trying to scrape by. Not exactly fun times. But I'd also found Devon and Felix and Oscar and Deah, and I wasn't about to lose them now. Not to Victor Draconi or anyone else. I wasn't about to abandon Mo, Claudia, and all the other captured Sinclairs when they needed me most. I was going to stay and fight for all the things I cared about—and for the future I wanted for myself.

My friends remained tense and quiet, but I started humming a soft tune, the same one that my mom used to hum whenever she was packing her coat full of monster supplies. Despite everything that had happened tonight, despite all the loss and grief and heartache, this was still exactly where I wanted to be.

The others gave me strange looks, wondering why I was humming, but they didn't say anything. A couple of minutes later, we rounded a corner and stopped in front of a brick building that took up this particular block. A stack of splintered books adorned a faded sign planted in the lawn that read CLOUDBURST FALLS LIBRARY—WESTERN BRANCH.

Devon grinned and let out a low chuckle, realizing exactly what I was up to. "Only you would think to come back here. Brilliant, Lila. Bloody brilliant."

I grinned back at him. "I do try."

Deah shook her head. "I don't get it."

"The library?" Felix frowned. "But this is where you lived before you came to work for the Sinclairs."

"Exactly," I said. "And no one knows that but us, so there's no way that the Draconis will even think to look for us here. Trust me, we'll be safe. At least for tonight. Tomorrow, we can figure out what our next move is. But right now, we're all about to drop from exhaustion. We need a place to lay low, and this is it. Now, come on."

I headed over to the side door that I had gone through so many times before. Seeing the locked door was like catching up with an old friend, and it took me less than thirty seconds to pick it open with my chopstick lock picks. We slid inside and I shut and locked the door behind us.

Felix pulled out his phone and used it as a flashlight again, but I didn't need any light to see by; I'd long ago memorized the library's layout. I led my friends down the aisles, past the shelves of books, and over to a door that led into a storage room. I picked open that door, then another one at the far end of the storage room, and we walked through the opening and down the steps to the library basement. I told everyone to stand still for a second, then went over and ran my fingers over the touch lamp that I'd set up in the corner.

Soft white light filled the basement, revealing a mini fridge, cases of bottled water, and a metal rack crammed full of canned and dried food, along with bottles of dark green liquid stitch-sting. Several battered suitcases full of clothes were stacked on top of each other, and two small cots covered with sheets and blankets were lined up against another wall, with a large, inflated air mattress lying on the floor in front of them.

And then there were the weapons.

Several duffel bags peeked out from underneath the metal rack, the cots, and even the corner table where the lamp was. The tops of the bags were all open, revealing the dull, ash-colored swords and daggers inside—the real, magic-filled black blades that Devon, Felix, and I had stolen from Victor over the past two weeks. The chill of magic emanating from the weapons filled the air, making it feel even cooler than it really was in the basement, but I didn't mind the sensation because it told me that no one had been near the weapons since the last time I'd come down here.

Claudia had asked me to take the weapons somewhere safe, and this was the first place I'd thought of.

The library had had one of its fundraising sales earlier this summer, right around the time I'd packed up most of my stuff and had moved to the Sinclair mansion. After the sale, I'd snuck back into the basement to check on the rest of my things, and the furniture I'd left behind had still been here, hidden behind boxes of old, used books that hadn't gotten sorted through and sold.

So I'd pulled all the furniture back out and put it right back where it had been before, as though I was still living here. Then I'd gone the extra step of bringing in the food, water, and other supplies, just in case my friends and I might need them some night.

Like tonight.

Devon looked around. "You've been busy."

I shrugged. "I wanted to put the weapons somewhere a little safer than a tree in the woods. Who would ever think to look for black blades in a library basement?"

Felix shook his head. "Not me, that's for sure."

Oscar flew up out of my coat pocket and hovered in midair in front of the metal rack. "I knew that you couldn't be eating all those bags of bacon-flavored beef jerky by yourself. I knew it!" He zipped back over to me. "You were stockpiling them, weren't you? Telling me that you were hungry and asking me to grab them from the mansion kitchen when you planned on bringing them down here the whole time."

"I did eat *some* of them." I grinned. "They are bacon-flavored, after all."

Oscar huffed, but a small smile lifted his lips.

"I can't decide if you're supersmart or superparanoid to

have brought all this stuff down here," Deah said. "I'm going to go with both."

"Both is probably right, but I'll take that as a compliment. Anyway, we should clean up and then try to get some rest. It's been a long night, and tomorrow . . ."

My voice trailed off, but I didn't have to finish my sentence. We all realized that we didn't know what was going to happen tomorrow. The light mood vanished and everyone quieted down again.

I handed out the extra clothes I'd stored down here, then led the others back upstairs and showed them where the restrooms were. It wasn't as good as taking a long, hot shower, but we cleaned the blood, dirt, and grime off ourselves as best we could. I even stopped up a sink in the men's restroom and filled it up with water so Oscar and Tiny could take a bath.

When we were mostly clean, we headed back downstairs to the basement to try to get some sleep. Devon and Felix took the air mattress on the floor, while Deah and I curled up on the cots. Oscar used some of the extra clothes to make a bed for himself and Tiny, right next to the bags of bacon-flavored beef jerky on one of the metal racks.

Once everyone was settled down, I ran my fingers over the touch lamp, casting the basement into darkness. One by one, the others drifted off to sleep, their breaths growing deep and even, but I lay on my cot, staring up at the cracks that zigzagged through the ceiling, replaying tonight over and over again in my mind, wondering what I could have possibly done that would have saved everyone at the restaurant and the mansion from Victor. Even though I'd known that it was coming, he'd still attacked my friends, my Family, and I had failed to save the people I cared about.

Just as I'd failed to save my mom four years ago.

My hand curled around the Sinclair cuff on my right

wrist, my fingers tracing over the small sapphire star embedded in the metal. The sharp points of the star pricked my skin, but the sensation soothed me because it told me that I was still alive and that I still had a chance to save my friends.

I'd kept Devon, Felix, Deah, Oscar, and Tiny safe, and I was going to make sure they stayed that way. In the morning, I would start figuring out how to find and rescue Mo, Claudia, and the rest of the captured Sinclairs.

And Victor . . . I was going to find some way to defeat him, to finally make him pay for all the horrible things he'd done to me, my mom, and my friends.

I wouldn't fail them again—no matter what.

My promise complete, I dropped my hand from the cuff, turned over onto my side, and finally let myself drift off to sleep.

CHAPTER THIRTEEN

"Ouch!"

A sharp *bang*, followed by that whispered word, made my eyes snap open sometime the next morning.

Had the Draconis found us after all? Were Victor and Blake here, ready to finish what they'd started at the restaurant last night? I lay still on my cot, although my hand had already wrapped around my mom's sword, which I'd slid under my pillow. My fingers curled around the hilt and my entire body tensed as I readied myself to leap up and start swinging the weapon at anyone who came near me.

"Be quiet!" another voice hissed. "Lila's still asleep!"

I knew those voices and I relaxed as I realized what was happening. Devon and Felix were trying to quietly get up but not having any success at it, since the basement was still pitch-black. I looked over at the clock sitting on the table in the corner. Just before noon. We'd been down here for almost twelve hours. I scrubbed my hands over my face. I felt like I could sleep for twelve more hours, but I couldn't afford to stay in bed any longer. Not if we wanted to get to Mo, Claudia, and the others in time.

So I reached over and hit the touch lamp with my fingers, flooding the basement with light. Devon and Felix froze at the bottom of the steps, while Deah let out a low groan, rolled away from the light, and pulled her blanket up over her head. On their shelf on the metal rack, Oscar and Tiny didn't move or stir at all, both of them still snoring in chorus, like a low drumbeat running through one of the pixie's beloved country songs.

"What do you think you're doing?" I asked, my voice thick with sleep.

The guys exchanged a guilty look, but they both turned to face me.

"We were going out to the Midway to see if we can spot any Sinclair guards or get any news about my dad and the others," Felix said.

I rolled my eyes. "Seriously? Whose dumb idea was that? The Draconis, especially Blake, are sure to be looking for any Sinclairs that they didn't kill or capture last night. They'll have guards posted all over the Midway. The two of you wouldn't last three minutes before getting spotted."

"Well, we can't just hide down here and do nothing," Devon said. "Not when Victor has my mom and Angelo and all the others. We have to find some way to save them before it's too late."

"And we will," I said. "But you guys are thinking that you can just walk through the Midway like everything's normal. Like you still have the full force of the Sinclair Family behind you when you don't."

Worry filled Felix's dark eyes, while a muscle ticked in Devon's jaw. I hadn't meant my words to be so harsh, but they were, because we all remembered the blood, bodies, and destruction at the Sinclair mansion. And we all knew that nothing would make Victor and Blake happier than capturing or killing us just like they had all the other Sinclairs.

I sat up and swung my legs over the side of the cot. Deah sighed, threw back her blanket, and did the same. Oscar and Tiny kept right on snoring, though.

"Listen," I said. "I want to find the others just as badly as you guys do, but we have to be careful. That's the only way we're all going to get through this in one piece. Victor . . . he's been planning this for a long, long time. He's sure to have thought about how things might go wrong and have contingency plans in place. He might not have expected us to switch out the black blades for fakes, but he's probably already regrouped and has a plan to find us, get the weapons back, and finish what he started. And he's got the guards to help him do it. All we have is each other and what's in this basement, so we have to be smarter about things, sneakier, and cleverer than he is."

Devon's hands tightened into fists, and he started pacing back and forth across the basement. "We can't just stay down here and do nothing," he repeated.

"I didn't say that."

"My mom and the others could already be dead," he said in a harsh voice. "Victor could have killed them last night while we were running all over town."

Devon stared at me, the red-hot needles of his pain and anguish stabbing me in the chest, while his aching desperation and helpless rage boiled in my veins. I felt the same way, but I pushed the sensations aside and focused on him.

"You saw Victor at the restaurant last night. You saw the look on his face when he realized that Claudia had stolen all of his precious black blades right out from under him," I said. "He won't kill her. Not until she tells him what she did with the weapons."

"He'll torture her to get the information. You know he will," Devon snapped, more anguish filling his eyes. "No doubt he's already started."

I got up and went over to him, taking his hands in my own, and making him stop pacing. "I know," I said in a low voice. "I know what Victor is capable of better than anyone else, and I wish I could have saved your mom from that. But Claudia is strong, and every second that she holds out gives us more time to save her. Okay?"

Devon stared back at me, pain and worry still shimmering in his eyes, but he finally nodded and squeezed my hands. "Okay."

I nodded back at him, then dropped his hands and looked over at Deah. "Can you think of any place where your dad might be holding Claudia and the others? Do you think they're up at the Draconi mansion?"

Deah shook her head. "No. If my dad—" She stopped and cleared her throat. "If Victor took all the other Sinclairs prisoner, then there's no place at the Draconi mansion big enough to hold them all. He'll have to keep them down here in town, probably at one of the Family warehouses."

"Which one?" Devon demanded, his hands clenching into fists again.

She gave him a helpless look. "I don't know. He has dozens of warehouses all over town. It could be any one of them, or someplace else that I don't even know about. I'm sorry, but Victor and Blake never talked to me much about the Family businesses. I guess my dad always knew that I wouldn't like what he was planning and didn't want to risk me messing things up. And I was always so busy training for the Tournament of Blades or watching out for my mom that I didn't pay much attention to anything else. I'm sorry. I wish I could be more help."

Felix walked over, sat down on the cot next to her, and slung his arm around her shoulders, pulling her close. "It's okay. I understand, and so does Devon. Don't you, Dev?"

Devon's lips pressed together for a second, but then his shoulders slumped and he nodded.

"So now what?" he asked, pacing back and forth again. "How can we figure out where the others are without getting captured ourselves?"

"Simple," I said. "Deah and I will go out to the Midway, snoop around, and see what we can find out."

"And how are you going to do that?" Felix asked. "Because the Draconis will come after you the second they spot you guys, just like they would Devon and me."

I went over to one of the suitcases full of extra clothes and dug through the piles of fabric inside until I found exactly what I wanted. I held up the T-shirt so that the others could see it. All three of them winced, especially Deah.

"Please tell me that you don't expect me to wear *that*," she said.

"Oh, you're going to wear it all right," I said. "And once you put it on, you're going to become practically invisible to the Draconis."

Deah groaned and flopped back down onto her cot. I just grinned.

"Are you sure this is going to work?" Deah asked. "I feel like I'm wearing a flashing sign that says, *Here I am! Come and get me!*"

"It'll work. Trust me."

Deah and I were standing in one of the alleys close to the Midway, along with Devon and Felix. We'd left Oscar and Tiny back in the safety of the library basement. Since it was Sunday, the library was closed, and after I'd told the others what I had in mind, we'd gotten ready, snuck out, and walked over here. Now we were hiding behind some dumpsters, reviewing our plan.

It was simple, really. Deah and I would wander through the Midway, eavesdrop on the Draconi guards, and try to pick up information about where Victor might be holding Claudia, Mo, and the others. When we were done, we'd come back here, meet up with Devon and Felix, and head back to the library to plan our next move.

"Well," Deah said, holding her arms out wide. "How do I look?"

Devon and Felix stared at her, then me, then back at her.

"Um, bright?" Felix said, trying to be nice.

I'd given Deah some clothes from my stash in the library, and she now wore gray sneakers, gray cargo shorts, and a T-shirt. But not just *any* T-shirt. One that was the boldest, most electric, neon blue you'd ever seen. A shirt that was so loud, bright, and colorful that it hurt your eyes to look at it for more than a few seconds. The words *The Pork Pit—Best Barbecue Ever* were done in sparkly silver sequins across the front of the shirt, adding even more glittering shine to it. A matching, neon-blue baseball cap perched on top of Deah's head, hiding most of her golden hair from sight and casting her face in shadow.

Deah glared at Felix, who shrugged back at her.

"What?" he asked. "I'm not the one who made you put on that ridiculous shirt. That was all Lila."

She turned her hot glare to me, even though I had on the exact same thing she did.

"And it will work," I said. "Trust me. Only the tourist rubes wear matching T-shirts and baseball hats, especially ones that are this color. The Midway guards, especially the Draconis, won't give us a second glance, and we'll walk right by them. They won't even think to actually look at our faces to see if we might be the people they're searching for. Trust me. This will work."

Deah sighed, but she finally nodded, agreeing with me.

"I still don't like this," Devon said. "It's risky, especially since you two don't have any weapons."

I shrugged. "I don't like it any more than you do, but only Family guards and workers have weapons on the Midway. Carrying around a couple of swords would tell the Draconis exactly who we are, and they'd be on us in a heartbeat. This way, we can nose around the entire Midway, Deah can point out the senior guards who might know something, and we can see what's what. We'll be fine."

Devon still didn't like my plan, but he didn't say anything else.

"Now, stay here until we get back," I said.

Devon and Felix both looked at each other, guilt flickering in their faces.

"Guys," I warned. "I don't need to worry about the two of you going off and getting captured while we're gone. Deah and I will have enough problems getting through the Midway and back here again. Promise me that you'll both stay right here until we get back. Okay?"

The guys both sighed, but they nodded.

"All right then," I said. "Here we go."

Devon opened his arms. I stepped into them and he hugged me tight.

"Be careful," he whispered. "I couldn't stand to lose you too."

"I'm always careful," I whispered back.

His arms tightened around me for a moment, as if he didn't ever want to let me go. But we both knew that this was the only way to find out where Mo, Claudia, and the others were. Devon sighed, pressed a kiss to my forehead, and dropped his arms.

Felix finished hugging Deah and she moved to stand beside me. I took one last look at Devon, while Deah did the same thing to Felix.

Then together, the two of us left the guys behind and stepped out of the alley and into the hot summer sunshine.

CHAPTER FOURTEEN

The alley led out to a street that was on the very edge of the tourist area, and we crossed it and entered one of the shopping squares. It was after two o'clock now, and people moved from one side of the square to the other, despite the sweltering July heat. No one gave Deah and me a second look, and we moved from that square over to the next one and the next one until we had reached one of the many entrances to the Midway.

I looked at Deah. "No matter what happens, we need to stick together. Okay?"

"Okay." Her fingers twitched. "I still wish I had a sword, though."

"I know. Me too." I drew in a breath. "Here we go."

Deah nodded at me, and together we walked out into the Midway.

At first, everything looked normal. People moving in and out of the shops, stopping at the food carts to get sweet and salty snacks, taking pictures of the stuffed monsters and other displays in the museum windows. The scents of popcorn and caramel apples filled the air, while kids shrieked, laughed, and ran circles around their parents.

But the deeper we headed into the Midway, the more I realized that something was seriously wrong.

Oh, the restaurants, shops, hotels, and other businesses were still open, but I only spotted a few guards from the Ito, Salazar, and Volkov Families patrolling through their designated areas. And the guards that I did see were in teams of three or more, all of them with their hands on their weapons, ready to draw their swords at the slightest hint of danger. My soulsight let me see and feel every bit of their worry, fear, and tension. The emotions punched me in the chest over and over again, with every guard I looked at.

We lingered by a few of the food carts, as though we were thinking about buying some funnel cakes and deep-fried fudge, and spied on a group of Ito guards, but they didn't talk to each other, and we didn't overhear anything that might tell us what was going on with the other Families.

Once again, I wondered what had happened to Poppy and her dad after the attack at the White Orchid last night, but it wasn't like I could go up to the Ito guards and ask. Not without raising their suspicions. I just had to hope that Poppy had made it to safety too.

Eventually, Deah and I wandered over to the Sinclair section of the Midway. It was far less crowded here than anywhere else, mainly because none of the businesses were actually open. All the carts, shops, and shacks were shuttered, dark, and locked up tight, and I didn't see any Sinclair guards patrolling through our section of the Midway—not a single one.

My heart sank. So it was as bad as I'd feared, and Victor had captured everyone but us. That made it even more important that we find out where he was holding the other Sinclairs before it was too late.

We stopped beside one of the closed Sinclair ice cream carts and I looked at Deah.

"Are you ready for this?" I asked.

She nodded. "Yeah. Let's get it over with."

I nodded back at her, and we slowly headed toward the Draconi section of the Midway.

The guards from all the other Families might have been nervous and on the lookout for trouble, but the Draconis were totally relaxed, strolling around in pairs, smiling, talking, and laughing with each other. They thought that they'd won, that they'd finally beaten all the other Families, and they were happy about it. Their wide grins and hearty chuckles made more white-hot rage burn in my heart. They weren't going to be happy for long. Not after everything they'd done. Not if I had anything to say about it.

Deah reached out and gripped my hand tightly, silently warning me not to let any of my true feelings show. I squeezed her hand back, telling her that I understood, and we moved even deeper into Draconi territory.

Deah flinched at every single guard we passed, but our matching T-shirts and baseball hats worked like the proverbial charm, and none of the guards gave us a second look, except to snicker at the outrageous, neon-blue color of our shirts and our apparently over-the-top love for barbecue.

We rounded a cart selling popcorn and candy apples. A few feet away, in the shade of a large blood persimmon tree, five Draconi guards were eating the snacks they'd just bought and laughing and talking to each other. Deah nodded, telling me that she recognized the guards and that they were high enough up in the Draconi Family to know something about where our friends were. She pretended to look at some sunglasses on another cart, keeping an eye out for more guards, while I crept closer and closer to the group in the shade.

"We finally taught the Sinclairs and everyone else a lesson," one of the guards crowed. "Victor has big plans for this town, and they were standing in our way."

All the other guards nodded their agreement.

"What are they going to do with all the Sinclairs?" another guard asked. "Victor can't keep them locked up forever."

My ears perked up, and I sidled a little closer, trying to hear every word he said.

The first guard shook his head. "I don't know. Right now, they're all in those cages at the warehouse. Maybe Victor will eventually let the Sinclair guards swear their loyalty to him. But you know he'll take care of Claudia Sinclair and all the other senior members of the Family first. He won't risk letting any of them go so they can try to regroup and rebuild their Family."

My fingers curled into fists, my knuckles cracking from the pressure. What the guard really meant was that Victor was planning to kill Claudia, something he'd been wanting to do for a long time. And now, he finally had her, Mo, and the others at his mercy. Dread rose up in my chest at the thought of losing Claudia and Mo the same way that I had my mom, but I forced the feeling aside. That wasn't going to happen. I wasn't going to *let* that happen. Never again.

"Well, I'm surprised he didn't just go ahead and do it last night, when we first brought her into the warehouse," another guard said.

The first guard shrugged. "Apparently, she still has something he wants. Something about those black blades that everyone was supposed to get. Victor's been working on her, along with that Kaminsky guy. You know, the one who owns that tacky pawnshop?"

The other men nodded.

"Anyway, Victor will get one of them to talk . . . sooner or later."

The guard let out an ugly laugh, and all the others joined in with him.

I squeezed my eyes shut, but not before two hot tears escaped and rolled down my cheeks. I'd known that Victor would torture Claudia, but to hear the guards so casually confirm it, and to realize that he was hurting Mo too. . . . It was almost more than I could bear.

In that moment, I wanted nothing more than to scream, wade into the guards, grab one of their swords, and cut them all down the same way they had the Sinclairs at the mansion last night.

But I couldn't do that. Not without getting myself killed or captured, along with Deah. Then there would be no way I could save Claudia, Mo, and the others. So I opened my eyes and forced myself to take slow, deep breaths, trying to get my raging emotions under control.

A minute later, the guards finished their snacks, said their goodbyes, and drifted away to start patrolling again. Frustrated, I whipped around and hurried over to Deah, who was still standing by that cart, trying on pair after pair of sunglasses.

"Anything?" she asked, worry darkening her eyes.

"The Sinclairs are in a warehouse somewhere, just like you thought, but the guards didn't say which one. Are you sure you don't have any idea where they could be?"

She shook her head. "I'm sorry, but no. Dad has a bunch of warehouses all along the river and in other parts of town. They could be anywhere."

"All right then. We'll just have to keep eavesdropping."

And that's exactly what we did, going around and around the Draconi section of the Midway, getting close to every single guard we could. After everything that had happened last night, they were a chatty bunch, almost as talkative as Felix, but while the guards kept mentioning the warehouse, none of them said where it actually *was*.

My frustration grew and grew, and Deah was just as tense and on edge as I was. We both kept our hats on, and our faces low and turned away from the guards, but every second we stayed in the Midway added to the risk of someone spotting and recognizing us. Still, we kept walking around and around in circles, trying to overhear something—*anything*—that might lead us to Claudia, Mo, and the others.

But we didn't hear anything useful, and thirty minutes later, Deah stopped and pulled a buzzing phone out of her shorts pocket. It was one of the cheap cell phones that I'd bought and stashed in the library basement, along with the rest of my supplies.

"It's Felix," she said. "He wants to know what's taking so long."

I sighed. "Tell him that we'll be back soon. I want to make one more lap around the Draconi section, just in case there are any guards we missed."

She nodded and texted him back. I waited until she'd finished, and then we started walking around again. But once again, we came up with nothing.

Just when I was ready to admit defeat and head back to the alley where Devon and Felix were waiting, a familiar, snide voice caught my ear.

"Dad didn't like using the warehouse so close to the lochness bridge, but we didn't have a choice with so many prisoners."

Deah heard the voice too, and we both stopped and looked at each other. I motioned to her, and we both slid behind a fudge cart, following the sound of the voice.

"But it won't matter. As soon as Claudia Sinclair gives up the location of the weapons, Dad will finish her off.

Then the rest of the Sinclairs will have to swear their loyalty to him—or else."

Blake—that was Blake's voice. I looked around, but I didn't spot him in the crowd of people, so I crept forward a few more steps, searching for him, with Deah right beside me.

"I don't see why Victor still wants those black blades so badly, when he already has most of the Sinclairs locked up," a guard chimed in.

"Dad wouldn't want the blades if they weren't important," Blake replied. "Once we have the weapons, we can wipe out all the other Families. Then this town will belong to the Draconis, like it should have all along."

Blake let out a low, ugly laugh. The sound made my skin crawl.

"I know what warehouse he's talking about," Deah whispered in my ear. "It's on Copper Street, not too far from the lochness bridge. Dad uses it to store T-shirts, sunglasses, and other cheap souvenirs to sell to the tourists."

I nodded. I knew the warehouse she was talking about. It was one of the few buildings in the bad part of town that still occasionally had guards patrolling outside—enough guards that even I had never dared try to break inside. It would be the perfect place to hold Claudia, Mo, and the rest of the Sinclair hostages.

"Let's go," I whispered. "We need to get back to Devon and Felix and tell them what we found out."

Deah nodded, and we both walked around the opposite side of the fudge cart. We'd just rounded the corner and were about to head over to one of the cobblestone paths when a couple of guys stepped in front of us. I managed to avoid them, but she spotted them a second too late.

"Oof!" Deah slammed into one of the guys going the opposite direction and bounced off his broad, muscled body.

"Watch where you're going," a low, familiar voice growled.

I froze, my breath hissing out between my teeth. Because Deah had just run into the very last person either one of us wanted to see right now.

Blake.

CHAPTER FIFTEEN

I hoped that Blake would just keep on walking, but of course he stopped, turned around, and glared at the person who had dared to run into him.

"I said watch where you're going," he snapped again, obviously waiting for some sort of apology.

"I—uh—um—" Deah sputtered, completely at a loss for words.

"Sorry! My friend is so sorry!" I said, pitching my voice light and high in hopes that he wouldn't recognize me. "She just didn't see you standing there!"

I stepped up to grab Deah's arm and pull her away from him, but Blake moved to the side, blocking me without even realizing it.

His face twisted into a sneer as he stared at her T-shirt. "That's the stupidest shirt I've ever seen. What kind of idiot wears a shirt for a barbecue restaurant?"

Deah dropped her head, but Blake leaned forward, trying to see her face underneath her baseball hat. He frowned, his eyebrows knitting together in confusion. Then his eyes widened as he realized that he was staring at his own sister.

"You!" he hissed, his hand falling to the hilt of his sword. "You're alive! You got away from the lochness after all! Guards! Guards!"

He yanked his sword free of his scabbard. Time to go. I stepped up, shoved my shoulder into Blake's, and sent him staggering back. Then I grabbed Deah's hand and pulled her away from her brother.

"Run!" I yelled at her. "Run! Run! Run!"

Together, Deah and I sprinted through the Midway, darting around people, food carts, and more. Behind us, loud curses rang out, and I could hear footsteps pounding on the cobblestone walkways as Blake and the Draconi guards chased after us. Even worse, Blake kept screaming for more and more guards the whole time.

And they answered his call.

We were still in the Draconi section of the Midway, and guards wearing blood-red cloaks and matching cavalier hats started converging on us from all sides. And since we were the only people running like our lives depended on it, we were easy to pick out of the crowd, especially with the neon-blue T-shirts and baseball hats we both still wore. Our disguises were useless now, so I ripped off my hat and tossed it aside. Deah did the same with her hat, but there was nothing we could do about our shirts.

My gaze darted left and right as I looked for some sort of escape route or at least a place to hide. But I didn't see anything. Just people and food carts and Draconis closing in from every direction.

A guard came up on my right side, swinging his sword over his head. I let go of Deah's hand, went low, and drove my shoulder into his stomach. The guard let out a loud *oof!* of pain and doubled over. I grabbed his sword out of his hand and whipped around. Deah had disarmed another guard, so she had a sword now too. She gave me a grim nod and the two of us started running again.

I'd always known how big the Midway was, how many acres it covered, but it seemed as though we would *never* reach the end of it, even though Deah and I were both sprinting down the cobblestone paths as fast as we could. People stared as we ran past, wondering who we were and why we were interrupting their vacation fun.

It was far hotter this afternoon than it had been last night, and sweat streamed down my face and spattered onto my T-shirt. My breath came in ragged gasps and a painful stitch throbbed in my side, keeping time to the steady *slap-slap-slap-slap* of my sneakers on the ground. Beside me, Deah's face was beet red, her mouth open wide as she tried to suck down as much air as she could. She was feeling the heat too, but we both kept running. We had to.

Eventually, *finally*, we reached the edge of the Midway and managed to dart onto a walkway that led out to one of the shopping squares. But this was a Draconi square, and Blake's shouts followed us, causing the guards here to turn and run in our direction as well. My head snapped left and right again, still looking for an escape route, but of course there wasn't one. So I looked around the square again, focusing on exactly where we were and what I knew about the surrounding area.

I pointed to the left. "This way! Follow me!"

I veered in that direction, with Deah right behind me. The guards kept chasing us, but they were wearing cloaks and hats, which weighed them down and made them even hotter and more miserable than we were, and we managed to put a little distance between us and them, something I was going to take advantage of. We ran past the buildings that fronted this side of the square and into another alley, darting past trash cans and leaping over loose soda cans, empty fast-food wrappers, and other garbage.

"Where are we going?" Deah yelled behind me.

"You'll see!"

We ran through that alley, then two more, and finally out into another shopping square, one that was in Sinclair territory. Of course, this square was deserted, since all the businesses here were closed, just as they had been out in the Midway, but that was okay because I was only interested in one particular business.

A large storefront took up the entire back of the square, and the sign over the front doors spelled out THE RAZZLE DAZZLE in ten-foot-high letters. On a normal day, the neon-blue letters would have been flashing, with the white stars that adorned the sign winking on and off, all of it creating a dazzling display. But the sign was dark today, as was the inside of the store. My heart clenched tight at the sight of the deserted store, but I sprinted over to the glass doors anyway.

"Mo's pawnshop?" Deah asked, skidding to a stop right beside me, her breath coming in ragged gasps just like mine was. "Are you . . . crazy? This is the first place . . . they'll think to look."

"Exactly."

I raised my stolen sword and smashed the point into first one door, then the other one, busting large chunks of glass out of both of them. I hated breaking anything at Mo's shop, but Blake and the rest of the Draconis would expect us to hole up inside, once they spotted the shattered glass. If enough of them went inside the store at once, it just might give us time to escape for good.

Once I finished breaking the glass, I jerked my head at Deah. "Let's go."

Not understanding why I'd bothered to smash the glass if we weren't actually going inside, she frowned in confusion but shrugged it off and followed me anyway.

I started to sprint over to the walkway that led out of the far side of the square, but I spotted a guy wearing a red cloak, checking his phone, heading in this direction. Another Draconi guard who'd been summoned by Blake. Before he could spot me, I changed direction, instead racing over to a blood persimmon tree that was close to the bubbling fountain in the center of the square.

"Now what are you doing?" Deah muttered.

"Up the tree!" I hissed. "Now! Start climbing!"

She gave me a look that said she thought I was totally crazy, but she took hold of the tree and started climbing.

"Faster! Faster!" I hissed again, climbing up right below her.

"Give me a second!" she sniped back. "I'm not as good at this as you are, remember?"

But Deah made it up the tree, with me following her. She wanted to stop after a few feet, but I made her climb higher and higher, until we were about thirty feet up in the tree, right in the center of all the thick green leaves. Hopefully, they would be enough to hide us from sight. If they weren't . . . I swallowed. I didn't want to think about that until I absolutely had to.

We'd barely settled ourselves back against the branches when the *slap-slap-slap-slap* of footsteps sounded, getting louder and closer with every passing second. Deah heard them too, and we both leaned forward and peered through the screen of leaves.

A few seconds later, Blake ran into the square, with his guards right behind him. When he didn't immediately see us, he stared across the square at the Draconi guard who had finally put his phone away and entered from the far side.

"Did you see them?" he called out. "Did they get past you?"

The guard shook his head, and Blake whipped around to face the other men.

"Search everywhere!" he barked out. "They have to be here somewhere. I want them found. Now!"

About half the guards spread out around the square,

peering into first one storefront, then another, while a couple of men went down to the street, scanning the sidewalks to see if we'd left that way. But what worried me the most were the three men who hurried over to search around the fountain, less than twenty feet from where we were hiding.

If one of them had sight magic and looked up into the tree . . . if one of them had a hearing Talent and noticed our harsh, raspy breaths . . . well, we were caught, simple as that.

Deah knew it too and she gave me a worried look, but I shrugged back. We were stuck up here, and there was nothing either one of us could do to change that—

Cheep.

For a moment, Deah and I both froze at the sound, our eyes wide as we stared at each other. Then we both slowly turned our heads and looked up.

A large nest made out of twigs, leaves, grasses, and colorful candy bar wrappers was perched in the crook of a branch a few feet above my head. I'd been so focused on climbing up the tree that I hadn't even thought to check whether any birds or monsters might be up here. But I didn't need my sight magic to see the tree troll standing on the branch right beside its nest.

As far as monsters went, tree trolls were pretty harmless, since they were only about a foot tall with charcoal-gray fur, long, bushy tails, and black webbing under their arms that let them catch wind currents and hop from one branch or tree to another. But this troll's emerald-green eyes were narrowed to slits, and it clutched a ripe blood persimmon in its long, curved black claws, ready to throw the fruit and drive us away from its nest. It could easily make enough noise to attract the attention of the Draconi guards still searching for us in the square below.

Cheep.

The troll chattered again, a little louder this time, although the noise sounded more questioning than angry. I stared at the creature and realized that three jagged scars slashed down its face. Relief flooded my body. I'd dealt with this particular troll before, so I knew that he was only protecting his family, hidden down in the bottom of the nest. Even better, I knew exactly what I could bribe him with.

Staring at the troll the whole time, I slowly reached into my shorts pocket and drew out a dark chocolate candy bar. It was all melted, mushed, and squished from the heat and all the running around I'd done, but the troll's eyes still brightened at the sight of it. I put my finger to my lips, asking the troll to be quiet, then held the chocolate bar up over my head.

The troll darted down the branch, snatched the candy out of my hand, and disappeared back into the bottom of its nest, out of my line of sight. A few seconds later, a couple of soft, *crinkle-crinkles* sounded as the troll ripped into the candy bar and passed it out to the mama and baby in the nest.

After that . . . silence. The trolls weren't going to make any noise to give us away.

Deah let out a sigh of relief. Yeah, me too—

"Hey! These doors are busted!" A shout drifted up from the square below.

Deah and I peered through the screen of leaves again. Blake raced over to the Razzle Dazzle, with all the guards hurrying to follow him, including the ones that had been close to our hiding spot. They didn't waste any time wrenching the locked doors open and storming inside.

Deah moved, like she was going to start climbing back down the tree, but I stopped her.

"Wait," I whispered. "It won't take Blake long to realize that we're not in there. We don't have time to climb down and get out of the square before he comes back out."

She gave me another worried look, but she nodded and eased back against the trunk again.

Sure enough, less than a minute later, Blake stormed back out of the shop. He looked around the square, his face twisting into an ugly sneer.

"Spread out!" he yelled. "Search every store in this miserable square! Find them! Now!"

The guards did as he asked, moving away from the Razzle Dazzle and running around the square, breaking windows, busting doors open, and searching every single storefront to make sure that we weren't hiding inside.

It didn't take the guards long to realize that we weren't in any of the shops, and they all converged around the fountain, waiting for Blake to tell them where to look next. One of the men stepped into the shade of the blood persimmon tree and tipped his head back, peering up at the branches above his head.

Deah reached over and clutched my hand, and I squeezed hers back. We both had our free hands on our swords.

"What are you doing standing in the shade?" Blake yelled. "Get over here, and keep looking!"

The guard winced and hurried back over to the others, but Deah and I both kept our hands on our weapons.

The guards searched the square for the next ten minutes, storming into all the shops over and over again, but they didn't find anything, and none of them came back over to the tree where Deah and I were hiding.

It quickly became apparent that they weren't going to find us, and Blake's face turned tomato red with anger.

"What is my dad even paying you for?" he yelled. "Idiots! You're all a bunch of idiots!"

Blake huffed and puffed and stomped around for another minute before he and the guards finally left the square to keep searching for us. Deah started to climb down the second they were gone, but I grabbed her arm again.

"They could always double back," I whispered. "Let's give them a few minutes to go somewhere else."

She nodded and we both held our positions, leaning back against the branches that supported us.

Truth be told, it was nice to just sit in the tree, rest, and catch my breath. The leaves provided some much-needed shade from the blazing sun, and a breeze danced through the branches, ruffling my ponytail and cooling the sweat on the back of my neck. The sticky-sweet scent of blood persimmons filled the air, creating a pleasant perfume.

While we were waiting, Deah's phone buzzed, and she pulled it out and checked the message.

"It's Felix again," she said. "He's worried that we're not back yet."

I looked around the square again, but all the Draconi guards were gone and had been for five minutes. It should be safe for us to climb down now. "Tell him that we're on our way back to the alley, and that we'll be there soon."

Deah nodded and sent him the message. Less than a minute later, her phone buzzed again. "He says that no one's spotted them; they're still waiting for us in the alley."

She put her phone away, and we both climbed down the tree. When we got back to the ground, we stopped and glanced around, but the Draconis were gone and I didn't see anyone wearing a red cloak patrolling out on the main street or roaming through the walkways that led into and out of the square.

Deah took the lead, hurrying over to the walkway that led out the far side of the square. I kept glancing back over my shoulder, making sure that no Draconis were sneaking up behind us. We reached the end of the walkway and rounded the corner.

Deah gasped and stopped short, making me slam into her back. I looked over her shoulder, wondering what had made her stop, and my heart sank.

Because Blake was waiting there, flanked by half a dozen guards.

CHAPTER SIXTEEN

Blake stared at me, a sneering grin twisting his face. "You know, you're not as smart as you think you are, Merriweather. I knew you had to be somewhere in that stupid square and that all I had to do was wait you out. And I was right."

I didn't respond, but my hand tightened around the hilt of my stolen sword, ready to swing it at the first Draconi who came near me.

Deah stepped forward, staring at her brother. "You don't have to do this, Blake. You could forget about the Draconis and come with us."

He gave her a look like she'd just said the dumbest thing ever. "And why would I want to do that? Dad is about to own this entire town, and I'm going to be standing right by his side when he does."

She shook her head. "And you don't care what Dad does to anyone else in order to get what he wants? Or what he makes *you* do?"

He gave her that same disbelieving look again. "Why would I care about any of that? We're the best and it's time everyone in this town realizes it, especially all the other Families."

"But Dad attacked all those people at the restaurant last night. And at the Sinclair mansion." Deah looked back and forth from her brother to the guards. "He ordered you and the other guards to slaughter everyone, and you just went along with it like it was okay. Why would you do that? Why would *any* of you do that?"

Some of the guards shifted on their feet, their cheeks suddenly red with shame, and dropped their gazes from her accusing one. But not Blake.

"Why *wouldn't* I do that?" he countered in a harsh voice. "I'm the Draconi bruiser. It's my job."

Deah shook her head again. "It's not your job to hurt and kill innocent people and pixies, but that's exactly what you did last night."

Blake's eyes narrowed, rage burning in their cold brown depths. "The more important question is why would *you* betray your own Family? Especially to side with the Sinclairs? Or are you so into Morales that you just can't think straight? Is that your excuse? Being blinded by love?"

He batted his eyelashes and clutched his hand to his heart as though he were about to swoon. All the guards laughed, but Deah's mouth flattened out into a harsh line.

"I'm not *blinded* by anything," she snapped. "And the only one not thinking straight here is you."

Blake rolled his eyes. "Whatever. The point is that you are no longer a Draconi. I don't even know why Dad wants us to take you alive."

Deah glanced at me, worry flashing in her eyes. We both knew that Victor wanted her alive because she was one of the best fighters in Cloudburst Falls. As long as Victor held Seleste captive, he could force Deah to do whatever he wanted. And that's if she was lucky. Victor could just as easily want to rip out her mimic magic and take it for himself.

Well, I wasn't about to let any of those things happen. Victor wasn't hurting Deah or anyone else I cared about. I shifted my stance, getting ready for the coming fight.

Deah opened her mouth to keep arguing, but Blake cut her off.

"Enough talk," he growled, waving his sword at the guards around him. "Get them!"

The men surged forward, raising their weapons high. If we ran, they would only cut us down from behind, so Deah and I stepped up to meet them, forming a strong, united front. We both whirled first one way, then the other, battling the guards and watching each other's backs.

One man screamed as I sliced my sword across his stomach, while Deah stabbed her sword into the leg of the guard closest to her. Two more guards stepped up to take their places, and we took them out as well, then the two after that. In less than a minute, all six of the Draconi guards were down on the ground, bleeding from the wounds we'd inflicted on them, and Blake was the only one left standing.

He stared at us for a moment, eyeing the blood on our swords and the guards moaning and groaning at our feet.

Then he turned and ran.

Deah and I looked at each other, then leaped over the injured guards and sprinted after him. Blake raced down the street, darted into an alley, and rounded the corner at the far end, disappearing from sight. I frowned, realizing that he was heading toward the parking lot reserved for the Families. Blake might be cruel, but he wasn't dumb. So why would he go there? There was nothing back there but cars, and no way for him to get to safety—

Too late, I realized what Blake was really up to. I grabbed Deah's arm, trying to stop her, but her momentum pulled us both around the corner.

And right into the ambush.

More than a dozen Draconi guards were waiting in the parking lot, all armed with swords. And Blake was standing in the middle of them, a smug grin stretching across his face. He'd known that we would chase after him, and he'd been ready in case the first group of guards failed to capture us. Now there were too many Draconis for us to fight our way through.

"Grab Deah and kill Merriweather," he called out in a casual voice, as though he weren't doing anything more important than ordering fast-food at a burger joint.

"Run!" I yelled at Deah. "Run!"

Together, we whirled around and raced out of the parking lot.

At least, we tried to.

I headed back toward the alley, but a couple of the Draconi guards ran in that direction, moving to cut us off. So I changed course, instead sprinting over to one of the Draconi SUVs parked in the lot, jumping up onto the hood, and then scrambling up onto the roof of the vehicle. A second later, Deah pulled herself up onto the car roof as well.

Blake waved his hand and the guards quickly surrounded the SUV, like sharks circling a lifeboat. My eyes darted left and right and finally up, looking for a way out of here.

There—over there. That would do quite nicely. It would have to, since it was the only chance we had.

"Now where do you think you're going?" Blake sneered. "You're trapped."

I ignored him and looked at Deah. "Follow me, and use your mimic magic to do exactly what I do."

She nodded.

I slid my stolen sword through a belt loop on my shorts so my hands would be free. Deah did the same thing. Then I drew in a breath, rocked back on my heels, and sprang forward, leaping over the guards' heads onto the roof of the next SUV over.

Thump.

My sneakers hit the roof and I stepped to the side, making room for Deah. A second later, she landed beside me, but I was already leaping onto the roof of the next vehicle . . . and the one after that . . . and the next . . . as if I was playing an enormous game of hopscotch.

Thirty seconds later, I was at the opposite end of the parking lot, with Deah right behind me and Blake screaming at the guards to catch us or else. The last car was parked up against one of the buildings that ringed the lot, so I was able to reach out, grab hold of a low roof there, and pull myself up onto it. Deah reached out and did the same thing, rolling to a stop beside me.

"Move! Move! Move!" Blake yelled at his men. "Get up there and follow them, you idiots!"

The guards hurried after us, but I tuned out their shouts, got to my feet, and raced over to the far side of the roof where there was another low overhang. I had a running start, which made it easy to leap, grab the overhang, and pull myself up onto the next roof.

The rest of the world fell away, and I focused on moving from one roof to the next, my legs churning, my arms stretching, my fingers grasping, and my muscles burning as I climbed up and up and up. Even though the Draconi guards were still shouting and chasing us, I couldn't help but smile the whole time.

This—this was what I *loved*.

The wind kissing my face, the *scrape-scrape-scrape-scrape* of my sneakers against the walls, the warm, rough feel of brick and stone under my hands. There was a freedom in it that I'd never felt anywhere else.

Behind me, a faint chill of magic gusted against my back like a cool, steady breeze. I pulled myself up onto another roof, then glanced back over my shoulder. Deah was staring intently at me, her dark blue eyes glittering in her face, as she used her magic to exactly mimic all of my movements, right down to the way my fingers flexed as I reached out for the next roof. I grinned and kept going.

We climbed up onto the highest roof in this section of buildings. Behind us, the guards were scrambling to catch up, so I stopped a second to look around, planning the rest of our escape.

I pointed out the route to Deah. "This way! Follow me!"

She nodded and fell in step behind me, her eyes still glittering with magic as she ran the exact same way I did.

Where I had climbed up before, now I went down, down, down, grabbing hold of the edges of the roofs and sliding down as far as I could before letting go and dropping to the next building. If not for the guards chasing us, I would have been having a great time.

Finally, I took hold of the lowest roof and hung in the air for a second before dropping back down to the street again. Deah jumped down right beside me, but she took her eyes off me, just for a second, and she landed awkwardly, tumbling to the ground, yelping, and clutching her left ankle.

"Are you okay?" I crouched beside her.

Her pretty face creased with pain, but she held out her arm to me. "I think I sprained my ankle. Help me up."

I did as she asked and the two of us started moving down the street where we had ended up, three blocks away from the parking lot. Deah tried to keep up with me, but she hissed every time she put any weight on her ankle and I ended up wedging my shoulder under hers and half dragging, half carrying her along.

Our slow pace gave Blake and the Draconi guards plenty of time to catch up with us.

Their shouts, which had faded to angry murmurs in the distance, grew louder and louder and closer and closer. I craned my neck around, then up. I didn't see any guards on the street behind us yet, but it was just a matter of time now, especially since a couple of them popped into sight on the rooftops, shouting and pointing in our direction.

We had to get out of sight of the men on the rooftops, so I dragged Deah into the first alley I came to—not realizing that it was a dead end. I cursed and whirled around, ready to head back onto the street, but Deah stepped away from me, even though she was wobbling on her feet the whole time.

"Stop—just stop, Lila. It's no use. I'm slowing you down." She lifted her chin. "You need to leave me behind."

My mouth dropped open. "What? You can't be serious! No—no way am I leaving you behind for Blake and the guards to capture."

She looked around a second, then pointed over to a rusty drainpipe that was attached to the alley wall. "You can climb up that, right? Get up onto the roof and then make it to safety?"

"Of course I can climb up that," I snapped. "I can climb up anything. But that's not the point. We can both make it out of here. I'm not leaving you behind. Now come on."

I started to take hold of her again, but Deah shook her head and hobbled away from me.

"My ankle is sprained. I can barely stand on it, much less run or try to climb with it. One of us needs to be the distraction while the other escapes. You know it as well as I do." She stared me in the eyes, letting me see and feel her rock-hard determination. "I'm the one who's injured, so I'm going to be the distraction."

"But—"

She gave me a grim look. "I'm Victor's daughter. You heard what Blake said. My dad won't kill me . . . right away." Her mouth twisted. "Not until he has a chance to blackmail me into doing his bidding again. Or to take my mimic magic for himself."

I opened my mouth, but she cut me off.

"But you, Lila? My dad will throw you into a cage with the rest of the Sinclairs. Or worse, execute you, if Blake doesn't go ahead and do it for him. So you need to go—right now." Deah pulled her sword free from a belt loop on her shorts. "I'll hold off Blake and the guards as long as I can. That should give you enough time to get back to Felix and Devon and tell them about the warehouse."

"But—"

She shook her head. "No buts. This is how it has to be and we both know it. Besides, Blake and my dad don't realize that you know about the warehouse. That means you, Felix, and Devon still have a chance to break in and rescue everyone, including me."

She tried to smile, but her expression twisted into a painful grimace, and she reached out and leaned one hand against the alley wall in order to take some of her weight off her injured ankle.

Deah looked at me again, her blue eyes as bright as Seleste's always were. "No matter what happens, I want you to know something—that you've been more of a friend, more of a family, to me in the last few weeks than Blake and my dad have ever been. I trust you in a way I've never trusted them, and I'm trusting you to rescue me, my mom, and all the other Sinclairs. Do you understand, Lila? I'm *trusting* you to save us all. Promise me you can do that. Promise me you won't let me down the way Blake and my dad always have."

Her gaze locked with mine again and I felt every ounce of her cold sorrow and aching regret. But mixed in with those tense, sad emotions was blazing conviction. She really did think I could save her, Seleste, and everyone else.

My heart twisted, but I stepped forward, grabbed her

hand, and stared back into her eyes, hoping that she could see my own determination.

"I promise," I whispered, squeezing her hand tight. "I'll find a way to rescue you and Seleste and all the others. Count on it."

She nodded. "That's all I needed to hear. Now go. Before it's too late for both of us."

Deah hesitated, then stepped forward and hugged me tight, just for a second, before letting go. She stared at me another moment, then raised her sword, turned around, and limped back down to the end of the alley. She looked up and down the street, searching for the guards. She froze for a second, then whipped around and started hobbling in the opposite direction. Excited shouts rose up in the distance. The guards had already spotted her.

I bit my lip, guilt, grief, fear, and worry churning in my stomach like acid, but Deah had sacrificed herself to save me, and I was going to honor her choice. So I took hold of the drainpipe and started climbing. A few seconds later, I was up on the roof. Even though I knew exactly what I would see, I still turned around slowly, dreading the sight.

Down on the street, Deah was still hobbling along, moving as fast as she could, with the Draconi guards shouting and running after her.

It took them less than a minute to catch up to her. The guards surrounded Deah, forming a tight circle around her and cutting off any potential escape. Blake swaggered up and said something to her that I couldn't hear. Deah glared at her brother, but she threw her stolen sword down at his feet. I winced at the harsh *clang-clang-clang* of metal hitting the sidewalk.

Blake barked out an order, and two of the guards stepped forward and clamped their hands around Deah's arms. She glared at Blake again, but he made a sharp motion with his hand and the guards dragged her away. A few seconds later, they rounded the corner and disappeared from my line of sight.

Gone. Deah was gone. Captured.

And it was all my fault.

CHAPTER SEVENTEEN

Blake and the rest of the Draconi guards spread out, still searching for me down on the ground, but I kept to the rooftops, so it was easy for me to avoid them. Ten minutes later, I slid down a drainpipe into the alley where Devon and Felix were waiting.

Felix looked up, his dark gaze locked onto the drainpipe, expecting to see someone else come sliding down it at any second. But of course she didn't.

"Where's Deah?" he asked.

I swallowed, trying to clear the guilt out of my throat, dreading what I had to tell him. When I spoke, my voice was a hoarse, ragged whisper. "She let herself be captured so that I could escape."

"What!" Felix yelled, his hands balling into tight fists, his bronze skin turning red with fear and fury. "How could you let that happen?"

I shook my head, tears stinging my eyes. "I'm sorry, Felix. So sorry—"

He snarled, turned away from me, and smashed his fist into the alley wall. Felix winced and shook out his hand, but that pain was small compared to the anguish filling his dark eyes. Devon squeezed his best friend's shoulder, then gathered me up into his arms, hugging me tight.

"It's not your fault, Lila," he whispered. "It's not your fault."

I hugged him back, leaning into his warm, strong body, even though I didn't deserve to be comforted right now. "Yes, it is," I whispered back. "Yes, it is."

"Tell us what happened," Felix growled. "Right now."

I pulled away from Devon, blinked back the rest of my tears, and told them about eavesdropping on Blake in the Midway, the guards chasing us, and finally Deah twisting her ankle and sacrificing herself so that I could escape. By the time I finished, Devon and Felix both had grim, worried expressions on their faces.

"I'm sorry, Felix," I whispered again. "So sorry. I tried to help her, I tried to convince her that we could both escape, but she wouldn't listen to me."

He sighed, his shoulders slumped, and some of the anger drained out of his body. "It's okay, Lila. I understand. Believe me, no one can make Deah Draconi do anything that she doesn't want to. I'm sorry I yelled at you."

I nodded, although the guilt continued to eat away at my insides.

"All right," Devon said. "What's done is done. Now that we know where the warehouse is, we can figure out how to get inside and break everyone out, including Deah. But first, we need to get out of sight. Now that Blake knows we're still alive, the Draconis will be combing the Midway and all the shopping squares searching for us. We need to get back to the library and regroup. Agreed?"

Felix and I both gave him tense nods. Devon nodded back at us, then crept to the end of the alley and looked in both directions. The street was clear and he gestured for Felix and me to follow him. Together, we left the alley behind.

* * *

Twenty minutes later, we were back in the library basement. We trudged down the stairs to find Oscar pacing back and forth on one of the metal shelves, his black cowboy boots *clack-clack-clacking* in time to his sharp, hurried movements. Tiny was lumbering along the shelf, as though he were also pacing, albeit at his much slower tortoise speed.

"There you are!" Oscar shouted. "I was so worried about you!"

The pixie zipped through the air, landed on my shoulder, and hugged my neck. I patted his back. He hugged me again, then zipped off my shoulder and hovered in the air in front of us. Oscar looked me over, then Devon and Felix. It only took him a second to realize that someone was missing.

"Where's Deah?" he whispered.

I sighed and flopped down on one of the cots. "She gave herself up and got captured so that I could escape."

Oscar gave me a sympathetic look, flew over, and hugged my neck a third time. "Oh, Lila. I'm so sorry."

I nodded, my throat closing up with emotion again. Oscar nodded back at me, then flew over to where Tiny was still lumbering along the shelf. The tortoise stopped and gave me a mournful look as well, as though he understood every word we'd said.

"Tell me about the warehouse where my mom and the others are," Devon said, pacing back and forth across the basement.

I drew in a breath and told him everything I knew about the warehouse, which frankly, wasn't much. Just that it was close to the lochness bridge, sometimes guarded, and that I'd never been inside.

"Mmm-hmm. Mmm-hmm," Devon said, absorbing the information and still moving from one side of the basement to the other and back again.

Felix sat down on the other cot. "Hey, man, stop pacing already. You're making me dizzy."

Devon finally stopped and looked at me. "If I create a distraction, just like Deah did, do you think you can sneak into the warehouse and free the others?"

"Sure. I can sneak into the warehouse if the guards are looking the other way. It's nothing that I haven't done before." I frowned. "What kind of distraction are you talking about?"

He pointed at the bags of black blades that were lying on the floor. "I'm talking about giving Victor exactly what he wants."

Felix shook his head. "No, no way, Dev. You show up with the weapons and Victor will just kill you and take the black blades for himself."

Devon's mouth flattened out into a harsh line. He straightened up and anger flashed in his green eyes. In that moment, he looked every inch the bruiser, the leader, he was. "I know he'll try, but he won't succeed. I'll meet Victor and offer to give him the weapons, while you and Lila sneak into the warehouse and free everyone. By the time Victor realizes what's happening, it will be too late for him and his guards to capture everyone again."

A cold fist of fear wrapped around my heart, squeezing tight. "And what about you? Because Victor will still have *you*. He'll kill you for double-crossing him. You know he will."

Devon looked at me, his eyes softening. "I know he'll try, but we'll figure out a way to get the best of him. Trust me, okay, Lila?" His face hardened again. "Besides, I'm the Sinclair bruiser. It's my job to look out for everyone else. It's the only thing I've ever wanted to be. So let me do my job now, when it matters most. Help me save our Family. Please."

We all looked at Devon, then at each other. Felix's eyes were dark and troubled, but he slowly nodded. So did Oscar and even Tiny. Finally, I did too.

I got up from the cot, went over, and kissed Devon. Then I drew back and stared up into his eyes. "I'm with you," I whispered. "Now and always."

Devon grinned. "I know you are, just like I'm with you. Now and always."

He moved over, opened one of the duffel bags, and started sorting through the weapons inside. Felix and Oscar both went over to help him, while Tiny peered down at them from his perch on the shelf. I stood back out of the way and watched them all work, my gaze locked onto Devon as he examined each weapon in turn.

I'd told him the truth—I was with him in his plan to save Claudia, Mo, Deah, and all the other Sinclairs. But I'd also made a promise to Claudia last night in the restaurant, the same promise I'd made to her the very first day I'd joined the Family. It might be Devon's job to protect the Sinclairs, but it was my duty to protect *him*, and that was exactly what I was going to do.

No matter what it cost me.

An hour later, we were still in the basement, all of us gathered around and staring down at Felix's phone.

"Are you absolutely sure you want to do this?" Felix asked, a bit of nervous tension creeping into his voice. "What if Blake is his usual jerk self and doesn't go for it? What then?"

"Blake will go for it," Devon said. "I'm sure of it. Besides, he's too afraid of his dad not to do exactly what Victor says, and we all know how much Victor wants these black blades. So make the call."

Felix nodded, scrolled through his contacts, and hit his

phone, putting it on speaker so we could all hear. A second later, it started ringing. We all tensed when someone on the other end picked up.

"Who is this?" Blake growled. "And what do you want?"

"It's Devon Sinclair," Devon replied in a cold voice. "And I want to talk to Victor."

Silence.

Then Blake let out a low, ugly laugh. "Finally calling to give yourself up? How sweet. You can join the rest of your loser Family in the cages my dad has them in."

A muscle ticked in Devon's jaw and it took him a moment to respond. "Tell Victor I have the black blades—the real ones that are filled with magic. Unless you want to be the reason why he doesn't get the weapons he wants?"

Blake hissed out a breath at the implied threat in Devon's words. He knew exactly what his dad was capable of.

"Call me back in ten minutes," he growled again and hung up.

So we waited ten minutes in silence, each minute seeming longer than the last, but the second the time was up, Felix hit Blake's number again. The phone rang three times before someone answered it.

"Mr. Sinclair," Victor's smooth voice oozed out of the phone. "I thought you might call with an offer, but I didn't expect it to be such an intriguing one."

"My offer is simple," Devon said. "The black blades in exchange for the safe return of my mom, Angelo Morales, William Reginald, Mo Kaminsky, and all the other Sinclairs you're holding hostage."

"And how do I know you'll give me the real black blades this time and not just more fakes?"

Devon drew in a breath. "Because I'm the one who stole them out of that secret room in your office. It took me two weeks to get them all, but believe me, I have them. I can send you photos or read off the codes that you put on the weapons, if you like."

Silence.

"That won't be necessary," Victor finally replied. "I assume you want the exchange to take place as soon as possible."

"Yes. And I want your assurances that you will not harm my mother or any of the other Sinclairs."

"Your mother is still in one piece . . . more or less," Victor purred, a note of sly satisfaction creeping into his voice. "Nothing's broken that a little stitch-sting can't fix." He paused. "Well, perhaps quite a lot of stitch-sting."

Devon's jaw clenched and his hands balled into fists, but he didn't respond to the obvious taunt. We all knew that Victor had been torturing Claudia to get her to give up the location of the weapons, but it was still horrifying to hear him talk about it, especially in such a cold, casual way.

"The same thing goes for Mr. Kaminsky," Victor continued in that same sly, satisfied tone. "Although I'll admit that I've been a little more . . . enthusiastic in my questioning of him."

I sucked in a breath, white-hot rage roaring through my body, but I clamped my lips shut and ground my teeth together to keep from screaming curses at him. No doubt that was exactly what Victor wanted. He'd hurt Claudia and Mo, and now he was hurting us by bragging about how he'd tortured them. Well, he was going to pay for it—all of it.

Victor laughed into the shocked silence. "The exchange happens tonight. Nine o'clock sharp. There's a warehouse on Copper Street. Do you know where that is?"

Devon looked at me, as surprised as I was that Victor wanted to meet where he was holding the Sinclairs. But I supposed it made sense. Victor would want to keep his prisoners as close as possible and his forces intact. He wouldn't want to risk going to another location with his guards and letting a single Sinclair escape while he was gone.

"Mr. Sinclair?"

"Yes," Devon said, his voice cold. "I know where that is."

"Good. Then bring the weapons there. I don't know how many guards you might have with you, but if my men see a single one, so much as the smallest pixie, then I will execute your mother right in front of you. Do I make myself clear, Mr. Sinclair?"

"Yes," Devon ground out. "Very clear."

"Excellent. Then we have an agreement. So nice doing business with you." Victor paused. "And Mr. Sinclair?"

"What?" Devon growled.

"Be sure to bring the real weapons this time. I would hate for anything to happen to your mother because you were stupid enough to think you could fool me with more fakes."

Devon opened his mouth, but Victor ended the call before he could respond. Devon let out a tense breath, and Felix turned his phone off.

"Now what?" Oscar muttered, twitching his wings and hovering in midair.

Devon sighed and ran a hand through his hair. "Now we try to get some rest before tonight."

CHAPTER EIGHTEEN

We hashed out our plan, gathered up our supplies, and made sure that everything was ready. Once that was done, there was nothing else for us to do, so we ate some of the bacon-flavored beef jerky and water I had stored in the basement, then turned off the lights and lay down, trying to get some sleep.

For a while, I lay there in the dark with the others, listening to Devon's and Felix's soft, even breaths, mixed in with Oscar's and Tiny's deep, rumbling snores. But I couldn't sleep, so I slid off my cot, crept through the basement, and eased up the steps, careful not to make them *creak* and wake the others. I opened the door at the top of the steps and went into the storage room, then out into the main part of the library.

It was still early, just after six o'clock, and the summer sun was still shining in the sky, streaming in through the windows and illuminating the shelves of books, magazines, and movies. At my passing, a few dust motes swirled through the air like lazy bumblebees before settling back down; everything was quiet, except for the faint hum of the air conditioning system.

I'd been sneaking in here at night for so long that it was strange seeing the library during the daylight hours, almost as if I'd never been in here before. So I wandered through the aisles, looking at all the books and running my fingers along their creased, well-worn spines. The air smelled faintly musty, like the books, but it was a familiar, comforting scent.

I thought about finding something to read or even getting a DVD out of the movie collection and popping it into the TV in the children's section, but I was too restless to sit down and watch something. Besides, the last two days had been like I was starring in my own personal action movie. Right now, I just wanted a little peace and quiet.

So I kept wandering around and finally ended up in the children's section after all, sitting in one of the kid-sized chairs, hunched over a small table, tracing my fingers over a star that had been crudely carved into the wood. Years ago, the very first summer we'd come to Cloudburst Falls, I'd used the sharp point of one of my bloodiron throwing stars to scratch the symbol into the table. I'd been obsessed with stars like the ones engraved in my mom's sword, and I'd drawn, carved, and scribbled them on everything back then.

My mom had been horrified when she realized what I'd done, and she'd made me go over to the librarians and apologize to every single one of them for scratching up their table, even though other kids had already put plenty of graffiti on the furniture. She'd also made me do chores all summer long to save up enough money from my allowance to buy the library a new table, although the librarians had ended up buying new books instead.

I smiled, tracing my fingers over the star and its grooves in the wood, which had been smoothed out by time. We'd been so happy back then. I wished my mom was still here with me. She would know what to do tonight. How to protect Devon. How to save everyone. How to finally defeat Victor.

But I wasn't my mom, and I had to figure all that out for myself. The thought made me miss her more than ever before.

"You look so sad," a voice called out. "What are you thinking about?"

I looked up to find Devon standing at the entrance to the children's section.

"My mom," I said. "She used to bring me here every summer when we stayed in Cloudburst Falls. It was one of my favorite places to visit with her."

Devon nodded, walked over, and sat down in the kid-size seat next to mine. "My mom's told me stories about Serena. Sounds like she was a really great person."

"She was," I whispered.

Devon reached out and put his arm around me. I scooted closer to him and laid my head down on his shoulder. We stayed like that for several minutes, just holding and leaning on each other.

"I know you're worried about tonight and what's going to happen," he finally said. "But I'm not."

I pulled back and looked at him. "Why not?"

He flashed me a grin. "Because I've got Lila Merriweather, thief extraordinaire, watching my back."

Sincerity shined in his green eyes, along with absolute certainty that we could rescue the others and not get captured or killed ourselves. It was a certainty I didn't feel and a confidence—a trust—I didn't deserve.

"Deah said the same thing to me right before she got captured," I said, my stomach churning with guilt again. "And look how well that turned out."

"Deah said that because she knows you'll do everything in your power to save her and all the others," Devon said. "Just like I know it."

He kept smiling at me, that certainty flaring a little brighter and hotter in his eyes, mixed with another, deeper emotion, one that took my breath away with its pure intensity.

Devon cleared his throat. "No matter what happens tonight, I want you to know something—I love you, Lila."

Tears stung my eyes, my throat closed up, and I couldn't speak. All I could do was just stare at him, wondering what I'd ever done to deserve such a great guy in my life. The answer? *Nothing*—nothing at all. But now that I had him, I was going to keep him safe—no matter what.

I cupped his face in my hands, leaned over, and kissed him, pouring all the emotion, all the feeling, all the love I had for him into this one kiss, this one moment. Devon's arms tightened around me and he pulled me over, so that I was sitting on his lap. All the while, we kept kissing, our lips, our mouths, our hearts fusing together time and time again, trying to make the most of right now, since we both knew this quiet would end all too soon—and that we might never be together again.

A minute later, we broke apart, both breathing hard and staring into each other's eyes again. I wanted to say those same three words back to Devon, and I opened my mouth to do just that. But at the last second, I chickened out.

"I . . . care about you too," I whispered. "So much that it scares me sometimes."

And it did. So much so that I didn't want to tell him I loved him too. I didn't want to say the words out loud. Because I'd loved my mom, and Victor had killed her. I didn't want to lose Devon the same way. Yeah, yeah, it was silly to think that just saying the words would put him in even more danger than he was already in, but I couldn't help feeling it would be a horrible jinx all the same. So I bit my lip and looked at him, trying to let him see what was in my heart as best I could.

A bit of disappointment flashed in his eyes, but it was

gone in an instant. Devon wrapped his arms around me, pulling me even closer. "I know exactly how you feel. But we'll get through this—together. You'll see. Everything will be okay after we get the others back."

I nodded and laid my head down on his shoulder again, listening to the steady *thump-thump-thump* of his heart. I didn't believe him about everything turning out okay, but I knew one thing for certain.

I was going to do everything in my power to make sure that Devon and the rest of my friends made it through the night.

Finally, around seven o'clock, we gathered up our gear and left Tiny behind to guard the library basement. Devon wasn't supposed to meet Victor until nine, but we were too tense to stay in the library any longer. Besides, the sooner we got to the warehouse, the more time we'd have to look around and hopefully spot any traps that Victor might have set for us.

I took the lead, since I knew the bad part of town a whole lot better than Devon, Felix, and Oscar did. The Draconi warehouse wasn't all that far from the library, and I stopped at one of the street corners. In the distance, I could see the lochness bridge arching over the Bloodiron River, but we couldn't go that way right now, since it was within view of the front of the warehouse and the Draconis would spot us coming. Devon would cross the bridge later on tonight, though, when he went to meet with Victor.

I led the others through the side streets and around the bridge, finally stopping in an alley across from and at the opposite end of the street from the warehouse. I bent down and peered around the corner at the warehouse, with Devon beside me.

The Draconi warehouse looked like any other in this

part of town—a sturdy building made out of faded red bricks that had seen better days. A door was set into the center of the building, framed on either side by a couple of large rectangular windows. Even though the sun hadn't started to set yet, lights blazed in the warehouse, the golden glow spilling out onto the street and highlighting the more than two dozen guards patrolling outside, doing a slow, steady circuit around the entire building. Through the windows, I could see more guards moving inside the warehouse, their red cloaks billowing around their shoulders.

"Victor certainly has a lot of guards here," Devon said.

"Of course he does," I muttered. "If he captures you, then he'll have all the Sinclair Family leaders *and* the black blades. He'll have everything he needs to exterminate the other Families and finally take control of the entire town."

"We're not going to let that happen, remember?" he said, flashing me a grin.

I made myself smile back at him, even though my heart wasn't in it. But I wasn't going to just let Devon walk straight into the monster's den without doing my part to help, so I studied the warehouse again, looking at the doors, windows, and all the other ways that I might sneak inside and rescue the others.

Given all the guards, going in through the ground floor was out, as it so often was, so I studied the upper level of the two-story warehouse. Windows lined that floor as well, but I didn't see any guards patrolling up there, so I moved on up to the roof. No guards up there either. The roof it was then. Now, how to actually get up there?

A rickety fire escape was attached to the side of the warehouse, but we couldn't get to it, much less actually climb up it, without being spotted by the guards. So I looked at the building next door, which seemed to be deserted, judging from the lack of lights and the busted out windows. A narrow alley ran between it and the Draconi warehouse, creating a five-foot gap between the two buildings.

Five feet. I could make that jump and so could Felix, who was coming with me while Oscar stayed behind to watch Devon's back. Once Felix and I were on the warehouse roof, we could find an access door and stairs leading down into the building itself. After we were inside, well, I didn't know what we would find, but Mo, Claudia, and the others were there and we were going to save them.

We *were* going to save them.

Devon and I eased back around the corner and moved deeper into the alley to where Felix was waiting, pacing back and forth, while Oscar hovered in midair beside him. Devon and Felix both wore black cloaks to help them blend into the shadows as much as possible, while a small one fluttered around Oscar's shoulders as well. I sported my mom's sapphire-blue trench coat like usual. We all had swords belted to our waists, and a black duffel bag was leaning up against the alley wall.

"Anything?" Felix asked. "Any sign of Deah and my dad?"

Devon shook his head. "No, just a lot of guards, but Victor has every single light in that place on. It has to be where he's keeping everyone, just like Blake said."

Oscar twitched his wings. "Now what?"

I drew in a breath. "Now, Felix and I get into position and see if we can sneak into the warehouse while Devon waits to meet Victor."

We all looked at each other, our faces serious, our bodies tense, our hands curled around the hilts of our swords, including Oscar with his needle-size pixie sword. The real danger was about to begin.

"All right then," Devon said. "Let's do it."

Devon and Oscar stayed behind in the alley to keep a watch on the guards and text Felix and me if anything changed. I led Felix out of the far side of the alley, around the block, across the street, and to the far side of the warehouse that was next door to the Draconis' building. I started to reach for the chopstick lock picks in my hair, but a breeze gusted down the street, and the door in front of us cracked open a couple of inches.

"That's weird," Felix muttered. "Why would it be open already?"

"I don't know," I whispered back. "But this is the only way we can get up to the roof, so let's go."

I drew my sword, opened the door, and stepped inside, with Felix behind me. There were no windows on this side of the warehouse, so he held his phone out, using it as a flashlight, but my sight magic let me see everything clearly.

Including the metal hooks hanging down from the ceiling.

They were spaced equidistant apart, and each one of them was located above a drain in the concrete floor. An eerie sense of déjà vu swept over me, one that only increased when the light from Felix's phone fell across a chair with thick, heavy ropes dangling off it.

"What happened in here?" he whispered. "Do you think the Draconis are using this warehouse too?"

"Nope."

"Why not?"

I looked up at the hooks dangling down from the ceiling. Several weeks ago, I had been tied to one of those hooks, strung up like a slab of meat about to be butchered. And I almost had been. I shivered, suddenly cold, despite the hot, humid air.

"Lila?" Felix asked again. "Why not?"

"Because this is the warehouse where Grant brought

me and Devon the night he kidnapped us and tried to take our magic."

He winced. "This has to be a bad sign, right?"

I shrugged. I didn't know what to make of the creepy coincidence any more than he did.

We moved on and eventually found a set of stairs that led up to the roof. The door at the top was locked and I had to pick it open, but that was easy enough. A minute later, we were out on the roof, keeping low and racing over to an old air-conditioning unit that was near the edge. Felix and I both crouched down and looked around the metal box, staring at the Draconi warehouse on the other side of the alley.

The roof was empty. No guards had been posted up here, which was both good and bad. Good because we could get onto the Draconi warehouse roof unseen, but bad because that meant all of the guards were most likely downstairs, guarding the prisoners.

I stood up and sheathed my sword, judging the distance from this roof over to the next one. About five feet, just as I'd thought from down on the ground. Felix peered over the edge of the roof at the thirty-foot drop below, his face pinched tight, his bronze skin suddenly pale.

"Um, Lila, are you sure this is such a good idea?" he asked.

"Don't worry about it," I said, backing up several feet. "All you have to do is take a good running start, get over to the edge, and then jump as hard as you can. Your momentum will do the rest. Easy peasy."

"Easy. Right," Felix said in a faint voice.

His face took on a greenish tinge, but he sheathed his sword and backed up so that he was standing right beside me.

I looked at him. "On three. One . . . two . . . three!"

We both started running toward the edge of the roof. I

reached it a second before Felix did and I dug my sneakers into the ground, pushing off as hard as I could. For a moment, it felt as though I were flying, my legs churning through the air as though I could propel myself even farther and faster with them. A soft, happy laugh bubbled up in my throat, but I swallowed it down.

Three seconds later, my sneakers hit the roof of the Draconi warehouse. A second later, Felix landed beside me, his feet barely on the edge of the roof, windmilling his arms for balance and trying not to fall backward. I reached out, snatched his black cloak, and pulled him toward me. He stumbled forward several steps before finally managing to right himself.

Felix doubled over, his hands on his knees, his face even greener than before, his breath coming in harsh, panicked rasps. "I never . . . want to . . . do that . . . again!"

I clapped him on the shoulder. "You did great. Now, let's go find your dad and the others."

At the mention of Angelo, Felix straightened up, wiped the sweat off his face, and drew the sword belted to his waist. He nodded at me, and we headed over to an access door that led down into the warehouse. Felix stayed by the door while I crept over to the far side of the roof, staring down at the street below. I watched the guards for a minute, then moved back over to the door.

"How does it look?" Felix asked.

"The same as before. The guards are still patrolling all around the warehouse. It doesn't seem like anyone saw or heard us leap over here. So let's get inside and get everyone out."

I reached out and tried the access door, but it was locked. Nothing I couldn't fix. I reached up, grabbed the chopstick lock picks out of my hair, and went to work. It was a simple lock and it took me less than a minute to pick it. Still, I winced at the *snick* of the door swinging open. I didn't know where the guards might be posted inside, but at least some of the Draconis had enhanced senses, so we needed to be as quiet as possible from here on out.

I looked at Felix, who nodded back at me and clutched his sword a little tighter. I drew my own weapon, feeling the star carved into the hilt pressing into my skin, just like the one on the library table had.

Thinking of my mom, I entered the warehouse with Felix right behind me.

CHAPTER NINETEEN

The access door led to a set of metal stairs that spiraled down, down, down into the warehouse. I crept down the stairs, stopping every few feet to look and listen, but I didn't hear anything, so I felt safe enough to keep going. Felix's harsh, raspy breaths tickled the back of my neck, but for once, he didn't start talking to fill in the silence. He knew how dangerous this was.

We reached the bottom of the stairs, which opened up into a long hallway. Felix pulled out his phone and checked the time.

"Twenty minutes until Devon is supposed to meet Victor," he whispered.

He sent a quick text to Devon, telling him that we were inside the warehouse. A few seconds later, his phone lit up with a new message.

"Devon is in position on the far side of the lochness bridge," Felix whispered again. "He says that he'll cross the bridge and be on the street in front of the warehouse right at nine o'clock, just like Victor wanted. Oscar is staying put in the alley down the street to watch Devon's back."

"All right then," I whispered back. "We need to find the others and free them before that happens. Come on."

We crept down the hallway, once again stopping every

few feet to look and listen. The deeper we went into the warehouse, the more faint murmurs I heard, although the voices were too far away for me to make out the exact words. Felix looked at me, nodding and clutching his sword and phone tight. He heard the murmurs too. Together, we moved on.

We reached another door at the end of the hallway. I picked that one open as well and we stepped out into the main part of the warehouse. We were on the second floor now, on a wide concrete balcony with a metal railing that ringed all four sides of the warehouse. I motioned for Felix to get down on his stomach, and together, the two of us slithered over to the edge of the balcony and peered down at the first floor of the warehouse.

Cages lay below us.

Three large cages took up a good chunk of the front of the warehouse. All the cages were lined with thick bars covered with a tightly woven mesh—ironmesh, if I had to guess—and all were filled with people and pixies. Most of the folks trapped inside were dirty and bloody, with cuts and bruises on their faces, arms, and legs, but my heart lifted when I saw that all of them were wearing silver Sinclair cuffs on their wrists. Far more guards and pixies were still alive than I'd dared to hope, given the destruction at the Sinclair mansion.

Draconi guards sporting blood-red cloaks and hats patrolled around the three cages, but not as many as I would have expected. If I had been Victor, I would have had more guards in here, watching my prisoners. But he had most of his men posted outside, waiting for Devon to show up with the black blades. Of course he did. Victor thought that the Sinclairs were beaten and that he'd already won. He was wrong.

"Look!" Felix whispered in an excited voice, pointing at one of the cages. "There's my dad! And Reginald too!"

Sure enough, Angelo and Reginald were in one of the cages. Reginald was talking to a group of pixies that were huddled together on a wooden bench, while Angelo was looking at a cut on the face of one of the Sinclair guards.

"Look!" Felix whispered again, pointing to another cage. "I see Deah and Seleste too!"

Deah was sitting on a wooden bench, curled into a tight ball, her knees against her chest, with one of her shoulders slumped up against the mesh-covered bars. No cuts or bruises marred her body, although she kept grimacing and rubbing her sprained ankle. Meanwhile, Seleste was moving from one side of the cage to the other, aimlessly circling like a goldfish in a bowl, her gauzy white dress fluttering around her.

Some more of the tightness in my chest eased. They were okay and Victor hadn't hurt or tortured them. This part of my family was still alive.

But my heart dropped when I realized that I didn't see Mo or Claudia anywhere in the cages. I looked once, twice, three times, but they weren't down below with the rest of the Sinclairs. So where were they?

"Hey," Felix muttered, echoing my troubled thoughts. "I don't see Claudia or Mo. Do you?"

I shook my head, and we both scanned the rest of the warehouse for them. Rows of wooden crates took up the back half of the building, and I spotted a long glass window set into one of the walls on the opposite side of the building. The window looked like it was part of some large office, and I leaned down a little more, trying to see through the glass. I could tell there were people in there, although not how many. But some of them were guards, given the red cloaks swirling around their bodies.

One of the guards moved away from the window and I spotted the edge of a man's shoe—black and patterned with white hibiscus flowers. The same kind of shoe that Mo had worn to dinner last night.

I waited, my breath in my throat, hoping that the shoe would move, wiggle, or give me some other indication that he was still alive. But it remained still on the floor. I hoped that meant that Mo was just unconscious or tied down. I wouldn't let myself think the worst—*I would not.*

"There," I said, pointing the room out to Felix. "Mo is over there, and I'm willing to bet that Claudia is in there with him."

He nodded, then checked his phone again. "Ten minutes until Devon is supposed to meet Victor."

"Let's go," I whispered. "We need to get into position before then."

He nodded and we eased away from the railing, crawled back over to the wall, and got up on our feet again. I pointed to a set of stairs leading downward, and Felix nodded and fell in step behind me.

We tiptoed down the stairs. Luckily for us, the stairs led down to the back of the warehouse, well away from the cages and guards near the front. I slid into a pool of shadow behind a row of crates, with Felix beside me.

"Now what?" he muttered.

"Now, we wait for Devon and his distraction and hope that none of the guards come back here in the meantime," I whispered.

He nodded, and we both tightened our grips on our weapons. Felix kept checking his phone, counting down the minutes, while I peered around the edge of the crates, staring at the cages in the distance, using my sight magic to focus in on the locks. They were all relatively simple, so it wouldn't take me long to pick them open. Good.

But the cages were spaced apart from each other, and I would lose precious seconds moving from one to another, not to mention trying to get over to the office to rescue Mo, Claudia, and whoever else might be in there with them.

The minutes crawled by and everything remained the same. Felix and me hiding, the guards patrolling, the Sinclairs staying quiet in their cages. Felix held up his fingers, telling me that there were three minutes until Devon was supposed to meet Victor.

And that's when one of the guards broke away from the others and headed toward the back of the warehouse—right where Felix and I were hiding.

We both tensed, but the guard was checking his phone so he didn't spot us. I gestured for Felix to slip farther back behind the crates, out of the guard's line of sight. I did the same, moving so that I could just look around the corner of the end crate and track the man's movements. The guard was walking fast and he'd be right beside us in less than a minute. There was nowhere else to hide or run to and absolutely no way that he wouldn't see us.

The guard drew closer . . . and closer . . . and closer.

Beside me, Felix sucked in a breath, getting ready to move just like I was. The guard would attack the second he saw us, and I'd have to come out swinging, take him out, and hope that I didn't make too much noise doing it. Not likely, but maybe if I was really lucky, I could sprint over to the cages and get at least one of them open before the other Draconis spotted me and realized what I was doing. If I could free some of the Sinclairs, that would improve the odds and give us all a chance to get out of here. If I couldn't free the others, well, I'd fight for as long as I could, even if I was horribly outnumbered by the Draconis.

The guard kept closing in on our position. Ten more seconds and he'd spot us and sound the alarm. I tensed and raised my sword, preparing to leap out and attack him—

"Hey!" one of the guards at the front of the warehouse called out. "The Sinclair kid is here!"

That made the guard in front of us stop, spin around, and sprint back in that direction.

Felix and I both breathed sighs of relief, but it was short-lived. More guards came pouring out from the side of the warehouse where the office was located, all of them lining up in a row along the front wall. Somewhere deeper in the warehouse, a door *banged* open, loud enough to make Felix and me jump, and steady footsteps rang out on the concrete floor.

A moment later, Victor Draconi stepped into view. Blake was with him, along with a couple of guards.

But the worst part was that Victor was holding a dagger in his hand, and it was glowing midnight black.

Felix spotted the dagger at the same time I did, and he hissed out a worried breath. "What is *that*?"

I shook my head. "I have no idea, but it can't be anything good."

Victor gestured for Blake to step forward. Blake was holding two dull, ash-colored swords that looked identical, and Victor waved his dagger over first one sword, then the other. Victor's weapon didn't do anything as it passed over the first sword. But as soon as it got within a couple of inches of the second sword, the midnight glow on the dagger intensified, pulsing darker than ever before, as if it were a magnet that was reacting to another magnet.

Victor nodded at Blake, who tossed the fake sword over to one of the guards and kept the real black blade for himself.

"That dagger must be some sort of tester," I whispered. "Some way for Victor to check and make sure that Devon is giving him the real, magic-filled black blades this time."

Felix gave me a worried look. "Well, let's hope there's enough magic in Devon's weapons to pass the test."

Earlier today in the library basement, we'd filled a duffel bag full of black blades—the ones with the weakest magic. We weren't stupid enough to give Victor any more power than we absolutely had to, so we'd left the stronger weapons hidden in the basement. And Devon hadn't brought all of the weapons with him either. For one thing, he couldn't carry them all by himself. Besides, we all knew that Victor would try to double-cross him, so we'd decided to hold on to as many of the weapons as we could.

But I hadn't expected Victor to have a way to actually test the weapons for magic. Worry twisted my stomach, but there was nothing I could do to help Devon right now.

Felix and I watched while Victor slid the dagger into a holster on his belt, hiding its midnight glow from sight, then strode over to the door at the front of the warehouse. One of the guards rushed to open it for him, and Victor stepped through it and out into the night, with Blake right behind him.

The guards hurried to fall in line and follow them, until there was only one man left behind in the warehouse. But even he stayed near the front, staring out the windows, watching what was happening on the street outside. In their cages, the Sinclairs turned so that most of them were facing in that direction as well, trying to figure out what was going on.

I looked at Felix and he nodded back. We wouldn't get a better chance than this. Together, we eased out from behind the crates and tiptoed toward the front of the warehouse, hugging the wall and keeping to the shadows as much as we could.

I motioned to Felix and we both crept toward the guard, who was still staring out the windows. We had almost reached him when one of the pixies spotted us.

"Felix!" she yelled in a high, squeaky voice.

The pixie clamped her hands over her mouth, realizing her mistake, but it was already too late.

Startled by the pixie's outburst, the guard whipped around, his hand dropping to his weapon. His eyes locked with mine and his surprised shock hit me like a jolt of electricity in my chest. He opened his mouth to shout a warning, but I was quicker.

I surged forward and slammed my fist into the guard's face. I didn't hit him all that hard, but he staggered back and his head snapped against the wall. He dropped to the floor unconscious. A lucky break for us. As soon as I was sure that he wasn't going to get back up anytime soon, I sheathed my sword and sprinted over to the closest cage, with Felix right behind me.

I yanked my chopstick lock picks out of my hair, bent down, and slid the tools into the lock. So much adrenaline was pumping through my body that my fingers trembled and the picks slipped out of the lock. I swallowed down a curse, then made myself draw in a long, deep breath and slowly let it out. My fingers steadied and I went to work on the lock in earnest.

Snick.

It popped open. One down, two to go. I left Felix to unhook the lock from the cage and open the door, even as I raced over to the second cell, where Angelo and Reginald were already standing by the door waiting for me. Ten seconds later, Felix was by my side with the first of the freed guards and pixies zipping through the air behind him.

"What are you doing here, son?" Angelo hissed. "It's too dangerous!"

Felix gave his dad a grim smile. "Believe me, I know. But no way was I leaving you or any of the other Sinclairs in here a second longer than necessary."

"Where are Mo and Claudia?" I asked, still working on the lock.

"In the office," Reginald said, worry making his English accent even more pronounced than usual. "Victor has been . . . talking with them ever since he brought us here last night."

"You mean torturing them," I spat out the words.

Reginald winced and nodded.

I redoubled my efforts on the lock, and a moment later, it too *snicked* open. While Felix opened that door, I raced over to the third and final cage where Deah and Seleste were. A few seconds later, I had it and the cage door open as well. I shoved the lock picks into my coat pocket.

"Darling!" Seleste said, striding through the open door and beaming at me. "I knew you'd rescue us!"

Deah limped up beside her mom and smiled at me. "I knew it too."

I grinned back at her. "Sterlings stick together, right?"

Her smile widened. "Always."

All the Sinclair guards, workers, and pixies came pouring out of the cells and gathered in a tight knot in the center of the warehouse. As soon as the guards were free, their eyes lit up with anger and they turned and glared at the front of the building, as if they were wishing that the Draconi guards would come back inside so they could show them what a real fight looked like.

"Now what?" Angelo asked.

"You, Felix, and Reginald stay here and keep watch. If Devon gets in trouble outside, you guys go out and help him. Meanwhile, let the guards help the injured folks and pixies out the back of the warehouse," I said. "I'll go get Mo and Claudia and come right back."

"But—" Felix started.

"Just do it!" I hissed, already turning and sprinting deeper into the warehouse.

CHAPTER TWENTY

I left the cages behind and headed down a long hallway that led to the office that I'd spotted before. I rounded a corner and found a door set into the wall. There was no time to be sneaky, so I put my shoulder down, twisted the knob, and barreled in, surprising the two guards who were inside.

The Draconi guards whirled around, not expecting someone to come bursting into the office, but I was already moving forward, swinging my sword. I took the first guard completely by surprise, slicing my sword across his stomach, then whipping back around and stabbing him in the chest. He crumpled to the floor.

I turned toward the other guard, but he moved away before I could attack him the same way I had his friend. I swung at him, but the guard ducked my blow, whirled back around, and slammed his fist into my face. He had a strength Talent, and blood filled my mouth from the hard blow, but the pain was worth it because that cold burn of magic exploded in my veins.

The guard came at me again, but I avoided his fist, then put my shoulder down and barreled into him the same way I had the door. With my extra surge of strength, I shoved him all the way across the office and slammed him into the wall. His head snapped back and he dropped to the ground unconscious.

I whipped around, wondering if any other Draconis might be lurking in the warehouse and come to investigate the noise, but none did so I turned toward the two people in the back of the office.

Mo and Claudia.

They were both tied down to chairs, with heavy ropes looped around their wrists and ankles. They wore the same black suits they'd had on at the White Orchid restaurant last night.

And they'd both been tortured.

Someone had badly beaten the two of them, maybe even more than one person, judging from the blood and bruises that covered their bodies. I hurried over and stopped in front of Mo, who had remained absolutely still through my fight with the two guards. For a moment, I thought he might be dead, but he slowly lifted his head and focused on me.

Up close, the damage to his face was even worse than I'd thought. Both of his eyes were blackened, his nose was broken, and his lips were swollen and split from where someone had punched him repeatedly. Every part of him looked like it just *hurt*, and my stomach roiled with a combination of grief, guilt, disgust, and rage. But his dark eyes were still sly and bright, and his gaze was steady on mine as I dropped down beside him.

"What did they do to you?" I whispered, tears filling my eyes.

Mo looked at me through his blackened eyes, and his face creased into a grin. "Nothing too bad, kid. Just some cuts and bruises. Why, I know pixies who can punch harder than Blake Draconi. Don't worry. Pour a little stitch-sting on my face and I'll be as right as rain. Promise."

He laughed, but it quickly turned into a choking cough and blood bubbled up out of his lips, dripped down his face, and spattered onto his black suit jacket, soaking into what was already there. The sight and sound tore at my heart, but I pushed my feelings aside and used my sword to slice through the ropes that bound him. Then I put my shoulder under Mo's and helped him to his feet.

He staggered forward and put a hand on a nearby desk to keep from falling. I watched him a second, but he managed to stay upright so I moved over to Claudia, who hadn't moved or spoken the whole time I'd been in the office.

Claudia's head was slumped down on her chest, so I couldn't see how badly her face had been damaged, but someone had sliced through the sleeves of her black suit jacket, and deep, ugly cuts crisscrossed her arms. It reminded me so much of my mom and how Victor had cut up her body before he'd killed her that white stars exploded in front of my eyes, blotting out everything else.

I blinked and blinked, trying to force the stars away, but it didn't quite work, and the image of Claudia's body wavered with that of my mom's, until I was seeing both of them side by side at the same time, each one of them bloody, broken, and beaten.

My stomach heaved and a screaming sob rose up in my throat, but I choked it down. Claudia couldn't be dead—murdered—like my mom had been. I couldn't be too late to save her. Devon would be devastated, and so would I.

Mo shuffled up beside me, reached out, and carefully laid a hand on her shoulder. "Claud? It's time to wake up now. Come on, Claud. Time to go home."

At his touch, she let out a weak cough and slowly lifted her head. I gasped. Her face was just as much of a mess as Mo's, and I could barely make out her green eyes in her bloody, swollen features.

"Mo?" Claudia said, her voice slurring. "What's going on?"

"Lila's here," he said in a gentle voice. "Everything's going to be okay now. You'll see."

Claudia looked over at me, her face creasing with confusion. "Lila? What are you talking about? That's Serena standing there. Look. She has on her coat and sword and everything."

My heart twisted, realizing exactly how badly she'd been beaten to make her confuse me with my mom, but I knelt down and took hold of Claudia's bruised, bloody hand. "We're going to get you out of here. I promise."

She smiled at me. "Okay, Serena. Whatever you say."

Then her eyes rolled up in the back of her head and she slumped forward in her seat, unconscious again. That was probably for the best right now.

I used my sword to cut through Claudia's ropes. I started to take hold of her, but Mo beat me to it. I don't know how he managed it, given his own serious injuries, but he bent down and scooped Claudia up into his arms.

"Don't worry, kid," he said. "I've got Claud. You lead the way out of here."

I nodded, and we left the office. I went first, with Mo carrying Claudia and shuffling along behind me, and we made it back out to the main part of the warehouse without any problem. Everyone who'd been injured was gone, along with the pixies, but Felix, Angelo, and Reginald were still here, along with several guards. The three of them hurried over to us the second we stepped into view.

Angelo gave Mo a quick once-over before turning his attention to Claudia. "We need to get her out of here," he said. "She needs stitch-sting and a lot of it. So do you, Mo."

I looked at Angelo. "I've got a stockpile in my library basement. Mo can show you where it is. Go. Now."

"What about Devon?" Felix asked. "He's still out on the street with Victor."

"I'll go out the front and get him away from Victor. Take the guards around to the west side of the warehouse and get ready in case we need help. Now go."

Felix nodded and he and the others hurried out the back of the warehouse. I whirled around and sprinted toward the front, peering out one of the windows.

Devon was standing in the middle of the street in front of the warehouse, with a black duffel bag lying at his feet. He had his sword drawn, even though the Draconi guards surrounded him on three sides. Victor and Blake were there too, standing in front of Devon, with more guards flanking them. The warehouse door was cracked open, letting me hear everything they were saying.

"I'm so glad that you decided to be reasonable," Victor said in a cool voice. "My son was getting rather tired of chasing you and your friends all over the Midway."

Devon shrugged, but Blake's cheeks turned a dark, mottled red with embarrassment.

"I got Deah, didn't I?" he muttered. "I told you I could get Merriweather and all the others too. I just needed some more time."

Victor arched an eyebrow at Blake, who clamped his lips shut, knowing better than to contradict his dad. He settled for shooting Devon an angry glare, as though it were Devon's fault that Blake hadn't managed to capture me along with Deah earlier today.

"Regardless, you're here now." Victor's gaze dropped to the duffel bag sitting at Devon's feet. "But apparently not with all the weapons, as we agreed."

"I want to see my mom and all the other Sinclairs first," Devon countered. "Then I'll turn the rest of the weapons over to you."

Victor let out a low, ugly laugh that made my skin crawl. "You stupid boy. As if I would ever agree to turn over your mother or any of the others for one measly bag of weapons and the faint promise of learning where the others are. I've waited too long and worked too hard to finally have your mother at my mercy to give her up for a little bit of magic."

"Not just a little bit of magic," Devon said. "How long did it take you to kill all those monsters and harvest their magic?"

Victor gave him a cold look. "Don't worry. You'll die much quicker than they did." He snapped his fingers. "Bring me the bag and the boy."

The guards started forward, but Devon brandished his sword, keeping them at bay—for now.

"That wasn't the deal," he snapped. "You do anything to me and you can kiss the rest of the weapons goodbye. You'll never find them, and I'll never tell you where they are."

A smile curved Victor's lips, but it was one of the most vicious expressions I'd ever seen. "I'm changing the deal. And you most certainly *will* tell me where every single one of my black blades are. You might last a day or two, like your mother has, but you won't be able to hold out forever. In the end, you'll be begging me to kill you."

Devon's face tightened, but he kept his sword raised and his gaze steady on Victor. The guards looked back and forth between the two of them, not daring to move or speak. The tension in the air between them practically crackled with electricity.

I had to help Devon, but I couldn't just go barging outside right into the middle of all the Draconis. They'd kill me in a second, then turn their swords on Devon. No, I had to be clever about things.

And the best way to do that would be by hiding in plain sight, just like Deah and I had out on the Midway.

The Draconi guard I'd knocked out earlier was still sprawled across the floor near the front of the warehouse.

So I rolled him over onto his side, stripped off his red cloak, and put it on over my blue coat. Then I grabbed his red cavalier hat from where it had fallen to the floor and stuffed my black ponytail underneath it. I also snatched the gold cuff off the guard's wrist and clamped it onto mine, above my own silver Sinclair cuff. Hopefully, no one would look at me closely enough to wonder why I was wearing the crests of two different Families.

Once my hasty disguise was complete, I opened the warehouse door another couple of inches and slipped outside onto the street with everyone else. All the guards were so focused on Devon and making sure that he didn't escape that no one gave me a second look. I eased up behind two guards, then slowly tiptoed to my right, moving around the circle of them until I was standing off to Devon's right. I'd only have one chance to break through the ring of men and get him to safety, and I wasn't going to fail. Not at this.

Devon was *not* going to die like my mom had.

I glanced around, looking at the part of the ring where the guards were the thinnest, then at the surrounding streets. I didn't see Oscar anywhere, but hopefully, the pixie was waiting for the best time to strike, just like I was. In the distance, Felix peered around the corner of the warehouse and flashed me a thumbs-up, telling me that the others had gotten to safety and that he and the guards were waiting back there. Now all I had to do was get Devon away from the Draconis, down the street, and around the corner, and we could escape with everyone else. Once we were all together, we could plan our next move and everything would be okay again.

Or at least as okay as it could get in the middle of an all-out mob war.

"Why do you hate us so much anyway?" Devon asked, stalling for time. "What did the Sinclairs ever do to you?"

Victor's mouth twisted and anger flashed in his golden eyes. "It wasn't all the Sinclairs. Just one of you. A girl named Serena Sterling. A long time ago, she interfered with my plans, tried to stop me from taking over this town. She actually succeeded too—for a time. But she's gone now, as dead as dead can be, and nothing is going to stand in my way. Especially not you, boy."

He snapped his fingers at his guards again. "Take him alive, and bring me the weapons."

That was my cue. Even as the guard closest to me raised his weapon, I stepped up and rammed my sword into the man's side. He screamed and fell to the ground, and I leaped over him and stabbed another guard, then another one, trying to take out as many men as I could before I lost the element of surprise.

And I wasn't the only one.

Out of the corner of my eye, I spotted a flash of silver. A guard yelped and clapped a hand to his neck, as though he'd been stung by a bee. But it wasn't a bee, it was Oscar with his pixie sword—one that was dipped in copper crusher venom. The guard's eyes rolled up into the back of his head and he fell to the ground convulsing. Oscar saluted me with his sword, then zipped through the air to stab another guard.

For a moment, the other Draconis were frozen in place, wondering what was going on and why one of their own was attacking them, but then I stepped up next to Devon and whipped off my cavalier hat, and everyone realized that I wasn't one of them.

"Lila!" Devon shouted. "Lila!"

I grinned at him. "At your service. Now what do you say we get out of here?"

He grinned back. "Why, I thought you'd never ask."

Devon moved so that we were standing back to back, and together we fought the Draconis, with Oscar darting in and stabbing the guards whenever and wherever he could. Everything else disappeared except for the feel of Devon's warm back pressed against my own, my sword in my hand, and the blur of red-cloaked guards in front of me. I whipped my sword back and forth again and again, clearing a path through the ring of men. All we had to do was break free of them, run down the street, get to the corner, and we'd be safe.

Unless Victor decided to unleash his lightning on us first.

I kept looking past the guards in front of me, waiting for him to do that very thing, but Victor stood back out of the way, his gaze locked on the bag of weapons still sitting in the street right in the middle of the fight, more interested in the black blades than anything else. Apparently, he thought his guards could handle us and he didn't feel the need to help them. Yet.

Devon cut down the man in front of him, finally slipping out of the ring of guards. He saw Felix waving to him at the corner and sprinted in that direction. I made a move to follow him.

But Blake had other ideas and he shoved his own men out of the way so that he could step up and fight me.

"I'm going to kill you if it's the last thing I do!" he screamed.

"Bring it on!" I yelled back at him.

Blake screamed, charged forward, and slammed his sword into mine. He hit my weapon again and again, trying to use his strength magic to overwhelm me so that he could ram his sword through my chest. But every time his sword struck mine, all he did was feed me more and more of his own power, until my body was so cold with magic that my breath frosted in the air.

As much as I wanted to stay and fight Blake, the most important thing right now was getting out of here. So I lashed out with my foot, tripping Blake and making him stumble past me. I turned to run, but another guard stepped up to block my path, cutting me off from Devon, who finally realized that I wasn't behind him. He turned around, halfway between me and Felix standing at the curb, with Oscar hovering in the air beside him.

Felix kept yelling and gesturing for Devon to run, but Devon only had eyes for me. He stopped, turned around, and started to head back to help me.

And that's when Victor finally decided to get into the fight.

He casually waved his hand, sending a streak of white lighting zipping down the street in Devon's direction. Devon's eyes widened, but he managed to throw himself to one side, out of the way of the blast. He got right back up on his feet, though, and started toward me again.

Felix sprinted down the street, grabbed him from behind, and started dragging Devon back toward the corner, even though Devon was struggling with every step. In the distance, I heard the low, throaty rumbles of several cars roaring to life. Angelo and Reginald must have found the Draconi vehicles parked on the streets around the warehouse. Mo would know how to hot-wire the cars, since he'd shown me the same trick long ago.

Victor waved his hand again, sending another streak of lightning at Devon, Felix, and Oscar, but it was an afterthought on his part, since his gaze was still locked on the bag of weapons, and they easily ducked the blast. The fight had moved away from the weapons and Victor headed in that direction, eagerness flashing in his golden gaze. He wanted the black blades first; then he would worry about killing us with his lightning.

Even as I raised my sword to engage the guard in front of me, another man stepped up beside the first one, further blocking my path. My heart sank. I'd never get to Devon now, not before the guards surrounded and overwhelmed me, but at least I'd saved him and the others. I'd done exactly what Claudia had hired me to do all those weeks ago—I'd protected Devon, protected the Sinclairs, protected my Family.

My mom would have been so proud of me right now.

That thought brought a smile to my face, despite my desperate situation, and I knew what I had to do.

"Go!" I yelled. "Devon, go!"

"No!" he screamed back. "I'm not leaving you!"

Even as Felix pulled him back, Devon started screaming at the Draconi guards to *stop*, *fall back*, and *drop their weapons*. Over and over again, he yelled out the simple commands, his voice crackling with his compulsion magic. Many of the guards followed his orders, compelled by his magic to do so, even though they didn't realize exactly what was happening. But as strong as Devon was in his magic, it still took a lot of power to force someone to act against their will, and he simply couldn't control them all. For every guard that Devon compelled, it seemed as though there were two more that charged at me, and soon, there were far too many for me to fight my way through.

Devon knew it too. For a moment, our gazes locked and his hot desperation and aching regret knifed me right in the heart. I forced myself to grit my teeth, throw off his emotions, and turn to fight the next guard who charged me.

"Lila!" Devon screamed again. "Lila!"

But I blocked out his anguished cries and kept moving, swinging my sword back and forth, and back and forth, cutting into every single guard that even thought about coming close to me. For a minute, maybe two, I managed to keep them at bay. But there were too many of them, and it simply wasn't going to be enough—I wasn't going to be enough.

Not this time.

But I fought on anyway. And every chance I got, I looked past the tangle of guards, the swirl of red cloaks, and the spatter of blood and focused on Devon, memorizing the sound of his voice, the lines of his face, and the exact evergreen color of his eyes. If this was the end, then I wanted him to be the last thing I ever saw—

Something slammed into the back of my skull, causing white stars to flash in warning in front of my eyes. I tried to blink the stars away, but it was no use. Before I even knew what was happening, my sword fell from my hand, tumbling end over end on the street, and I felt myself dropping down to meet it.

I stuck my hands out, trying to break my fall, but it was no use and the cobblestone street rushed up to meet my face.

Then nothing but darkness.

CHAPTER TWENTY-ONE

For a long time, there was just darkness—just a soft, soothing darkness that I was floating along in.

For some reason, I dreamed or imagined that I was in the middle of the Bloodiron River, with cool water all around me, drifting along on my back like an otter. Every once in a while, something would gently brush against my arm or leg or even my cheek, and I realized that it was a lochness tentacle, almost as if I were some sort of toy boat that the creature was playfully pushing down the river. But I didn't mind. It was almost . . . fun.

I could have stayed in the dream—or whatever it was—longer, but harsh reality eventually intruded, the way it always did.

The first thing I was aware of was the pain in my head and face, where I'd been hit from behind and had fallen onto the cobblestones. It was a dull, steady ache, one that made it hard to open my eyes and actually focus on anything, but I slowly managed it. Everything was hazy and distorted at first, but I kept on blinking and blinking until my surroundings solidified. Then, once they had, I wished I was still unconscious.

For the third time this summer, I woke up as someone's prisoner. Heavy ropes wound around my wrists and ankles, binding me to a chair. I looked around, expecting to be back in that office in the Draconi warehouse where Claudia and Mo had been held, but instead of a desk, filing cabinets, and other office equipment, all I saw were gray cinderblock walls and meat hooks dangling from the ceiling, along with a single bare bulb that cast out weak, flickering light.

I was in the abandoned warehouse next door, the same one I'd woken up in when Grant had kidnapped Devon and me several weeks ago. Did the Draconis own this warehouse too? Either that, or they just didn't want to dirty up their own space when they killed me.

And they *were* going to kill me—I had absolutely no doubt about that.

Still, I must have been really out of it because a giggle rose up in my throat. Here I was in this dark, creepy warehouse again, more or less right back where I'd started at the beginning of the summer. I'd always thought that bad things came in threes, but this was getting ridiculous—

A pair of fingers snapped in front of my face, making me jerk back in surprise. The sudden motion made more pain blossom in my head and face, and I couldn't help but groan.

"So, you're finally awake . . . *Lila Sterling*."

I froze at the sound of my real name, then slowly turned my head.

Victor Draconi stood in front of me, his arms crossed over his chest. Something silver glinted in his right hand and I realized it was my Sinclair cuff. He must have found it when I'd been knocked out. And judging from his cold, cold glare, he knew exactly what it meant and who it had belonged to.

Victor stared at me for a second, then started circling, examining me from all angles. Blake stood off to the side, his arms also crossed over his chest as he smirked. He finally had me exactly where he wanted me. Good for him—very, very bad for me.

I forced myself to ignore the pain and focus. Victor might have removed my Sinclair cuff, along with the gold Draconi one I'd swiped from the guard, but I still wore my mom's blue trench coat, and her star-shaped sapphire ring still glimmered on my finger. I shifted in my chair, feeling the edge of my black leather belt and the three throwing stars hooked to it dig into my stomach.

Once I'd taken stock of everything I still had, I moved on to the one thing I didn't—my sword.

I didn't spot it anywhere. Victor wasn't wearing it, and I could see the dragon crest stamped into the hilt of Blake's sword, which was belted to his waist. There weren't any other chairs or tables in here, and the weapon wasn't lying on the concrete floor anywhere.

What had happened to my mom's sword?

Tears burned my eyes at the thought that her sword was gone, that someone had swiped it off the street when I'd been unconscious, stealing it the way I'd stolen so many other things over the years. Well, that was certainly some cruel, poetic justice. But I forced myself to blink away my tears. Now wasn't the time to mourn what I'd lost. Not if I had any hope of escaping.

So I looked around the warehouse again, this time searching for Draconi guards, but I didn't see any—not a single one. I wondered why none of the guards were here to keep an eye on me. Then again, I supposed that Victor didn't need any guards, given how much magic he had. Even as he circled around me, I could feel the cold chill of power radiating off his body and I knew it was from the lightning magic he possessed. I wondered if he was going to kill me with it. Probably. The thought chilled me even more.

My own transference power stirred weakly in response to his magic, although not enough to give me the strength necessary to break through the thick ropes tying me down. Still, I slowly started flexing my hands and arms, trying to create at least a little slack in the ropes. The long sleeves of my coat hid the furtive motions.

Victor kept circling around me. Every *tap-tap-tap-tap* of his polished black wingtips on the concrete sounded like a nail being driven into a coffin—my coffin.

Finally, he stopped circling and stood in front of me again. "So," he said in a cold voice. "You are Serena Sterling's daughter."

There was no point in denying it, so I lifted my chin. "Yes, I am. Lila Sterling. That's my real name."

Blake's eyes narrowed with confusion. "Sterling? But that's Seleste's last name."

I looked at him. "Seleste and my mom were sisters. That makes Seleste my aunt and Deah my cousin."

His lips twisted into a sneer. "So Deah betrayed her Family for you and Morales? I always thought she was dumb, but I didn't realize she was such a complete idiot." He glanced over at his dad. "Did you know about Seleste and this Serena Sterling person?"

"Of course I knew," Victor said. "The sight magic that runs in the Sterling Family is the only reason I married Seleste. I wanted her visions without the trouble of taking her magic and actually experiencing them myself."

He shuddered a little, as if the thought of doing and saying all the odd things that Seleste did made him ill. My hands curled into tight fists. At that moment, I wanted nothing more than to punch Victor in his smug face for daring to mock Seleste, even if he would electrocute me with his lightning magic on the spot. Part of me was wondering why he hadn't done that already, why he hadn't just gone ahead and killed me when I'd been unconscious. Or maybe he had something worse in mind. I swallowed, my mouth suddenly dry. I didn't know what could be worse than being electrocuted, but I'm sure Victor had thought of it long ago.

His gaze flicked over my face, then my long, blue coat. I stayed absolutely still, not even daring to flex my hands under his intense scrutiny.

"Yes, yes, I see it now," he murmured. "Same features, same black hair, same Sterling blue eyes. I would know those eyes anywhere."

He bent down, his face so close to mine that I had no choice but to look him directly in the eyes. His golden gaze was bright yet cold and empty at the same time, as though I were looking at a picture of a handsome man instead of at an actual real, live person. I could see the monster lurking underneath, though. I wondered what Victor saw when he looked at me. Part of me didn't want to know.

"Tell me, girl," he said. "What kind of magic do *you* have?"

My stomach clenched at the eagerness in his voice, but I shrugged. "Sight magic, like my mom. And a bit of strength. Moderate Talents, at best."

Victor stared at me, but I looked right back at him, keeping my face flat and blank, even as my stomach churned and churned. He was going to kill me, no matter what kind of magic I had, but I couldn't let him guess anything about my soulsight or especially my transference power. Otherwise, he would rip the Talents out of me and make himself that much stronger, which was the last thing I wanted.

He arched an eyebrow as if he didn't believe me. "Ordinary sight and strength magic? That's it? Those are all the Talents you have?"

"That's all I've ever seen her use," Blake said, although Victor wasn't paying any attention to him.

I shrugged again. "What were you expecting?"

He started circling around me again. "Oh, I don't know. Perhaps something like Devon Sinclair's compulsion magic."

My hands curled around the arms of my chair. "I don't know what you're talking about."

Victor let out a soft, sinister laugh. "You know *exactly* what I'm talking about. Very noble, the way he kept screaming at my guards, trying to compel enough of them so that he could save you. I imagine that's the reason Claudia took you in. So you could protect Devon from me. Did you know that I tried to kidnap him years ago to determine exactly what kind of magic he had? But of course, your meddling mother was there, and she killed all my men before they even had a chance to bring Devon to me."

"I know," I snapped. "I was in the park that day too."

"Hmm. Yes, I suppose you were. I always thought it was stupid of Serena to come back to Cloudburst Falls. I was rather surprised to learn that she'd been doing it for years." He paused. "Before that final summer, of course."

I didn't respond, but my hands clenched into fists again. Victor moved so that he was standing in front of me again.

Blake frowned, looking back and forth between his dad and me. "Wait a second. Are you talking about that woman in that ratty apartment a couple of years ago? That was *her* mom?"

I stared at him, my face as cold as Victor's. "Her name was Serena, and you should remember her. You were there when your dad killed her, when he cut her to pieces."

"And where were *you*, Lila?" Victor asked. "Why, I would think such a loving, devoted daughter would have immediately come to her mother's defense, but you weren't there. I'd heard rumors that Serena had a child, and I was always so disappointed that I didn't get the chance to kill you in front of her before I finished her off. Why weren't you there that day?"

Every word out of his mouth was like a knife to my heart, which was exactly what he wanted, but I kept my face blank. I wasn't about to give him the satisfaction of realizing how guilty I felt that I hadn't been with my mom that day, even if I would have died right alongside her. White stars winked on and off in front of my eyes, but I forced them away. I couldn't afford to think about my mom right now or how Victor had hurt her. Still, I had to clear the emotion out of my throat before I could speak again.

"She knew you were coming for her after she spoiled your plan to kidnap Devon, so she sent me out for ice cream. Of course I didn't realize it at the time." My voice came out as a harsh rasp and I had to force out the next words. "I was on my way back to our apartment when I heard her start screaming."

Even now, four years later, I could still taste the strawberry cheesecake ice cream that I'd been eating, still feel the two cones slip from my hands, still hear their soft splatters against the lochness bridge even as I started running, trying to get to my mom in time. . . .

More white stars flashed on and off in front of my eyes, but I ruthlessly blinked them back. Now was not the time to get thrown back into the past. Not if I wanted to survive whatever cruel torture Victor had in mind. I needed to stay sharp, stay focused, and not remember how he had utterly destroyed my world that hot summer day.

"So you found your mother's body, and then did what? Stayed in town and hid all this time?" he asked.

I shrugged a third time, even as I started flexing my

hands and arms again, still trying to get some slack into the ropes that tied me down. "It wasn't like I had the money to go somewhere else."

"No," he murmured. "I suppose you didn't."

Victor stared at me again, the cold curiosity in his eyes crystalizing into something hard and ugly. "But you've meddled in my affairs one too many times, just like Serena did. She should have stayed away. I warned her that if she ever came back to town, I would kill her, but she just didn't listen."

"Why did you hate her so much?" I wanted to scream out the words, but my voice came out as a choked, ragged whisper instead. "Why did you kill her?"

He looked down his nose at me. "We all grew up together. Me, Serena, Claudia, Seleste, even that fool Mo Kaminsky. The Families were much friendlier back then. I always thought my father was too soft, playing so nicely with everyone else. He could have easily taken control of the town and crushed all the other Families, but he preferred to live in peace. He said there had already been too much bloodshed over the years and he wanted it to stop."

"But you didn't want it to stop."

"Of course not," Victor said. "The Draconis founded this town. We're the ones who built it up out of nothing. The Sinclairs just rode along on our coattails, copying every single thing we did. Cloudburst Falls belongs to the Draconis, to *me*, and no one else."

The cold vehemence and ringing conviction in his voice made me shiver, and even Blake shifted on his feet, as though this side of his father made him uncomfortable.

"So I came up with a plan to take control of the Draconis and then all the other Families," Victor said. "I'm sure you can guess what that plan was, since you've interfered in things just like your mother did."

For a moment, I didn't understand what he meant, but

then I thought of that secret room in his office, and the answer came to me.

"Black blades," I whispered. "Your plan was the same back then as it is now. You were going to give black blades filled with magic to everyone who was loyal to you so you could attack and overwhelm all the other Families."

"Precisely—until your mother found out what I was doing."

I stared at him, and Victor started pacing back and forth in front of me.

"Your mother snuck out into the woods one day to meet your father, and she stumbled across one of my monster traps," he said. "Naturally, she let the monster loose, but that's not all she did. She destroyed that trap and all the others I'd set in the area. Serena always had a soft spot for the monsters. I can't imagine why."

But I knew why. "Because they were just monsters, just animals like any others. They didn't deserve to be trapped, tortured, and killed just because you wanted their magic."

Victor waved his hand. "A foolish, childish sentiment. Magic is the only thing the monsters have that's worth taking. Magic is the only thing that's worth *anything*."

I could have argued with him, could have told him how the monsters were beautiful and special in their own unique ways, how they should be respected and protected, instead of tortured and slaughtered, but I decided not to waste my breath. He hadn't listened to my mother back then, and he wouldn't listen to me now. Victor was too blinded by his greed, his thirst for power, to hear anything but the twisted desires of his own dark heart.

Blake shifted on his feet again and then shuffled back a step, eyeing his dad with a wary expression, as if he'd never realized exactly how depraved his father was.

"Serena realized that I was the one who had set the traps and that I was killing the monsters for their magic. She found the black blades I had hidden away, the ones I was going to use to rise up against my father and take control of the Draconi Family." Victor stopped his pacing and looked at me, his handsome face twisting with rage, even all these years later. "She went down to the lochness bridge and threw them all into the Bloodiron River—every last one. She cost me *years* of work, and I had to start all over."

So that's why Victor hated my mom. She'd stolen all his black blades and monster magic to stop him from killing people back then, and I'd done the same thing again now. And I was going to die for it, just like she had. Like mother, like daughter, after all.

"After Serena got rid of my black blades, I decided I wasn't going to risk doing something like that again. At least not immediately," Victor said. "Instead of relying on a stockpile of weapons, I decided I would start taking magic for myself. And not just monster magic, but Talents from other people. Power that would *last*, instead of burning out in a few hours the way monster magic does. And it worked. Far better than I ever dreamed."

He held out his hand, and a ball of white lightning sparked to life in the center of his palm, crackling and spitting and hissing as though it were a living thing. I could feel the raw, electrical energy across the short distance that separated us, and my transference magic stirred again, wanting to reach out and tap into that power. My stomach roiled and bile rose up in my throat. The lightning was the most monstrous thing I'd ever seen because it was the direct result of people's pain, suffering, misery, and death.

"You see," Victor purred, a sly smile curving his lips. "There comes a point when you can amass so much magic, you go beyond mere *Talents*, mere speed or strength or enhanced senses. You can eventually take so much magic from so many people that you can physically manifest it—call the power up in any way, shape, or form you like."

He stepped forward so that he was standing right in front of me, the lightning still crackling in his palm. "I've always been fond of electricity."

I shuddered and leaned my face and body as far away from him as I could. All the while, I kept flexing my hands and arms, harder and faster than before, still trying to get some slack in the ropes that bound me to the chair. I had to get out of here—soon—before Victor electrocuted me to death where I sat.

This . . . this must have been what he'd done to my mom. He must have stormed into our apartment that day and stunned her with his lightning the way he had Claudia at the White Orchid restaurant. Then, when my mom couldn't fight back, he had slowly moved in for the kill, cutting her up just because he wanted to, just because it amused him, just because he wanted to make her suffer.

Victor stepped back and the lighting vanished, although I could still feel the electrical echoes of it in the air all around me, pricking my skin like dozens of tiny pixie swords.

"Your mother coming back to town and keeping Devon Sinclair from me was the final straw, the last insult in a long string of them," he said. "At every turn, all the years we were growing up together, Serena Sterling was always there, always standing in my way and taking the things I wanted."

Another thought popped into my mind. "Like the Tournament of Blades? Mo told me she beat you in the tournament one year."

His eyes glimmered with fresh anger. "Not just that one

year, but every single year from the time we were kids. But she wasn't the only one who stood against me. So did your father."

"Luke Silver," I whispered. "You killed him too."

"Luke was the Draconi Family bruiser, my right-hand man," Victor said. "At least until Serena came along. He got all moony-eyed over her, and nothing I said or did could break her hold over him."

"He loved her and she loved him," I snapped. "There's nothing wrong with that."

He shrugged. "Love is a concept I've never understood. A sappy, foolish emotion at best, but it completely turned Luke against me, and he started seeing things from Serena's point of view. Started wanting to protect the monsters instead of taking their magic."

"Why did you kill him?" I asked.

He shrugged again. "Luke helped Serena get rid of my black blades. Told her exactly where I had hidden them. He betrayed me for love, for *her*, and that's why he had to die. I killed him first, so that she would suffer even more. I was going to kill her too, but she managed to leave town before I got the chance."

By this point, Blake's eyes were bulging, his mouth was hanging wide open, and he was staring at his dad as if he didn't even recognize him anymore. Blake might be a cruel bully, but Victor was completely, utterly ruthless. The only thing that Victor cared about was how much power he had and how he could use it to bend others to his will. I wondered if Blake was finally starting to realize that—and that he was just as expendable to his dad as everyone else.

"You'll never get away with this," I said. "The other Families know what you're up to now. They'll find a way to stop you. Claudia will find a way to stop you."

Victor let out a low, amused chuckle. "Claudia won't be

a problem for much longer. I've challenged her to a duel, and she's already accepted." He paused. "Then again, she had to, since I told her that I would order my guards to start killing anyone associated with any of the Families—guards, workers, and pixies—if she didn't."

I gasped and my heart clenched tight with fear. Victor had easily knocked out Claudia with his lightning magic at the restaurant and I had no doubt that he could kill her with it. With Claudia dead, the other Families would bow down to Victor and there would be no one left to stand against him. I couldn't let that happen, but I didn't know how to stop it either. Especially since my own future was so uncertain at the moment.

"Anyway, I've dallied here with you long enough," he said. "Tell me, Lila, do you know how your father died?"

"Of course I know," I snapped. "My mom told me all about it. How you sent him out to some building owned by the Draconis to deal with a copper crusher, only there was a whole nest of them inside. They attacked and killed him before he even knew what was happening."

Victor actually smiled at me, his face creasing with happiness. "Excellent. I was hoping Serena had told you that story. It will make this so much more satisfying."

My heart dropped and fear spread through my body. "What do you mean?"

He gestured out at the empty warehouse. "Because this is the building where your father died. This warehouse has been in the Draconi Family for years. We've housed various businesses in here, shipping and storage companies and the like. Even a butcher at one point. But none of them ever lasted long. Do you know why?"

I shook my head. I had no idea what he was getting at.

"Because of the copper crushers," Victor said. "This is one of their favorite spots in all of Cloudburst Falls. It's why the town founders named this area Copper Street.

I'm not sure exactly why the crushers like it so much. Maybe because it's close to the river. Anyway, every couple of months, I would have to send guards down here to clean them out. You know how vicious crushers can be, especially when there's a whole nest of them. We lost more guards than it was worth to keep the businesses open, so finally, I just let the crushers have the warehouse. Every once in a while, though, I come back here and leave a meal for them. And tonight, Lila, that meal is going to be you."

Panic shot through my body, and my head snapped from left to right and back again, wondering if the copper crushers were already creeping up on me. For a moment, I didn't see anything, but slowly, glowing, ruby-red eyes began to appear, like lights winking on, one after another, in the darkest, blackest shadows of the warehouse. A second later, a faint *rasp-rasp-rasp* sounded, as though something large and heavy were sliding across the floor.

Victor laughed, the sound soft and sinister, chilling me to the bone. He was going to leave me tied up here in the middle of the warehouse. Once he and Blake were gone, the copper crushers would slither across the floor and make a meal out of me, just like he'd said. The oversize snakes would wrap their coils around me and slowly crush me to death—and that's if they didn't bite and poison me with their venom first.

Either way, I was dead. I'd thought that nothing could be worse than Victor cutting me up and ripping my magic out of me, but this . . . this was *horrifying*.

He smiled at me again, pleased by the fear filling my shocked face. Blake curled his hand around his sword and glanced around, as if he was afraid that the crushers would shoot out of the shadows and eat him too.

Victor held up my mom's Sinclair cuff. "This didn't do your mother any good. Despite all her friends, her precious Family, even her sight magic, she still died in the end, just like you're going to."

He threw the cuff down onto the floor, and it rolled end over end before spinning to a stop a few feet in front of me. Victor stared at me, his golden eyes as bright as any monster's.

"Enjoy your life, Lila Sterling—what little is left of it."

Then he turned and strode out of the warehouse, leaving me to the copper crushers.

CHAPTER TWENTY-TWO

Instead of following his dad out of the warehouse, Blake stayed frozen in place, peering into the shadows, his eyes wide, his hand still on the sword belted to his hip. As cruel as he was, even Blake was shocked by what his dad was going to do to me.

"Blake!" I hissed. "Help me!"

He stared at me, and for the first time, a bit of fear flickered in his eyes. I didn't know if it was because of the copper crushers lurking in the shadows or if Blake had finally realized that if his dad could do this to me, he wouldn't hesitate to do it to Blake if he ever displeased Victor. He stared at me and opened his mouth to say something, maybe even that he was sorry, but he never got the chance.

"Blake!" Victor called out in a loud, commanding voice. "Let's go! Now!"

Blake kept staring at me, and for a moment, I almost thought that he was wavering, that he was actually going to step forward and do something to help me.

"Blake!" I hissed again. "Please!"

"Son!" Victor called out again. "Move it! Right now!"

And just like that, the moment passed. Blake shook his head, then turned and ran out of the warehouse. The door banged shut behind him. A few seconds later, a car cranked to life on the street outside, then drove off.

As soon as the last rumbles had faded away, things began moving and stirring in the shadows in earnest. More and more ruby-red eyes winked open, all staring steadily at me. Dark shapes moved on the floor, and a series of low, ominous *clack-clack-clacks* sounded as the crushers swayed back and forth, making the rattles on the end of their tails chime together in a dark, deadly chorus.

And slowly, the monsters slithered out into the light.

I'd always thought of copper crushers as a cross between copperheads, rattlesnakes, and pythons—only much, much deadlier—and the first snake I saw only confirmed my opinion. Its eyes were that rich, jewel-toned, ruby red I'd noticed before and burned even brighter than the overhead light, as though two hot coals had been set into its eye sockets. Its skin featured a large diamond pattern and gleamed like polished copper, giving the monster its name.

But the creature's size and strength were what made it truly dangerous. The first copper crusher I spotted was at least twenty feet long and three feet thick, which made it easily capable of squeezing me to death. Two others were sliding across the floor toward me as well, their long, black tongues flicking out. They could smell my fear and knew that I was going to be an easy dinner for them, unless I found some way to escape. And still more crushers were waiting in the shadows behind these three.

Once again, I strained and strained against the heavy ropes that tied me down to the chair. I'd managed to get a little slack in them when Victor had been talking to me, but not nearly enough. I was stuck, like a fly trapped in a sticky web, waiting for the spider to come and gobble me up—or snakes, in this case.

Sweat beaded on my forehead, trickling down my face

and neck and spattering onto my long coat. If a pack of tree trolls, rockmunks, or some other monsters had been coming at me, I would have patted down my coat pockets, looking for dark chocolate, white pebbles, or some other small tribute to give them so they would leave me alone.

But copper crushers were one of the few monsters that you couldn't reason or bargain with. It wasn't because they were inherently vicious or evil or anything like that. They just didn't care about anything other than sleeping, eating, and stalking their prey. I hadn't realized it before now, but the creatures reminded me of Victor's snarling dragon crest. Maybe that's why he liked them so much—or at least let them do his dirty work for him.

I forced my gaze away from the slow, slithering snakes and glanced around the warehouse, searching for something, anything, that would help me get out of here. But there was nothing. Just the chair I was sitting in, the snakes creeping toward me, and my Sinclair Family cuff glinting on the floor—

My cuff.

My gaze locked on the silver cuff, zeroing in on the small sapphire glinting in the middle of the metal. I'd run my fingers over that cuff a hundred times since Claudia had given it to me earlier this summer, and each and every time, I'd felt the points of the star-shaped sapphire dig into my skin. I didn't know if the points were sharp enough to saw through the ropes, but it was worth a shot. Without any magic around to steal, I just wasn't strong enough to break through the ropes binding me to the chair. So this was my best—and only—option.

My wrists and ankles were both tied to the chair, so there was no way I could stretch out my feet and slide the cuff closer. Even if I had been able to do that, it would have still been down on the floor and utterly useless to me. So I'd just have to go down to it instead.

I started rocking back and forth in my chair, trying to build up enough momentum to tip myself over. From there, I could scoot over to the cuff and hopefully get my hand on it. But the chair was old, sturdy, and heavy, and it didn't rock as easily as I wanted it to. I planted first one foot, then the other, on the floor, pushing off as hard as I could.

And slowly, the chair started to wobble, even as the copper crushers slithered closer and closer to me.

"C'mon," I muttered. "C'mon, c'mon, c'mon . . ."

Slowly, very, very slowly, the chair started to rock back and forth and I used the momentum to go faster and faster, but I couldn't quite get it to tip over. With a loud, desperate scream, I pushed off with my left foot, harder than ever before, and finally managed to tip the chair over with me in it.

My head smacked against the concrete floor, reigniting the ache in my face and skull and causing white stars to flash in front of my eyes, but I blinked them away. I couldn't afford to waste a second right now, not when the crushers were still creeping up on me.

My face was level with the cuff and the light from the bare bulb overhead made the star-shaped sapphire glimmer like a drop of blue blood against the silver. Now I just had to figure out a way to actually get my hand on it. So I dug my right foot into the concrete floor, pushing as hard as I could. The chair was heavy and it didn't want to move at first, but I kept straining and straining, and it slowly started sliding across the floor, taking me with it one slow inch at a time.

But I wasn't the only thing moving on the floor—so were the copper crushers, slithering closer and closer all the while, their ruby-red eyes narrowed in thought as they considered the best way to go about eating me. My gaze locked with one of the monsters and its gnawing hunger squeezed my chest, just the way the crusher wanted to squeeze the life out of me.

More sweat poured down my face, my heart pounded, and my entire body ached from straining so long and hard, but I finally scooted myself up far enough to get my right hand level with the cuff. I'd created just enough slack in the ropes to reach out and snag the cuff with my fingertips. I dragged it closer, feeling the star-shaped sapphire prick my skin the way it always did. I quickly bent my wrist back as far as it would go, pressed the points of the star against the rope, and began to saw through it.

The sapphire wasn't nearly as sharp as I'd hoped, and it was slow going. But I kept sawing and sawing, even as the copper crushers slid closer and closer to me. The snakes were taking their time, enjoying my panic, fear, and desperation, but it wouldn't be long now before one of them came close enough to wrap itself around my legs and sink its fangs into my body. The monster's venom would paralyze me long enough for the snake to fully coil its body around my chest and crush my ribs. Death would come quickly after that.

More sweat slid down my face, my wrist ached, and my fingers started to twitch, shake, and cramp from being forced into the same awkward position for so long, but I kept on sawing. My world had shrunk to two things—digging the sapphire star into the ropes and watching the ruby-red eyes of the copper crushers grow bigger and bigger as they slowly slithered toward me.

I don't know how long it took before I finally felt the slightest bit of give in the rope. I quickly tested it, wondering if I'd just imagined the sudden slack, but I could move my hand more than before. Not much more, just a fraction of an inch, but it was progress. All I had to do was get one hand free, then I could grab one of the throwing stars still attached to my belt and use it to cut through the rest of the ropes.

I kept sawing and sawing, and more and more of the rope slowly started fraying and loosening. I let go of my cuff, flattened my hand down as much as it would go on the chair arm, and then yanked it back as hard as I could.

I almost cried when my hand slipped under and free of the ropes.

Once my right hand was free, I reached down and snagged one of the throwing stars off my belt. The points of this star were razor-sharp, and it only took me a few seconds to slice through the ropes on my left wrist, then the ones on both my feet. I reached out, grabbed my cuff, and slapped it back onto my wrist.

The copper crushers realized that they were about to lose their midnight snack, and they surged forward, moving faster. I scrambled up and tried to run away from them, but one of my feet got tangled in the ropes and I fell back down onto my knees.

My head snapped up and the ruby-red glow of the nearest crusher's eyes filled my vision. I instinctively raised my arm, trying to protect myself, and the crusher lashed out, sinking its fangs deep into my left hand. I screamed at the sharp sting of the bite, even as something cold spurted into my veins—the copper crusher's venom.

I screamed again and tried to yank my hand free, but the crusher clamped down hard and held on, cracking the bones in my hand, even as another one slithered forward and started coiling around my ankles. And there was a third monster waiting just behind the other two, ready to join in and drag me all the way down to the ground. Once that happened, the crushers would make quick work of me.

I was still holding on to my throwing star with my right,

uninjured hand, so I lashed out with it. The sharp points of the star sliced into the head of the crusher that was biting me, leaving a jagged, bloody wound behind and causing the creature to finally let go of my hand. It flopped down onto the floor, hissing and writhing with pain and anger.

But the second snake was still coiling itself around my ankles, so I sliced out with the star again, cutting it as well. That crusher loosened its grip, and I kicked it away from me.

I was screaming and crying and shrieking now, and I lashed out with the throwing star over and over again, digging it into every single part of the snakes that I could reach. The creatures hissed and shook their rattles at me, but they retreated. Not far, but enough for me to finally get back onto my feet and stagger away from them.

I whirled around and the copper crushers slowly started slithering in my direction again, still determined to make a meal out of me.

I brandished my throwing star at them, though it didn't frighten the creatures. But I'd more than had enough, so I turned and sprinted for the warehouse door.

Blake had left the door open and I staggered out of the warehouse, salty sweat cascading down and mixing with the tears streaming over my face. My heart pounded, my breath came in short, ragged gasps, and my body felt strangely numb and heavy from the copper crusher's venom coursing through my veins. So numb and heavy that I couldn't even feel the stinging bite or the broken bones in my left hand anymore. Still, even beneath the numbness, I could sense the magic in the venom making me stronger, wanting to be used in some way.

"Hello?" I called out. "Is anyone out here?"

But my voice was nothing more than a hoarse croak, and

no one answered me. Victor and Blake were long gone, and so were any guards they had stationed outside. I looked at the warehouse next door, the one that the Sinclairs had been held in, but it too was dark and I didn't see any guards patrolling outside. Of course the Draconis were gone. There weren't any prisoners inside to watch anymore.

I didn't know what time it was, but it must have been after midnight because the moon hung so low it almost seemed as if I could reach up and pluck it out of the sky, like a blood persimmon dangling from a tree. The stars seemed to pulse all around the moon, each one a pinpoint of light stabbing into my brain. For some reason, the pain made me giggle.

I had to get away from the warehouse in case the copper crushers slithered outside after me. So I put my head down and focused on putting one foot in front of the other, even though my legs felt heavier and heavier with every single step.

I don't know how far or what direction I walked, but somehow I found myself on the street outside the apartment building where my mom had been murdered. It, too, was dark and abandoned, like everything else in this part of town. At least, that's where I thought I was. I couldn't really tell since white stars kept exploding over and over again in front of my face. I dimly remembered something my mom had told me about how copper crusher venom could cause hallucinations and convulsions. Combine that with my soulsight magic and transference power, and my body was going haywire right now.

Still, I managed to stumble over to the side of the building where a rusty, rickety drainpipe clung to the brick wall, the same drainpipe I'd used to climb into and out of our apartment that summer, instead of trudging up and down the stairs. I put one hand on the drainpipe, intending to climb up it so I would at least be out of reach of the copper crushers down on the ground. But my strength gave out, my fingers slipped off the metal, and I landed on the dirty asphalt.

Those white stars kept exploding over and over again, faster and faster, and brighter and brighter, until they merged into a solid wall of white in my mind, showing me dreams, memories, and visions. So many that I didn't even know if they were my own or not . . .

I was standing on the lochness bridge, eating ice cream, just as I had four years ago, when the first of my mom's screams tore through the hot summer air. But I wasn't that young girl anymore. I was all grown up now, wearing my mom's coat and ring and carrying her sword.

I dropped the ice cream and ran, ran, ran, trying to get to her in time, just as I had back then. I moved faster than I ever had before, and an instant later, I was at our apartment building. I threw open the front door and charged up the steps, taking them two and three at a time, trying to save my mom from the horrible fate that I knew awaited her at Victor's hands. Before I knew it, I was in the hallway on our floor. I put my shoulder down and barreled through the door into our apartment.

"Mom!" I yelled. "Mom!"

But she wasn't here.

I whirled around and around, but she wasn't here. No blood, no body, no trace of my mom at all.

"Mom!" I yelled again. "Mom! Where are you?"

"Right here, Lila."

Startled, I whirled around again. The motion made my head spin, and suddenly I wasn't in our tiny apartment anymore. Now I was standing on the balcony outside my room at the Sinclair mansion. It was night and everything was calm and quiet, except for the lights of the Midway, which flared, flashed, and flickered in the valley far, far below.

My mom was standing on the balcony with me, her elbows on the stone ledge, staring down at the lights. The wind tangled her black hair and made it float like mist around her shoulders, but I focused on her eyes. They were as blue as I'd ever seen them, each one like a bright blaze of magic in her face.

In an instant, the Midway lights dimmed, the moon and stars disappeared, and storm clouds further blackened the sky. In the distance, white lightning crackled from cloud to cloud, making me think of Victor's horrible magic. I shivered and focused on her.

"Mom?" I whispered. "Are you really here? Or is this just a dream?"

She turned to face me, a smile stretching across her face. "Probably a little bit of both. Mixed in with the copper crusher venom, of course. These things often are, you know."

I shook my head. "Now you're talking in riddles like Seleste always does."

My mom's smile faltered. "Seleste," she whispered. "I miss her so much. And you too, Lila."

She stepped forward and cupped my cheek with her hand. I leaned in to her touch. So warm, so soft, so alive. *Nothing at all like the cold, dead, bloody hands I remembered from that day in our apartment.*

"Why are you here? Why now? Am I . . . dead?"

She laughed, her face creasing with amusement. "Of course not, silly. It would take more than a little copper crusher venom to do you in. It's pure magic, you know. Most people can only handle so much magic, so much power in their body at one time. The venom stops their hearts, and then everything else inside them just shuts down. But you're different, Lila. Your transference magic makes you different. You can handle the venom."

"So I'll live then," I said, trying to crack a joke and make her laugh again. "Good to know."

She did laugh again, the sound warming my heart, then dropped her hand from my face. "You always were one to look on the bright side of things."

Mom turned and stared out at the view again. I scooted up so that I was standing right beside her. It reminded me of so many other times and places we'd done this. Whenever we would hike up to the scenic overlooks on Cloudburst Mountain, or go down to the beach that ringed Bloodiron Lake, or just stand on the lochness bridge, staring down at the rippling surface of the water, watching it rush by. My heart squeezed tight, but I didn't say anything. I didn't know if this was real or not, but either way, I didn't want this moment to end. If I could have stayed here forever, I would have.

But finally, the quiet was too much for me to bear.

"So what happens now?" I asked. "How can I stop Victor?"

My mom looked at me out of the corner of her eye. "How do you *think you can stop him?"*

*I bit my lip. "I don't know. He has so much magic, so much power. That lightning of his . . . it's like nothing else that I've ever seen before. I knew he had a lot of Talents, but to be able to wield raw magic that way . . . it scares me." My voice dropped to a whisper. "*He *scares me."*

I'd never admitted that to anyone before, not even myself, but I looked at my mom, knowing she would understand.

"His magic always scared me too," she said. "But what scares me even more is how close Victor is to getting everything he's always wanted. Even if the other Families band together with the Sinclairs, he won't rest now until he slaughters everyone who opposes him."

"I know," I whispered, my stomach twisting at the thought. "He'll kill Devon, Claudia, Mo, Felix, Oscar, and all the rest of my friends. Deah and Seleste too. And he won't stop there. He'll go after the monsters too. As many of them as he can until he has every single scrap of magic he can possibly get."

"Unless someone stands up to him," my mom said. "Unless someone stops him."

She stared at me, her blue eyes as dark and serious as I'd ever seen them.

"Me?" I asked. "You really think that I can beat Victor? How?"

"By doing what I trained you for all along, Lila." She arched her eyebrows. "By doing what you do best."

I snorted. "I don't think Victor is just going to stand by and let me steal his magic the way I would break into someone's house and snatch a diamond necklace."

My mom kept staring at me, a small smile playing on her lips. She didn't say anything else, but she gave me this wise, knowing look, like I'd just said the perfect thing to solve the riddle of how to defeat Victor.

My eyes narrowed. "Wait a second . . . you really think I can steal *Victor's magic? How do you expect me to do that?"*

She nodded. "The same way he stole everyone else's."

I frowned, not understanding what she meant. My mom stepped forward and folded me into her arms. The scent of lilacs, her favorite perfume, filled my nose, and her arms felt warm and strong around me, as though she really were hugging me, even though I knew that was impossible.

But she drew back all too soon. She smiled at me again, then reached up and brushed my hair back off my face.

"I'm so proud of you, Lila," she whispered. "Always remember that."

Then she dropped her hand from my face and stepped back. I reached for her, but somehow I couldn't move.

"Mom!" I yelled. "Mom! Come back!"

She smiled at me a final time, and then it was as if the stars started falling from the sky like flakes of snow. Each one pulsed with light as it hit the balcony. Together, their combined glow grew brighter and brighter until it formed a solid wall of white in my mind again, a wall that separated me from my mom—

"Lila?" a soft voice called out. "Lila? Wake up, honey."

A hand touched my shoulder and I gasped, my eyes snapping open.

Claudia Sinclair was standing over me.

CHAPTER TWENTY-THREE

Claudia put her hand on my shoulder, coaxing me to lie back down. "Easy," she whispered. "Easy now, Lila. There might still be some copper crusher venom running through your veins. Just relax."

I nodded and did as she said, propping myself up against the pillows. I looked around and realized that we were in a bedroom. It was just as finely furnished as my own room at the Sinclair mansion, with one main difference—bunches of purple wisteria perched in crystal vases throughout the room, along with beautiful white orchids. Several paintings of wisteria flowers hung on the walls and the symbol was also carved into every piece of furniture that I could see.

I frowned, not understanding what was going on. "Where are we?"

"The Ito Family mansion," Claudia said. "Hiroshi has agreed to join forces with us. So have the Salazars."

"And the Volkovs?" I asked, already knowing the answer.

She shook her head. "They're staying out of things. At least until they see who wins—us or Victor."

I nodded again. "What happened? How did you find me? How did I get here?"

"It was Seleste, actually. She kept insisting that she saw

you outside an old apartment building close to the lochness bridge. Told everyone who would listen that that's where you would be. That you were sitting there waiting for us to come find you. So Devon, Deah, and Felix went and looked for you. And they found you, right where she said you would be."

I shook my head. "I don't remember any of that."

"I know. Devon said you were muttering as if you were talking to someone, but that you didn't speak to or recognize any of them." Claudia looked at me. "Was it Serena?"

I blinked. "How did you know that?"

She gestured at my hand. "Not only does copper crusher venom cause hallucinations, but it also has the unique magical property of letting us see the thing we want most to see. In your case, I guessed that would be Serena."

I looked down at my hand, but the two deep, red puncture wounds from the crusher's fangs were gone. So was the pain in my face and head. In fact, all my cuts, bumps, and bruises had been healed, including the broken bones in my hand, and I felt perfectly fine. Felix and Angelo must have used their healing magic on me, along with a whole lot of stitch-sting. But I was well and whole again, except for the old, familiar ache in my heart, one that seeing my mom had only intensified.

"We were standing on the balcony outside my room at the Sinclair mansion, looking down at the Midway," I whispered. "She looked so beautiful, just like I remember. And the way she smiled at me, talked to me, it was like she was *really* there."

"Maybe she was," Claudia murmured.

"What do you mean?"

She shrugged. "Sight magic is a very powerful thing, especially in the Sterling Family. Seleste can see the future, Deah can see people well enough to copy their every movement with her mimic magic, and you can actually see into people's hearts with your soulsight. Who's to say that you can't see something else? Sometimes, the living and the dead aren't that far apart, especially in a place like Cloudburst Falls."

I didn't know if I believed all that or not, but my mom had seemed so real to me in the dream or vision or whatever it had really been. If nothing else, seeing her again, even if it was only a figment of my imagination, had given me a little peace. I was comforted by the idea that she was in a better place, in some other version of Cloudburst Falls where she was alive and well and watching over me.

"So what happened after the fight at the warehouse?" I asked. "Where did you guys go? And how did you end up here at the Ito mansion?"

Claudia sat back in her chair, lacing her fingers together and making her silver Sinclair cuff flash on her wrist.

"I was pretty out of it myself, but the others took me to your library basement. Angelo and Felix used their magic and your supply of stitch-sting to heal me, Mo, and everyone else who had been injured," she said. "The guards and pixies told us what had happened at the mansion, so we knew that we couldn't go back there, but there wasn't room for all of us in the library basement. So I reached out to Hiroshi, hoping that he had escaped the restaurant. He had and he suggested that we join forces. I agreed and, well, here we are."

"And Devon and the others?"

She gestured to an empty chair that had been pulled up close to the other side of my bed. "He was sitting right there, watching over you, until I finally made him go get some sleep," she said. "Everyone's fine, thanks to you."

I nodded, tears pricking my eyes. I'd hoped that Devon had escaped with the others, but it was such a relief to hear that he had. That he was all right. That everyone was okay.

For now.

"And this is fine too."

She leaned down, picked up something from beside her chair, and raised it where I could see it.

My mom's sword glinted in her hand.

My breath caught in my throat, and Claudia reached over and laid the sword down on the bed beside me. I eagerly traced my fingers over the stars engraved in the blade, then the single one carved into the hilt. I'd thought that my mom's sword had been lost in the fight with the Draconi guards, that it was another piece of her that had been ripped away from me forever. But to see it here, now, to hold it in my hand again. . . . My heart lifted and tears scalded my eyes.

"How . . . who . . ." So many emotions were rushing through me that I couldn't even get my questions out.

Claudia realized what I was asking. "Oscar," she said. "He couldn't save you from the Draconis, but he managed to dart in, scoop up your sword, and fly away with it before they could stop him."

Despite their small size, pixies were quite strong and could lift and carry several times their own body weight, but this . . . this was *amazing*. A truly incredible feat on his part. I didn't know how I would ever repay Oscar for saving this piece of my mom for me.

I ran my fingers over the sword a final time, then focused on Claudia again. "So what happens now?" I asked. "Victor told me that he challenged you to a duel. That you either had to face him, or he would order his guards to kill anyone who has anything to do with the other Families."

She grimaced. "So he did. A one-on-one magic battle. Winner take all. You should like this. He wants it to take place on the lochness bridge."

I frowned. "Why would he pick that spot?"

Claudia shook her head. "I don't know."

"You can't face him. He'll kill you with his lightning magic. You know he will."

A wry smile curved her lips. "Concerned about me, are you, Lila?"

"Of course I am. I've grown rather used to living in a mansion, eating all the bacon I want, and sleeping in a nice, warm, soft bed every night. I'd hate to have to give that up just because you went and did something as silly as getting yourself killed."

She laughed, but her face turned serious again all too quickly. "Well, Victor didn't give me much choice, did he? I can't just stand by and do nothing while he slaughters innocent people. I have to face him. I have to stand and fight, and I have to protect my Family and everyone else as best I can for as long as possible."

I drew in a deep breath, staring at all the stars on my mom's sword, knowing what I had to do now. Maybe I'd always known, ever since I'd started working for the Sinclairs. Or maybe I'd realized it even before then, the day my mom had been murdered.

"And what if you didn't face Victor yourself? What if you chose someone else to do it for you?"

Claudia looked at me, her eyes sharpening with understanding. "You . . . you actually want to fight Victor." She shook her head. "No, Lila, I can't let you do that. Protecting the Sinclairs is my job, my responsibility. You saved Devon at the restaurant, and you kept him safe, just as I asked. In fact, you've done every single thing I've asked of you this summer. I'm not going to ask you to do this too. Facing Victor is my duty and my sacrifice to make, not yours."

"And he's the one who tortured and murdered my mom just because she got in his way, just because she dared to stand up to him, just because she tried to protect the monsters and everyone else from him," I said. "He told me all about it—how she stole and destroyed the first stash of black blades he had all those years ago."

Claudia nodded. "Serena never told me all the details, but I thought it must have been something like that. Even back then, when we were kids, Victor was always hungry for power. I just never thought he would go to such horrible lengths to attain it."

"I can beat him," I said. "That's what my mom told me in my dream . . . or whatever that was. I can take away Victor's magic, his Talents."

She frowned. "And how can you do that?"

"I have no idea, but stealing is what I do best. Lila Merriweather, thief extraordinaire, remember?" I grinned and waggled my eyebrows at her. "I'm sure I can figure it out. I always have before."

Claudia laughed, but the sound quickly faded away, and her face turned serious again. "But you never had to battle Victor before. He's stronger and more cunning and ruthless than anyone else you've ever fought."

Everything she said was true, but I shrugged, not letting her see how scared part of me was deep down inside. Scared that I would end up just like my mom—dead at Victor's hand.

"You don't have to do this for me," she repeated. "I am perfectly capable of taking care of myself."

"I know," I said. "But I'm not doing it for you. I'm doing it for *me*—for me and my mom and every monster and every person that Victor has ever hurt."

She stared at me, her green eyes locking with mine. She didn't have my soulsight magic, so she couldn't feel my emotions the way I could her worry and fear, but she could easily see the determination etched in my face.

Claudia stared at me for a long, long time. Then she finally nodded. "So be it then," she said. "I'll let Hiroshi and the others know."

"So be it," I echoed.

Claudia left my room. According to the clock on the nightstand, there were still a couple of hours to go until dawn, so I went back to sleep. After all the stress, worry, and tension of the past few days, it was nice to know what I had to do now—even if Victor would probably end up killing me, just like he had my mom.

I woke up the second time to find Oscar pacing back and forth on the nightstand, his cowboy boots *clack-clack-clacking* out a steady, soothing rhythm. Tiny was on top of another table, nestled in a bowl full of lettuce, happily and steadily chewing his way to freedom as though he was in a prison of delicious greenery.

I got out of bed and went over to where the tortoise was. "Looks like someone's already had his breakfast."

I scratched the top of Tiny's head. He huffed his thanks, then went straight back to his lettuce. I liked a tortoise who had his priorities straight.

Oscar fluttered over, landed on the table, and gave me a critical once-over. "How are you feeling?"

I put my arms up over my head and stretched from side to side. "Tired. Sore."

"No more hallucinations?" he asked.

I shook my head. "Nope, no more crazy dreams or visions or whatever."

My stomach rumbled, reminding me that it had been a very long time since I'd eaten. "So . . . please tell me that they have some bacon in this joint."

Oscar laughed. "Now I know you're all right." He flew up and hugged my neck before zipping over to the door. "This way."

I scratched Tiny's head one more time, then followed him.

Like the Sinclair and Draconi compounds, the Ito mansion was richly furnished, with bits of gold, silver, and copper flashing everywhere, along with precious jewels. Walking through the halls was also a bit like strolling through a beautiful, elegant greenlab; there were trees, plants, and flowers practically everywhere, from bonsai trees perched in large clay pots in the corners to white orchids in crystal vases on the tables to clusters of purple wisteria flowers nestled in alcoves in the walls. The Ito wisteria crest was also stamped, carved, embroidered, painted, and chiseled into many of the pots and vases, along with the rest of the furniture.

Oscar led me down a long hallway that opened up into a dining hall very similar to the one at the Sinclair mansion. Lots of tables, lots of floor-to-ceiling windows, and lots and lots of food set out, with pixies fluttering through the air, hurrying to replace empty trays with fresh, full ones. Among the breakfast staples, I spotted pancakes, eggs, and plenty of bacon, along with pitchers of orange, apple, and other juices.

It was a good thing there was so much food, given how many people were crammed in here. Silver and bronze cuffs flashed on everyone's wrist, some stamped with the Ito wisteria flowers, some with the Salazar hacienda, and of course, many with the Sinclair hand-and-sword crest. It looked as though the survivors from all three Families had gathered here. It made sense. Nobody wanted to be by themselves with Victor and the Draconis out there. I wondered what the Volkovs were doing. Probably holed up in their own compound, waiting to see who won the war between us and Victor, just like Claudia had said.

Oscar flew off to talk to some of the Sinclair pixies, and I headed straight for the buffet tables and heaped a plate high with food, especially bacon. I grabbed a glass of apple juice, then turned around, looking for my friends in the crowd. Finally, I spotted Poppy Ito waving to me from a table in the corner and I headed in that direction.

Devon, Felix, and Mo were sitting together as usual. Angelo and Reginald were here too, talking to each other in low voices, and there was one other addition to the table that surprised me—Claudia.

She was sitting next to Mo, laughing and smiling at him. It was the friendliest that I'd ever seen her be to him, and Mo, well, he preferred teasing Claudia more often than not. I wondered what all had gone down between them while they'd been locked up in Victor's office, if maybe they'd finally let the past be the past and had agreed to a fresh start. I didn't know, but it eased some of the hurt and ache in my own heart.

"Lila!" Poppy said, getting to her feet. "I'm so glad you're okay!"

I put my food down and hugged her. "And I'm glad you're all right too. I was worried about you, after everything that happened at the restaurant."

She gave me a somber look. She shook her head and turned away, but not before I saw the glimmer of tears in her dark eyes, and I realized that Poppy was missing her friends and all the members of her Family who hadn't made it out of the restaurant alive. I looked around the room, grief, fear, and anger punching me in the chest one after another as I locked eyes with various people.

Victor—Victor had done this.

He had hurt every single person in this room in some way, and he wouldn't be happy until we were all under his thumb with his gold cuffs shackled around our wrists. Well, that wasn't going to happen, and he was finally going to pay for all the horrible things he'd done. I just had to figure out how I could actually steal his magic. But there was another question that troubled me almost as much.

Once I had his magic, what would I do with it?

But I didn't have time to dwell on my worries because the rest of my friends got to their feet, came over, and hugged me as well. Angelo, Reginald, Mo, Felix, and Devon, who pressed a kiss to my forehead.

"I was so worried about you," he whispered, holding me tight.

"I know," I whispered back. "But you found me, and you saved me."

He nodded. "With Seleste's and Deah's help."

He tilted his head to the side and I realized that my aunt and cousin were sitting at the far end of the table. At first, I wondered why they were sitting down there all by themselves, but then I realized that not everyone was happy they were here. More than a few folks gave them suspicious, hostile glares, especially Deah. She stared down at her plate, pretending she didn't notice people glaring at her, but I could see how tight and tense her shoulders were.

I looked at Devon and Felix, then jerked my head in Deah's direction. They nodded and grabbed their plates. Together, the three of us, plus Poppy, sat down with Deah and Seleste in a silent show of support. That got some folks to turn away and focus on their food again, especially since I glared at them just as harshly as they had been staring at Deah and Seleste.

"Lila! Darling!" Seleste said, leaning over, putting her arm around my shoulder, and hugging me tight. "So nice to see you up and about this morning. Nasty things, those copper crushers."

I thought of those ruby-red eyes creeping closer and closer to me. I couldn't hold back a shudder. "You have no idea."

Seleste arched her eyebrows.

"Well, I guess you do, since you probably had a vision of it. Thanks for telling my friends where to find me."

She fluttered her hand at me. "Don't be silly, darling. That's what family is for."

I nodded and looked across the table at Deah, who was staring back at me. When she realized that I was really all right, some of the tension in her face eased.

"I'm glad you're okay," Deah said.

She hesitated, then leaned over, reached out, and squeezed my hand. I nodded at her and squeezed back.

Felix opened his mouth to start talking, the way he normally did, but my stomach let out a loud rumble, drowning him out before he could get started.

He looked at me, an amused grin on his face. "Hungry much?"

"You have no idea," I said, reaching for the first strip of bacon on my plate.

While I shoveled food into my mouth, my friends told me about finding me outside the old apartment building last night.

"You should have seen yourself," Felix said. "You were just leaning up against the side of the building and staring off into the distance, mumbling like you were talking to someone who was sitting right next to you. It was actually kind of funny."

Devon, Poppy, and Deah all shot him warning looks.

Felix shrugged. "Well, it was, even if Lila was poisoned with copper crusher venom at the time. I kind of wish I had recorded it on my phone for blackmail purposes."

He winked at me. I rolled my eyes and shoved another piece of bacon into my mouth.

The others kept talking while I ate and then made several trips back over to the buffet table to refill my plate, especially my bacon supply. I had just polished off the last of my pancakes and my final strip of bacon when Claudia rose to her feet and moved to the front of the dining hall, along with Roberto Salazar and Hiroshi Ito. Everyone slowly quieted down and turned to face the heads of their respective Families.

"Everyone knows the horrors of the past few days," Hiroshi said. "You all know that Victor has attacked us, all of us, and that he will keep right on attacking until either he is defeated or we are."

Uneasy murmurs rippled through the dining hall, and once again, several folks turned and gave Deah and Seleste harsh glares. Deah squared her shoulders, lifted her chin, and glared right back at them, not scared of anyone, while Seleste smiled and waved her hand, as though she was reconnecting with old friends. At least that got some folks to look at her with puzzled expressions instead of angry ones.

"Victor has proposed a truce, of sorts, along with a meeting," Hiroshi continued. "During the day, all the Families will stand down and go about their normal routines. All the guards and workers are to return to their regular stations on the Midway, and all businesses are to be open as usual, so as not to alarm or alert the tourists to the problems we're having."

I snorted. Victor might want all the other Families defeated and under his thumb, but he loved money almost as much as he did magic. Of course he would want all the businesses to be open during the day in order to get as much cash from the tourist rubes as he could.

"Victor might have called a truce, but I want everyone to be extra careful," Roberto Salazar chimed in. "No one goes anywhere alone and I want at least one guard with every worker. Understood?"

Everyone nodded and murmured their agreement.

"As to the meeting," Hiroshi said. "I'll let Claudia address that."

Claudia nodded at him, then stepped forward, her hands clasped in front of her, staring out over the sea of faces. "Victor has demanded that I fight him in a duel, or he will order his men to attack everyone associated with the other Families—guards, workers, even pixies." Her mouth hardened and anger flared in her eyes. "I have chosen to accept his challenge. The duel will take place tonight, and the winner will take control of both of our Families."

Shocked gasps rang out through the crowd, and worry and tension tightened more than one person's face, including my own. In an instant, people started shouting, each one trying to be heard over the other.

"No way!"

"You can't do that!"

"He'll kill you!"

More and more shocked gasps and murmurs sounded, but Claudia held up a hand, asking for quiet.

"I've agreed to the duel because it is the best way to avoid more bloodshed," she said. "We all know that Victor is the main threat. Most of the Draconis are decent folks, like everyone in this room. It's not their fault that they work for a man who wants to destroy us all."

More looks were directed at Deah and Seleste, but this time there was some sympathy mixed in with the glares.

"Victor challenged me to a duel, but I have decided to choose a champion for myself, for the entire Sinclair Family." Claudia paused. "And that champion is Lila Merriweather."

My friends whipped around, staring at me, their eyes wide and their mouths gaping open in shock. But they weren't the only ones looking at me now. Every single person and pixie in the dining hall regarded me with a mixture of shock, surprise, and wary hope. It was the hope that made my throat tighten, my spine straighten, and my chin lift—hope that I could finally end the threat that Victor posed to all of us.

Devon was the only one who wasn't surprised by Claudia's announcement. He stared at me and slowly nodded his head, blazing conviction and rock-hard certainty flashing in his eyes. He knew how important this was, not just to the Sinclairs and the other Families, but to me personally. He knew that this was my chance to finally make Victor pay for murdering my mom.

And he believed that I could win.

That meant so much to me, more than he would ever know. I reached my hand out across the table and Devon threaded his fingers through mine. I smiled at him and he winked back at me.

"The duel is to be held at midnight tonight at the lochness bridge, well away from the Midway and all the shopping squares," Claudia said. "Victor will be there, and I'm betting that so will all of the other Draconis. If the duel doesn't go his way, I have no doubt that Victor will order his men to attack us, to try to wipe us out so he can take control of the town anyway. I'm asking for volunteers to come to the lochness bridge to make sure that doesn't happen."

She had barely finished speaking before guards from all three Families started shooting to their feet, raising their hands, and declaring that they wanted to be there tonight. Mo got up and started going around the room, taking down the name of everyone who wanted to come to the duel, as well as pairing up folks to go work down on the Midway today.

But the most surprising thing was that people started coming over to *me*.

One by one, they approached me, saying how proud they were of me and wishing me good luck. And it wasn't just the Sinclairs. Members of the Ito and Salazar Families came over and offered their thanks as well. Once again, the faint hope shining in all their eyes took root in my own heart. My throat closed up with emotion and all I could do was just nod at everyone, shake their hands, and accept their soft touches and pats on the shoulder.

I might have started working for the Sinclairs in order to get revenge on Victor, but now, I was truly a part of the Family. And I was going to protect my Family the best way I could.

Or die trying.

CHAPTER TWENTY-FOUR

One by one, all the guards, workers, and pixies left the dining hall to head down to town and their assigned stations, but my friends and I stayed behind in the Ito mansion.

Poppy led us to one of the game rooms, complete with a pool table and a large-screen TV, but none of us felt like relaxing or goofing off. Not when we knew what was coming tonight. But Poppy popped in an action movie and we all sat down on the couches and pretended to watch it. Eventually, the others started talking, but I got up and went out onto one of the balconies.

The Ito mansion was a little lower down on Cloudburst Mountain than the Sinclair compound, but the view was just as spectacular. It was a little after noon and the summer sun was shining in the clear blue sky, but the neon lights of the Midway still glowed, pulsed, and flashed down in the valley below, as though they were competing with the sun to see which could shine the biggest and brightest.

I put my elbows down on the warm stone ledge, thinking about everything that had happened over the past few days. A few minutes later, the door behind me whispered open and Devon stepped outside to join me. He leaned his elbows down on the ledge as well, and the two of us stood there together, our shoulders touching. We didn't speak for a few minutes.

"I know why you feel like you have to do this," he finally said, looking at me. "Why you have to face Victor. I understand. But I want you to know that you won't be doing it alone. I'll be right there with you, every single step of the way."

He reached over and squeezed my hand, and I laced my fingers through his.

"I know," I said. "And I love you for that."

I hadn't said the words to him before when we'd been together in the library, and I'd almost died last night. I could still die tonight. So I wasn't going to let another second pass without telling him how I felt, potential jinxes be damned.

He blinked, as if shocked by my words, but then his whole face lit up, shining brighter than the sun and all the Midway lights combined. "You love me?"

For a moment, I felt unsure, since the words had just slipped out, but it was too late to take them back now, and I didn't want to anyway. I nodded, staring into his eyes. "Of course I do. You're kind, thoughtful, considerate, supportive, and you always think about others before yourself. Not to mention the fact that you're handsome and charming *and* you live in a mansion." I grinned. "You're a hard guy *not* to love, Devon Sinclair."

My voice was light and teasing, but the look in Devon's eyes was anything but. That hot, hot spark in his green, green eyes erupted into the most beautiful thing I'd ever seen. A wave of love washed over my heart and spread throughout my entire body, bringing a dizzying rush along with it. Without a word, Devon stepped forward, cupped my face in his hands, and pressed his lips to mine.

It was a soft kiss, just a brief touch of his lips against mine, but I felt more in this one kiss than I had in any of our others because I loved him, and I knew that he loved me too.

All too soon, we broke apart, but Devon opened his arms and I stepped forward and laid my head on his shoulder. And we stayed like that, wrapped in each other's arms, for a long, long time.

The rest of the day passed by in a blur, as Claudia, Mo, and the others planned who would be on the lochness bridge with me, where the rest of the guards would be positioned, and what everyone should do depending on who won the duel. All too soon, their plans became reality, and it was time for me to face Victor.

According to reports, the truce was holding down on the Midway and none of the Ito, Salazar, or Sinclair guards or workers had been attacked by the Draconis. The Volkovs were keeping to themselves and staying out of things completely, just the way Claudia had predicted.

Around nine o'clock that night, I was back in the guest bedroom, putting on my gear for the evening. For once, I wasn't wearing my mom's trench coat. Instead, tonight I'd opted to wear a black cloak in honor of the Sinclairs. In fact, I was wearing the same outfit that I had during the Tournament of Blades—black boots, black pants, and a white sleeveless silk shirt, topped by the black cloak. I hadn't bothered with a black cavalier hat, though. I hated wearing those hats. The stupid feathers always fell down into my face.

"You look good," Oscar said, fluttering around me the way he had been ever since I'd come back to the bedroom. "Just like a Sinclair."

I nodded and finished pulling my black hair back into its regular ponytail. I thought about sticking my chopstick lock picks through my hair like usual, but I didn't want to lose them during the fight, so I left them in one of the pockets of my mom's coat, along with her ironmesh gloves.

I looped my black leather belt with its three bloodiron throwing stars around my waist and tucked several quarters into a hidden slot on the belt, just in case I needed to pay the lochness's toll. I didn't know how the monster would feel about a duel taking place on its bridge, but I wanted to be prepared.

For the final touches, I slipped my mom's star-shaped sapphire ring onto my finger, then slid her black blade into the scabbard hanging off my belt.

I stared at myself in the mirror over the dresser. Oscar was right. I did look like a Sinclair, especially with my silver cuff flashing on my right wrist. But I also thought that I looked like a Sterling—like my mom. And that made me happier than anything else, because I knew that she would be proud of me, no matter what happened with Victor tonight.

Even if I still didn't have any idea how to defeat him.

Still fluttering around my shoulder, Oscar looked at me in the mirror. I turned and held out my hand. He flew forward and landed on my palm, his cowboy boots tickling my skin.

"No matter what happens tonight, I want you to know how much I care about you," I said. "And what an amazing friend you've been to me this summer."

A soft, almost reproachful snort sounded, and I looked over at Tiny, who was on the same table as before.

"And you too, Tiny," I added.

The tortoise nodded and went back to eating the fresh pile of lettuce that Oscar had brought for him earlier.

Oscar looked at me, tears shining in his violet eyes. "Don't you dare do that," he snarled in his twangy voice. "Don't you dare say goodbye to me. It's the same thing your mother did the day she left the Family. I never saw her again after that."

"Don't worry. I'm not saying goodbye, and you *will* see me again."

I kept my voice strong and my eyes steady on his, as though I really did believe every word. But I didn't. Not deep down inside where it really mattered. I thought of Victor's lightning and I had to hold back a shudder. I still didn't know how to stop him from electrocuting me with his magic, much less how to actually steal his power. But Oscar didn't need to know that.

No one needed to know that.

"I'm going to find a way to stop Victor," I said, still keeping my voice strong. "Do you trust me, Oscar?"

Tears streaked down the pixie's cheeks, but he swiped them away and nodded his head. "I trust you."

"Good," I replied. "Then there's nothing to worry about. Mo's sent me out on way tougher jobs than this. I survived Grant and Katia and everything else that's happened this summer. I'll get through this too."

Oscar nodded and gave me a tentative smile. He zipped up, landed on my shoulder, and hugged my neck tight. I hugged him back, careful not to crush his wings.

And just like with Devon, we stayed like that for a long time while Tiny looked on in approval, slowly chewing his lettuce.

I scratched Tiny's head a final time, then left the guest bedroom with Oscar riding on my shoulder. My friends were all waiting in the dining hall, along with the Sinclair guards and members of the Ito and Salazar Families, and we all went outside.

I got into the back of an SUV with Devon and Felix. Angelo was driving, with Mo sitting in the front seat and

Oscar perched in the cup holder. Devon reached over and grabbed one of my hands, while Felix took the other. I looked at them both and smiled, and we stayed like that for the rest of the ride down the mountain.

It was only ten o'clock, but Claudia wanted everyone to get into position early, just in case Victor had any tricks or traps planned. Angelo parked the SUV a couple of streets over from the lochness bridge, and the other vehicles stopped as well. People poured out of the cars, every single one of them carrying at least one sword or dagger, and they all crept through the streets as quietly as possible. I hung back with Devon and Claudia, who was getting updates on her phone from the other guards.

Mo was here too, staring off into the night.

"What are you thinking about?" I asked.

He shook his head. "I'm thinking about the night that Serena left town. It was just like this one."

We both looked up. When we'd left the Ito mansion, the moon and stars had been out in full force, but now, heavy clouds cloaked the sky and lightning flashed in the distance. It reminded me of Victor's power, something that made me shiver.

Mo looked at me and smiled, although I could see the sadness in his eyes. "Serena would be so proud of you," he said in a soft voice. "And I am too. You are everything that she ever wanted you to be. Smart, strong, brave, resourceful. I wish that she was here to see you for herself."

I thought of the strange dream I'd had when I'd been poisoned by the copper crusher venom. "Maybe she is here . . . somewhere. Watching over us."

He nodded. "That's what I like to think too, kid."

Mo slung his arm around my shoulders, pulling me in for a quick hug. I put both arms around him and hugged him back even tighter.

Someone cleared her throat and we broke apart to find

Deah and Seleste standing behind us. Deah was dressed just like I was—as a Sinclair. Black boots, black pants, white shirt, black cloak. No cuff glimmered on her wrist, but it was obvious which side she was on. I was happy that it was ours.

Seleste wore another one of her gauzy white dresses, but her long hair was done up in braids with black and blue ribbons running through her golden locks.

Seleste grabbed my hands and looked into my eyes, although her own gaze was distant and far away. "Remember what I said, darling," she whispered. "Don't be afraid of the lightning."

"Kind of hard not to be when Victor's going to fry me to a crisp with it," I muttered.

But instead of being concerned, Seleste gave me another serene smile, patted my cheek, and twirled away, making her braids and ribbons flutter like butterflies dancing around her shoulders.

I shook my head. At least someone was confident about my winning. I wondered if Seleste had seen me defeating Victor in one of her visions. I even thought about asking her how I could possibly do it, but I decided not to. She'd only speak in vague riddles that would likely confuse me more than I already was.

Deah's dark blue eyes, so similar to mine, flicked over me, her gaze lingering on the black blade belted to my waist. She was wearing her own Sterling Family sword with its cluster of three stars carved into the hilt.

"Good luck," she said.

"Thanks." I paused. "I know this has to be hard for you. Everyone rooting for me to . . . beat your dad."

The right word was *kill*, but I didn't say that. It would have been cruel, and people had already been mean enough to Deah and Seleste over the past few days.

She shrugged. "I've always known that he wasn't a nice

man. But these last few days . . . I know what kind of person he really is now."

Her voice was calm and steady, but anguish glimmered in her eyes. Her dad had broken her heart, and it was a deep, ugly wound that she would carry with her the rest of her life.

Deah chewed on her lip. "Do you think that . . . do you think that you'll actually kill him?"

"I don't know. I don't imagine he'll give me much of a choice, especially since he'll be doing his best to kill me."

She let out a short, humorless laugh. "No, he won't give you a choice. Just like he didn't give those monsters or all the people he killed a choice." Her face hardened, and she looked at me again. "So you do whatever you have to in order to protect yourself. Use every single low-down, dirty trick you know. Because that's exactly what he'll do. He won't fight fair. He *never* fights fair."

Deah blinked back the tears shimmering in her eyes and gave me a sharp nod. Her warning delivered, she hurried over to where Seleste was now twirling around Mo and Claudia.

I went over to Devon and Felix. They both gave me somber looks, but they kept on talking, as though we were all just out for a late-night stroll instead of one final battle to determine who took control of Cloudburst Falls—for good.

Felix glanced down at his phone. "The Ito and Salazar guards are in position, hidden in the buildings and alleys on all the surrounding side streets on the opposite side of the bridge. So Victor won't be able to use his own guards to flank and overwhelm us. We've got your back, Lila. All you need to focus on is Victor. Don't worry about anything else."

I flashed them both a smile, forcing myself to hold the expression on my face. "Me? Worry? Please. Besides, if I don't beat Victor, maybe you can talk him to death instead."

Felix rolled his eyes, but he smiled back at me. He opened his mouth to say something else, but Claudia strode over to us, her face serious, her phone in her hand.

"The Draconis have pulled up on the opposite side of the bridge," she said.

I nodded, knowing that it was finally time for my battle with Victor, the same one my mother had fought before me. But now, here, tonight, I was determined that the outcome would be different. That I would finally be able to end Victor's reign of terror.

For my mom, for me, and for my Family.

"Are you ready?" Devon asked.

I drew in a breath and wrapped my hand around my mom's sword, sliding it free of the scabbard and staring at all the stars running down the black blade. Her symbol, the Sterling Family symbol, and now, my symbol too.

"I'm ready," I said, tightening my grip on my sword. "Let's settle this—once and for all."

CHAPTER TWENTY-FIVE

Claudia signaled everyone to be on high alert. Then she started walking toward the lochness bridge. Mo was right beside her, with Angelo and Reginald on her other side. I walked directly behind Claudia, with Devon, Felix, and Deah flanking me and Oscar flitting around our shoulders.

Even though it was midnight, the July air was warm and humid, and the clouds had darkened in the time we'd been out here, now hanging so low that I felt like I could almost reach up and touch them. Despite the thick clouds, there was plenty of light to see by, thanks to the old-fashioned iron streetlamps at either end of the lochness bridge and the lightning crackling in the sky, getting closer and closer with every passing second. It wouldn't be long before the storm was here.

I just wondered if I'd be dead before then or not.

But I kept my face blank and didn't let any of my worry and uncertainty show. More and more Sinclair guards fell in step behind us, and together, as one group, we walked toward the lochness bridge, where the Draconis were already waiting.

Several dozen Draconi guards lined the opposite side of the bridge, all of them wearing their blood-red cloaks and hats, with their hands on the swords belted to their waists.

Victor and Blake were standing in the middle of the guards. Blake was dressed like all the others in a red cloak and hat, but Victor wore a long-sleeved red silk shirt, black pants, and glossy black wingtips. The really interesting thing was the fact that he didn't have a weapon strapped to his waist like everyone else. No sword, no dagger, no blade of any sort. Odd. I would have thought that Victor would have been carrying some sort of weapon to make it easier for him to kill me.

Then again, he had his lightning magic. He didn't need anything else.

Claudia stepped out onto the bridge and stopped, looking over her shoulder at me. "Are you sure about this? You can still change your mind. I can still go out there and face Victor instead."

I drew in a breath and slowly let it out. "No, I want to do this. I *need* to do this."

She nodded. "All right then."

I took off my cloak and handed it to Felix. Devon reached out, threaded his fingers through mine, and squeezed my hand. I turned to face him, focusing on the blazing conviction and rock-hard certainty shining in his eyes, and letting his emotions flood my chest, letting them comfort me and add to my own determination to defeat Victor.

We didn't speak, but we didn't need to. Not after everything that had happened the past few days.

I stared back at Devon, letting him see just how much I cared about him, just how much I loved him. I pressed a quick kiss to his lips, then slipped my hand out of his and joined Claudia on the bridge.

Together, the two of us walked out to the middle of the span. I glanced over the side, but the surface of the river remained smooth and calm below. I wondered if the lochness would help me again, since the monster had already saved me twice before. But three times might be asking too much of it, especially against Victor.

Victor strode out to the middle of the bridge as well, with Blake by his side. Both of them blinked at the sight of me standing next to Claudia.

"So you survived the copper crushers," Victor said, his eyes narrowing in thought. "How did you manage that?"

I shrugged. I wasn't about to explain myself to him.

"What is this?" he asked, turning to Claudia. "Why is she here?"

Claudia raised her chin and stared back at him, her features as cold and hard as his were. "Lila has volunteered to represent me, to represent the entire Sinclair Family."

"Are you actually sending this girl out to do your fighting?" He let out a low, ugly laugh. "You really think *she* can beat *me*? What a fool you are. I killed Serena and I'll be happy to do the same to her daughter. Then you'll have two Sterlings to mourn instead of just one."

Claudia's lips pressed together into a tight line, but she ignored his cruel taunt. "Do we have an agreement or not?" she snapped.

Victor studied her a moment, then his gaze flicked to me. It only took him a second to decide that he could beat me. "Agreed. As previously arranged, the winner of the duel will take control of both our Families—and do whatever they like with the losers."

He whirled around and stalked back over to his guards, filling them in on the terms of the duel. But Blake stayed in the middle of the bridge, staring at me as if he had never seen me before.

"I thought you were dead," he muttered. "You *should* be dead. Those copper crushers should have killed you."

I looked at him, trying to reason with him for Deah's sake. "You know that your dad is going to turn on you one day, right? You'll do something to displease him, and he'll order one of his men to kill you, just like he ordered you to capture Deah. Victor doesn't care about anything or anyone other than himself. Even if he beats me, even if he takes control of all the other Families in Cloudburst Falls, it still won't be enough for him. He'll start thinking about what other Families and other towns he can take over. Nothing will *ever* be enough for him."

A bit of doubt flickered in Blake's eyes, overcoming his usual arrogance. But his uncertainty quickly vanished and he gave me the same sneer he always did.

"That's never going to happen," he said. "My dad loves me. Besides, I'm the Draconi bruiser, his right-hand man. He can't run the Family without me. He's told me so himself."

"Just like he told Deah and Seleste how much he loved them?" I asked.

Blake blinked, as though it had never occurred to him that he might be just another tool for Victor to use, the way he had used Deah and Seleste all these years. He opened his mouth to say something, but the sharp, ringing *tap-tap-tap-tap* of Victor's wingtips on the cobblestones had him clamping his lips shut again.

Victor stopped in the middle of the bridge. He looked at me, then went over and placed three quarters on the center stone, the one marked with three Xs, before stepping back out into the center of the span.

"You didn't think I would forget to pay the lochness toll, did you, Lila?" He smirked, seeing my disappointment. "Your mother taught me better than that."

I really had been hoping he would forget about the toll, just as Grant Sanderson had all those weeks ago, and that the lochness would make Victor pay for his oversight. But of course Victor wouldn't make things that easy.

So I dug my own set of quarters out of the hidden slot on my belt, walked over, and placed them on the center stone, careful to keep them away from his. I waited a few seconds, wondering if the lochness might appear to take its tribute, but the surface of the river remained smooth and calm, so I moved back over to the center of the bridge.

"You can do this," Claudia whispered, her eyes steady on mine. "Just remember Serena and everything she taught you."

"Always," I whispered back.

She squeezed my hand, then turned and walked to the end of the bridge, where Devon, Felix, Mo, Oscar, Deah, Seleste, and all the other Sinclairs were waiting.

Victor murmured something to Blake that I couldn't hear, and Blake nodded and looked past me. I glanced over my shoulder and realized that he was staring at Deah and Seleste. I wondered what Victor was telling Blake about his own sister and stepmother, if he wanted Blake to try to capture them—or worse—if he lost the duel. Part of me didn't want to know. It would only remind me of how cruel Victor was.

And how he was most likely going to kill me.

Blake nodded at whatever Victor told him. He smirked at me a final time, then stalked to the opposite end of the bridge so that he was standing with the rest of the Draconi guards.

Victor turned around and strode forward until he was right in the center of the bridge. I let out a tense breath, then stepped up to meet him, leaving about five feet of space in between us.

"I'm going to enjoy this, Lila," he purred, his voice showing the first hint of warmth I'd ever heard. "Just as I did with your mother."

He was trying to make me angry, get me to fly into a rage and do something stupid, like recklessly charge at him. But I forced myself to ignore his horrible words and take slow, deep, steady breaths. He wasn't going to rile me up that easily. He wasn't going to win that easily.

He wasn't going to kill me that easily.

"Good," I said. "I hope you do enjoy this."

He arched a golden eyebrow. "Really? Why is that?"

"Because it's going to be the last thing you ever enjoy."

Instead of being concerned, his face creased into a wide smile, and he let out a low, deep belly laugh. The sound reminded me of the copper crushers slowly slithering toward me, their rattles shaking and their scales scraping against the concrete floor of the warehouse. But I stood my ground, not letting Victor see my fear and disgust.

"You certainly are confident," he said. "Just like your mother was. And I'm going to kill you, just like I killed her."

His golden eyes glimmered with a sinister light. My gaze locked with his and my soulsight kicked in, showing me just how much he meant every cruel word—and just how cold, dark, and empty his heart truly was.

In that moment, I almost felt sorry for him. Victor Draconi would never know true love or happiness or anything else. All he cared about was magic and the power it gave him over others. Even if he beat me here tonight, even if he killed me and took control of the Sinclair Family, it wouldn't be enough for him. Nothing would ever be enough for him, just as I'd told Blake.

My hand tightened around my sword. But he wasn't going to win.

"This ends tonight," I said, raising my sword into an attack position.

Victor gave me a thin smile. "The only thing that's ending tonight is you, Lila. I'll see to that."

"Then let's get on with it," I snarled.

He shrugged. "As you wish. But don't say I didn't warn you."

Instead of reaching for his magic right away, Victor just stared at me, his golden eyes glowing in his face as he studied everything about me, from my face to the cuff on my wrist to the way I slowly twirled my black blade around and around in my hand.

"That sword isn't going to save you," he said. "I don't even need a weapon to kill you."

"We'll see."

He looked at me another second, then turned around as though he were going to walk away. I knew it was a trap, but he was giving me an open shot at his back and it was too good a chance to pass up. So I raised my sword high, ready to bring it down on top of his head.

But I hadn't taken three steps toward him before he whipped back around and reached for his magic. A ball of lightning popped into his hand, and I barely managed to duck out of the way as he sent it streaking through the air toward me. The lightning hit one of the streetlamps at the end of the bridge, making white sparks shoot up into the night sky.

Claudia, Devon, Mo, and all my other friends ducked out of the way as well, along with the Sinclair guards, and several hoarse shouts rose up in surprise. The sparks had barely winked out before the wind started to pick up, and more and more lightning flashed in the sky. A low rumble of thunder sounded, and a few raindrops spattered against my cheeks. The storm was almost here.

But it was nothing compared to the power that Victor was calling up.

White lightning crackled in both of his hands now, and I could feel the cold burn of magic in the air, even though I was still standing five feet away from him. His magic was stronger than any I'd ever felt before, but I supposed that was to be expected given how much power he had running through his veins. I wondered how many people he'd killed just to make himself stronger. So many people and creatures dead, just because of one man's relentless thirst for power.

Victor kept calling up more and more magic. Then he unleashed it, hurling ball after ball of lightning at me, as though it were winter and we were having a snowball fight in the middle of the lochness bridge. With all the Talents he'd stolen, I expected him to be faster, to throw so much magic at me so quickly that I wouldn't be able to avoid it, but Victor kept his movements slow and steady. And I realized that he wasn't trying to kill me. Not just yet. No, he wanted to play with me first. I was the mouse to his cat right now, another creature caught in one of his traps with no hope of escaping.

I ducked the lightning and tried to move forward so that I could hit Victor with my sword. But he easily held me at bay, the lightning getting closer and closer with every blast and making static electricity gather around my own body. My transference magic stirred in response, eager to soak up Victor's magic, and I could feel myself getting stronger with each ball of lightning that zipped past me. But I could also feel exactly how powerful he was. Sure, I had my transference power, had the ability to absorb magic, but not that *much* magic. Not at one time. It would kill me outright.

Still, I had to try. So with every blast of lightning, I forced myself to bob and weave and duck, creeping closer and closer to Victor all the while. A few more raindrops spattered against my face, but the storm seemed to be waiting to see who won our fight, just like everyone else gathered around the bridge.

Victor knew I couldn't get close enough to hit him with my sword, much less actually kill him with it, and he threw back his head and laughed, the lightning in his hands crackling in time with his dark chuckles.

"What's the matter, Lila?" he called out over the spark, hiss, snap, and sizzle of his lightning. "Not what you were expecting?"

Instead of answering him, I eased forward another step, then two, then three. He realized what I was up to and he shook his head.

"You stupid, stupid girl," he said. "Thinking you could actually beat me. All you've done is gone and gotten yourself killed, just like your mother before you."

I didn't think it was possible, but Victor summoned up even more of his power, so that his lightning fully illuminated the lochness bridge, blazing brighter than the noontime sun. And he finally did what I'd been dreading all along. He added his speed Talent to the mix, drew his hands back, and hurled his magic at me before I could even think about ducking out of the way.

A second later, the lightning slammed straight into my body.

CHAPTER TWENTY-SIX

The lightning hit me square in the chest, knocking me back five feet and making me lose my grip on my sword, which clattered to the cobblestones. I landed flat on my back in the middle of the bridge. For a moment, I didn't feel anything. Not heat, not electricity, not pain, nothing.

Then the lightning zipped over my body, sinking deep inside me, and I started screaming.

And I didn't—couldn't—stop.

Every single part of me burned with hot, unending, electrical pain. My legs flailed, my fingers twitched, and my teeth chattered together from the shocking jolts of power. I bit down on my own tongue by accident and blood filled my mouth. Sweat streamed down my face, and I felt like every nerve ending in my body was on fire. White stars flashed on and off in front of my face faster and brighter than they ever had before. Or maybe that was just the lightning flashing over me again and again. I couldn't really tell.

It wasn't that the lightning just hit me and that was the end of it. Oh no. That would have been too *easy*. The lightning crackled over my body again and again, never stopping, never weakening, not even for an instant. It coiled around and around me like a copper crusher, as though it were a monster with a mind of its own and it wouldn't be satisfied until I was burnt to a crisp.

Through the dazzling white flashes, I realized that Victor was slowly advancing on me, the lightning streaking from his fingers, through the air, and straight into my body. But all I could do was writhe on the ground and scream and scream and scream some more.

I was dimly aware of my transference power flaring to life, and the familiar chill of magic surging through my body the way it had so many times before. But it had never, ever been this intense, this painful before, and I realized that Victor's magic was greater than my own. He was going to kill me, and there was nothing I could do to stop him. Right now, it was all I could do to suck down air between my screams, much less actually get to my feet and fight back.

Victor kept coming closer and closer to me. Even through the lightning, I could see his golden eyes, glowing brighter than any monster's. He was a monster all right, through and through. His power might be pure white energy, but his heart was as black as the darkest night.

I kept screaming as the lightning flashed over me again and again. I was dimly aware of people yelling, Devon and the rest of my friends, most likely, but they couldn't do anything to help me. They couldn't even step onto the bridge right now without getting electrocuted themselves.

Victor stopped beside me, looming over me and giving me a triumphant sneer, lightning still pouring out of his hands in steady, crackling waves. His face twisted with sly satisfaction, and he drew in a breath, as if preparing himself to unleash a final wave of magic that would end me once and for all.

And that's when the lochness decided to strike.

Just as Victor raised his hands to finish me off, a long,

black tentacle whipped through the air, then slammed straight into his chest. The blow knocked Victor back and made him lose his grip on his magic, the lightning dimming to white sparks flickering around his hands.

But it didn't stop him for long.

Even as the lochness reared back its tentacle to lash out at Victor again, he scrambled to his feet and gave the waving tentacle a cold, unconcerned look.

Then he unleashed his magic on the monster.

Lightning erupted on Victor's fingertips again, but this time, instead of pouring into me, the magic streaked across the bridge and straight into the lochness. Not only that, but the harsh, crackling power zipped down the long, black tentacle, traveling over the side of the bridge and all the way into the water below.

The thought of Victor hurting the lochness gave me the strength to roll to my side, push myself onto my hands and knees, and then stagger up to my feet. Every part of me still hurt, twitched, and burned with electrical pain, but I managed to stumble over to the side of the bridge.

By this point, Victor's lightning had lit up the entire surface of the river, perfectly outlining the lochness's enormous, octopus-like body in the water below. Perhaps I only imagined it, but I thought I could even see the creature's two sapphire eyes, staring up at me, silently begging me for help.

"Stop it!" I screamed. "You're killing it! You're killing the lochness!"

Even if Victor had heard me, he didn't care, and his face was twisted into a snarl, his eyes shining with absolute, bitter hate. In that moment, I realized that he despised the monsters just as much as he had my mom. He was going to kill the lochness, just because he could, unless I did something to stop him.

I didn't think—I just acted.

I grabbed my mom's sword from where it had fallen and stumbled forward again. I tried to raise the weapon to attack him, but it was all I could do to hold on to the sword, and I ended up just slamming my body into Victor's instead, knocking us both down.

His head snapped back against the cobblestones and the blow stunned him enough to make him lose his grip on his magic again. Lightning still crackled around his body, though, and mine too, washing over both of us in wave after white-hot wave.

Only this time, it didn't hurt nearly as much as before.

Part of me wondered why, especially since the lightning kept crackling and crackling around me, even though it wasn't actually sinking into my body and burning me alive anymore. I looked down, and I finally realized what was different this time.

I was holding my mom's sword in my hand.

And it was glowing the blackest midnight imaginable.

The blade practically pulsed with darkness that was as intense as Victor's white lightning. I'd always thought you had to get blood on a black blade in order to make it glow, but that didn't seem to be the case. At least, not with Victor and his lightning. Maybe that's because it was blood magic in a way—power born of all the blood that Victor had cut out of others in order to steal their Talents and make them his own.

And I realized something important. Even with my transference power, I wasn't strong enough to absorb his magic, but my black blade *was*.

And I finally realized how I could steal Victor's magic—the same way he had stolen everyone else's, just like my mom had said.

Victor shook off the hard blow, shoved me off him, and scrambled back to his feet. When I got back up onto my feet as well, surprise flickered in his face, as though he'd never expected me to survive for this long. For the first time since I'd known him, Victor actually looked a bit disheveled, his blood-red shirt untucked, his golden hair rumpled, his handsome face streaked with dirt.

Behind him, at the far end of the bridge, Blake and the Draconi guards shifted on their feet, glancing at each other, unease and uncertainty flashing in their eyes. I doubted that anyone had knocked Victor down in years, much less someone from another Family like me.

I risked a quick glance over my shoulder to find the Sinclairs all staring steadily back at me, their hands holding their swords high overhead, just like the Family crest, in a silent show of support. Devon, Felix, Mo, Deah, even Oscar with his pixie sword. All saluting me, all supporting me, all urging me on.

Claudia stepped forward, raised her own sword even higher, and nodded at me. I nodded back, tightened my grip on my sword, and turned to face Victor again.

"I'm sick of you Sterlings!" he hissed. "This is the end of you!"

He reached for his power again, gathering more and more magic around himself until the entire bridge looked like it was in the center of a lightning storm. But this time, instead of cringing or ducking out of the way, I faced Victor and his magic head on.

Don't be afraid of the lightning, Seleste's voice whispered in my mind.

And I finally realized what she meant. That magic was magic, no matter what form it was in or who was wielding it. Black blades—bloodiron—didn't care what magic belonged to which person. All they could do was soak up power. It was the person wielding the weapon that decided what to do with that power. As long as I had my mom's sword in my hand, I could withstand Victor's magic.

So that's what I did.

I stood my ground and held my sword out in front of me even as Victor's lightning slammed into me again. But this time, instead of shooting into my chest and knocking me back, the lightning went straight into my black blade.

The sword soaked up that initial blast of magic and then all the ones after it, absorbing the magic as fast as Victor could summon it up, like a literal lightning rod in my hand. But my mom's sword wasn't the only thing soaking up power. So were the three black blade throwing stars attached to my belt.

And so was I.

That cold burn of magic filled my veins, more intense than ever before. My breath frosted in the air and my entire body became as cold as a blizzard. With every breath, I felt myself growing stronger and stronger, until I was more powerful than I had ever been before. In that moment, I felt like I could do *anything*—take on every single Draconi, swing my sword at a hundred enemies, even reach down and tear the lochness bridge apart with my bare hands.

I forced all that magic, all that power, out into the cuts, bruises, and burns on my body, using Victor's own power to repair all the damage he'd done to me with his lightning strikes.

In an instant, my skin smoothed out, my muscles quit twitching, and my breath came easier. So I kept going, channeling the magic through my whole body until I was completely healed, as if I'd never even been injured to start with.

But I was even better than that now—I was even *stronger.*

I didn't duck or hide or run from the lightning. Not anymore. Instead, I embraced it in a way that I had never fully embraced my transference power before. I had always kept my Talent hidden for fear that someone would try to take it away from me, would try to cut it out of me, but not anymore, not now. Instead, I became like the black blade in my hand—hungry for magic, eager for every single scrap of power I could soak up.

Slowly, I began to walk toward Victor.

It wasn't easy—far from it—especially not with the lightning still crackling around my body, trying to drive me back and rip the sword from my hand at every turn. But I channeled the magic in my veins, pushing it out into my hands, arms, and legs, making them rock steady and stronger than ever before, and I held on to my sword and crept toward Victor, one small step at a time. All the while, the black blade in my hand grew colder and colder, and its midnight glow blacker and blacker until it seemed to snuff out Victor's magic before it even left his hands.

Victor finally realized that I wasn't burned to a crisp, that I had found a way to endure his magic, and that I was still coming for him. His golden eyes widened and his mouth fell open in surprise.

And he actually *stopped*.

He dropped his hands to his sides, although the lightning continued to crackle on his fingertips.

"You," he sputtered. "You're—you're not dead yet. You're not even *close* to being dead."

"Now you're catching on," I rasped.

His eyes widened again, more shock swirling through his gaze, but the emotion was quickly replaced by cold calculation. He took a step back, looked over his shoulder, and made a sharp motion with his hand.

"Attack!" Victor screamed. "Attack! Kill the Sterling girl! Now!"

CHAPTER TWENTY-SEVEN

Even though Victor and I were supposed to be the only ones participating in the duel, the other Draconis stepped onto the bridge, with Blake leading the charge, just like always. All the magic coursing through my veins heightened my senses and I could hear every single harsh, raspy slide of their swords leaving their scabbards and every single one of their footsteps on the bridge.

And the answering sounds behind me.

I didn't have to turn around to know that my friends had stepped onto the bridge behind me. Even as the Draconis crept closer to me, I spotted Devon and Deah out of the corner of my eye, leading the Sinclairs. My friends eased up beside me, careful to stay away from my sword, which was still glowing that eerie, midnight black.

Victor realized that his guards weren't rushing to attack me like he wanted, and he glared over his shoulder at Blake. "You fool!" he yelled. "What are you waiting for? Kill her! Now!"

Blake hesitated a moment longer, then sprinted toward me. My gaze flicked back and forth between him and his dad. Victor wasn't able to kill me outright with his magic, so he was once again ordering someone else to do his dirty work for him.

"That's it!" Victor said, urging his son on. "Kill her! Now!"

Blake let out a loud roar and quickened his steps, an evil grin stretching across his face at the thought of finally cutting me down. I gritted my teeth, trying to figure out how I was going to channel all the magic roaring through my black blade and body right now and fight him off at the same time.

But I didn't have to worry because his sword never touched me.

In an instant, Deah was by my side, using her sword to block her brother's.

"Leave her alone!" Deah hissed.

"Stay out of this!" Blake screamed back at her.

He tried to charge past her to get to me, but Deah whipped around, stuck her foot out, and tripped him, making Blake topple to the cobblestones. He snarled and scrambled right back up onto his feet, lashing out with his sword at her this time.

"Come on! Come on! Come on!" Blake screamed at the guards who were still hanging back. "Do you want to win or not?"

And with that, the fight was on. With an angry roar, the Draconi guards stormed ahead, and the Sinclairs rushed forward to meet them.

For a moment, there was just *noise*.

Swords clanging together, people yelling, boots scraping against the cobblestones. Maybe it was all the magic pulsing through my sword and body, but I thought I could hear the hiss of every single blade as it sliced into someone's skin and the resulting spatter of the blood on the cobblestones.

From the corner of my eye, I spotted my friends. Devon

fighting two Draconi guards, Felix and Angelo taking on two more, Mo and Claudia standing back to back, him using his tall, strong body to throw the guards around while she used her cold touch magic to freeze any that came near. I even spotted Oscar zipping through the air, the Sinclair pixies following him like a swarm of bees as they dive-bombed first one Draconi guard, then the next, stabbing the men and women with their poison-tipped, needle-size swords. It was a full-out mob war, in every sense of the word.

Except for Victor and me.

Even though we were still standing in the center of the bridge, no one dared to approach the two of us. Not with the white lightning still crackling around his hands and the black blade still glowing in mine.

"How are you doing this?" he demanded. "What power, what Talent, do you have that lets you withstand raw magic?"

"Wouldn't you like to know?" I growled back at him.

"Oh, soon I will," he promised. "You might have siphoned off some of my magic, but I can cut it right back out of you again, one slice at a time."

"Never!" I hissed back.

Victor stepped forward, once again calling up his lightning and throwing it at me, and I shrieked as a fresh wave of his power rolled over me. It was all I could do to stand upright, much less withstand and channel another brutal assault of magic. But I gritted my teeth and forced myself to put one foot in front of the other, creeping closer and closer to him. The black blade was soaking up as much of his power as it could, but all the magic crackling through the air around me was overloading my system, just like the copper crusher venom had. I had to do something to get rid of the excess power or the magic would burn me to a crisp from the inside out, in a way worse than Victor's lightning had.

So I surged forward, drew back my left fist, and punched him in the face, putting as much strength into the blow as I could, both physical and magical.

I screamed as my hand passed through the lightning still crackling around his body, and I screamed again as my fist slammed into his face. For a moment, there was just a bright blaze of magic, hotter and whiter than any that had come before it. The burst of power was so intense that it stunned everyone on the bridge, and they all threw their hands up over their eyes and staggered back, just trying to get away from the two of us.

Victor staggered back as well, and his lightning magic was snuffed out completely. He brought his hand up to his lip, then stared at the bit of blood glistening on his fingertips. His eyes widened, as though it had been so long since he had seen his own blood that he couldn't even remember what it looked like anymore. Then he glared at me, his eyes narrowing to slits. But instead of summoning up more magic, Victor raised his fists and came right back at me.

His lightning hadn't burned me to death, so Victor decided to change tactics and use his Talents in a different way. This time, he used all that power to make himself impossibly fast and strong, slamming his fists into my face and stomach over and over again, like a boxer working a heavy bag, his movements almost too fast for me to follow, much less defend against.

Pain exploded in my body, blood filled my mouth, and the force of the hard, repeated blows made me double over. But once again, I channeled the magic still running through my veins and my black blade and sent all that cold, cold power shooting outward, healing the areas of my body that Victor had damaged.

He snarled and charged at me again, but I used his own trick against him, sending the magic down into my legs and forcing myself to move quicker than he did. I managed to sidestep him, and we both whirled around, facing each other again.

Instead of attacking me, Victor actually smiled, as if he were happy that I'd taken his punches and was still standing.

"You . . . you have transference magic," he said in a high, giddy voice. "That's why you aren't dead yet. You're absorbing all of my power and taking it for your own, and your black blade is helping you do it."

His eyes narrowed again and I could see the hunger in his golden gaze, even more intense than that of the copper crushers who'd tried to eat me. "And now, your power is going to be *mine*."

I thought he might try to blast me with his lightning again, but instead, Victor whipped around, waded into a group of guards, and grabbed a sword from one of them. He pushed that guard aside, his strength still so great that he made the other man fly back ten feet, hit the side of the bridge, and flip over into the empty air. The guard screamed as he plummeted toward the river below, but Victor didn't give him a second thought.

Instead, he raised his sword and attacked me.

Victor was using his speed magic again and I barely managed to raise my own sword in time to stop him from splitting my skull open. Once they realized that the two of us were finally fighting sword to sword, the rest of the Sinclairs and Draconis raised their own weapons and went at it again, with even more screams, shrieks, and shouts tearing through the night air.

But I only had eyes for Victor, and he for me. Back and forth we fought on the bridge, our swords crashing together time and time again. High, low, side to side to side.

We whipped our blades back and forth, and back and forth, both of us using magic to make ourselves as fast and strong as possible, and both of us evenly matched in that regard.

Victor was a good fighter, one of the best I'd ever been up against, cold, calculating, and ruthless, but I was just a smidge better, and he knew it. So he did what anyone would do in this situation—he decided to fight dirty.

While our swords were locked together, he snapped up his hand and slammed his fist into my jaw. He put the full force of his lightning magic into the blow, making me scream and white stars flash in front of my eyes again. I stumbled back, but for once, my sight magic deserted me and I could barely see Victor standing in front of me, much less actually fend off his blows.

And that's when he stabbed me.

Victor slipped past my defenses and rammed his sword into my side, making me scream with pain. The stars finally faded enough to let me see his gaze locked onto his sword in my side and all the blood pouring out of the deep wound.

"Mine," he whispered. "Your magic is going to be *mine*."

Despite the pain pulsing through my body, I managed to snarl back at him. "Never!"

I shoved him away and Victor stumbled back, tearing his sword out of my body as brutally as he could and making me scream again. Before I even had time to catch my breath, he came right back at me, swinging his sword, wanting to cut me again and rip my magic out of me, one bloody slice at a time. All around us the fight raged on, but I blocked out the shouts, screams, and everything else, knowing that this was the most important battle of my life.

Victor and I kept fighting. Well, really, he fought. I just parried his blows, clutching one hand to my side to try to slow the blood loss. With every blow, I grew weaker and weaker, and he pressed his advantage, concentrating his strikes on my sword hand. I knew what he was trying to do—knock my weapon away so he could stab me through the heart and take my magic for himself.

But I wasn't about to let that happen so I tightened my grip on my sword, channeling the magic still pulsing in my black blade into my hands, arms, and legs so that I could keep on fighting. But I was still losing, and it was only a matter of time before Victor snuck through my defenses again and gutted me. He lashed out with a particularly hard blow and I staggered back, almost flipping over the side of the bridge.

"If you give up now, I will make your death relatively painless," Victor said, slowly approaching me. "One blow to your heart and it will all be over."

I let out a harsh, bitter laugh, realizing it for the trick it was. "You're such a liar."

He shrugged. "Certainly. I'm going to enjoy cutting you to ribbons, just as I did your mother."

Once again, white stars flashed in front of my eyes, but they weren't caused by any lightning or other magic. No, these stars were part of my soulsight, letting me look back into the past and see my mom's body, bloody, beaten, and broken on the floor of our small apartment.

White-hot rage roared through me, more rage than I had ever felt before. This time, the cold burn in my veins had nothing to do with magic, but everything to do with my desire to stop Victor, to finally hurt him the same way he had hurt my mom.

Even as I raised my sword again, Victor used his speed magic to step up and pin me against the side of the bridge. He pressed the tip of his sword against my throat. I froze, my own sword raised in midair.

"Drop your weapon," he hissed, pressing his sword a little deeper into my neck, breaking the skin there and making blood trickle down my throat. "Now."

I slowly laid the sword down on the bridge ledge. I waited, wondering if Victor would tell me to take off my leather belt with its three throwing stars as well, but he just sneered at me, cold triumph gleaming in his eyes. So slowly, very, very slowly, I dropped my hand down to my side, inching my fingers toward my belt. Victor hadn't won yet, and I could fight dirty too. All I needed was one moment of opportunity and I could finish what my mom had started all those years ago.

"I'll admit that you put up a good fight," Victor said, staring at me. "I didn't expect you to have transference magic and be able to siphon off my magic into your black blade. That will be my bonus for killing you, and taking it from you will just be *fun*."

I didn't respond, although I kept crawling my fingers toward my belt.

"You might have stolen some of my magic, but I'll use your black blade to put it right back inside my own body again," he said, his voice ringing with triumph. "Where it *belongs*."

I still didn't say anything as my fingers reached one of the throwing stars on my belt and curled around the metal.

"Goodbye, Lila Sterling," Victor sneered. "And good riddance to the Sterling Family once and for all—"

Even as he crowed about how he was going to kill me, I shoved his sword away from my throat. The blade cut deep into my palm, but I ignored the stinging pain, yanked the throwing star off my belt, and swiped it across his face. The star sliced his cheek, making him scream, stagger back, and lower his weapon.

Using the last of the magic in my veins, I grabbed my sword off the ledge, stepped up, and stabbed him straight through the heart with the black blade.

Victor screamed as my mother's sword plunged deep into his chest. He staggered back, but I went with him, keeping a tight grip on the black blade. I was going to end this—now.

And that's when his magic started pouring into me.

It was small at first, a single spark of white lightning erupting from his chest, zinging along the length of the sword, and traveling up to my blood-covered hand. The second that spark came into contact with my blood, a whole cascade of sparks erupted, until it seemed as though Victor and I were standing in the middle of a giant fireworks display.

He gasped in surprise and so did I, but we were connected by the sword in his chest and all I could do was stand there and gape, as though I were outside my own body and watching all this happen to me from someplace far, far away.

When Grant Sanderson had tried to take my magic, he'd been determined to cut me to pieces to get my power just because he wanted me to suffer. But you could also take a person's magic by stabbing him once straight through the heart with a black blade. That's what I'd done to Victor, not because I wanted to take his magic, but simply to end the fight. But apparently, he had so much magic, so much raw power, it was literally bursting to get out of him.

So it did—traveling straight into me.

I saw the lighting, the power, the magic, streak from Victor, up my black blade, and into my body, felt the cold burn of it in my veins, felt it gather around my own dark heart, squeezing, squeezing tight. Once again, every single part of me burned with hot, electrical pain. My legs flailed, my fingers twitched, and my teeth chattered together just like they had before. It hurt terribly—worse even than when Victor had been trying to electrocute me—but all I could do was stand there as the magic flooded into my own body.

The sharp, continuous jolts of power and pain seemed to go on forever, although they couldn't have lasted much more than a minute. But finally, they eased up and then stopped altogether, and the white sparks went out, although I could still feel the cold chill of them in the humid night. My breath frosted in the air, as white as snow, and I felt the icy sting of power flowing through my veins, stronger than ever before. The midnight-black glow on my sword slowly lightened, then vanished altogether, until the weapon was once again its usual, dull, ash-gray color.

Victor stared at me with wide, gaping eyes. "You . . . you . . . took it all . . ." His voice failed him.

He staggered back and this time I let him, my sword sliding free of his chest. Victor wobbled on his feet for a second, then he hit the side of the bridge, fell down, and toppled over onto his side. Blood oozed down his chest and trickled onto the cobblestones, turning them a glossy, sickening scarlet. All the while, Victor kept staring at me, his golden eyes getting darker and darker, a glassy sheen slowly covering the accusation in his gaze.

And just like that, the cold light was snuffed out of his eyes and his head lolled to the side.

Dead—Victor Draconi was dead.

And I had taken all his magic for my own.

The greatest—and most terrifying—thing I'd ever stolen.

CHAPTER TWENTY-EIGHT

Despite the magic rippling through my body, I was exhausted. My feet slipped out from under me, and I landed on the cobblestones. I looked up, expecting to see lightning flashing overhead and for the impending storm to finally descend, but to my surprise, the rain clouds had disappeared, revealing the moon and stars. I was going to take that as a good omen.

My final battle with Victor had frozen everyone in place and startled them all into absolute silence, except for Devon, who hurried over and dropped down beside me, with Oscar buzzing around our shoulders.

"Lila! Are you okay?" Devon asked, gently cupping my face in his hand.

All I could do was nod. I didn't even have the strength to speak right now.

Slowly, all the guards, Sinclairs and Draconis alike, crept forward. So did the Ito and Salazar guards who'd come up behind the Draconis on the opposite side of the bridge. A few whispers broke out as they realized that Victor was dead, but they quickly faded away and everyone was still and quiet again. The guards all kept staring from me to Victor and back again, shocked that I had actually done it, that I had actually killed him and ended the threat he represented to the Families and everyone in Cloudburst Falls—mortal, magick, and monster alike.

"No!" a loud, anguished voice cried out. "No! Dad! No!"

Blake sprinted forward, fell to his knees, and shook Victor's shoulder, but of course, Victor didn't wake up, and he never would again. Once Blake realized that his dad was really and truly dead, he scrambled to his feet and whipped around to me, hate filling his eyes.

"You! You killed him!" he snarled.

Blake raised his sword and charged at me, but once again, Deah was there to swing her blade into his and stop him from hurting me.

"That's enough, Blake!" she snapped, pushing him away from me. "It's over. Look around you. Don't you see? It's over!"

And it was.

Dead guards—Sinclairs and Draconis alike—littered the bridge like crumpled dolls. More Sinclairs were standing than Draconis now, but both sides had sustained heavy losses. Members of the Ito and Salazar Families had been killed as well, since they'd engaged the Draconi guards from behind.

Blake looked around. For a moment, I thought he would stand down, but his mouth tightened into an ugly slash, and more and more anger, hate, and disgust filled his eyes.

He glared at me. "You!" he screamed again. "This is all your fault!"

"Blake! Stop!" Deah yelled. "It's over!"

She moved in front of her brother again, trying to stop him from attacking me, but he used his strength magic to barrel right past her. Deah hit the cobblestones hard, but she scrambled around, trying to get back up onto her feet in time to stop Blake from killing me.

But she didn't have to because Felix was there.

Felix stepped up and slammed his sword into Blake's, knocking him away from me. But Blake just wouldn't give up.

"I'm going to kill you, Morales!" he screamed. "You and all your stupid friends!"

Blake charged at him again, but Felix slid to the side at the last second, just the way I'd taught him during our training bouts. But Blake was too committed to his charge to stop and he ran right into the side of the bridge, where his momentum flipped him up and over the side into the water below. Blake screamed as he plummeted toward the river.

Then . . . silence.

Deah got back up onto her feet and rushed over to the ledge, staring down into the river. So did Felix. After several seconds, he turned and shook his head at me. Deah kept staring down at the river, tears shimmering in her eyes, and Felix gently put his arm around her shoulder. She let out one small cry and choked the others back, although a few tears slid down her face. Despite everything, Blake had still been her brother and Deah had loved him, along with Victor.

The seconds ticked by, and no one moved or spoke. Finally, Claudia strode forward, moving past me, Devon, Oscar, Felix, and Deah until she was standing in the center of the bridge in front of the remaining Draconis.

"Victor is dead and his cruelty along with him," she called out in a loud, strong voice. "My champion has won the duel. By law, that makes you all part of my Family now."

The Draconis grumbled, shifted on their feet, and looked back and forth between each other and Claudia. They didn't know what to do now that Victor was gone.

"I do not believe that you are bad people," she called

out again. "You just had a bad leader. I don't want to hurt you, any of you. We've all lost friends over the past few days, and there's been more than enough bloodshed here tonight. It's time to end this cycle of violence, this mistrust and suspicion between the Families once and for all. Don't you agree?"

More mutters, along with a few murmurs of agreement this time.

Claudia looked out over the crowd again. "I'm offering you all a choice. Strip off your red cloaks and hats, take off your gold cuffs and weapons, and join my Family. Not because we have beaten you, but because you want a fresh start, for yourselves and all of Cloudburst Falls. A place where we can finally live together in peace, without the threat of war constantly looming over us."

Claudia didn't have Devon's compulsion magic, but her voice boomed through the night, and more and more of the Draconis started nodding, agreeing with her. Several even started doing exactly as she asked, pulling off their cloaks and hats, throwing down their weapons, and slipping the gold cuffs off their wrists. One by one, the Draconis cast off the remnants of their old Family and embraced their new one.

Slowly, they walked across the bridge, stopping to bow their heads to Claudia, then headed past her, taking their place in the ranks with the Sinclair guards. The Sinclairs eyed the newcomers with more than a little suspicion, but no more fights broke out and I knew that we were finally on our way to a real, lasting peace.

Claudia looked over and nodded at me. I nodded back and she turned away to start seeing to the wounded guards, Sinclairs and Draconis alike. The Itos and Salazars also crossed the bridge, with Hiroshi Ito and Roberto Salazar ordering their guards to tend the injured as well.

"Help me up," I said. "I have to check on someone."

Devon put his arm around my waist and slowly lifted me to my feet, with Oscar still buzzing circles around us. With Devon's help, I slowly shuffled forward and peered over the side of the bridge. Down below, a lone tentacle rose up out of the water and waved at me. I waved back, but then my strength left me and I would have slumped back down onto the cobblestones if Devon hadn't steadied me.

In an instant, he'd lowered me back down onto the ground, his eyes wide with concern. "Lila! Are you okay?"

"I think so," I said. "Except for the stab wound in my side. That's three times now that I've been stabbed this summer. Why do the bad guys always get me there?"

I laughed, but it was a weak sound, and more white stars flashed in front of my eyes, telling me I was close to passing out.

"It's okay," Oscar said, hovering in midair in front of my face. "Relax, Lila. Just relax. We'll get you healed up and everything will be fine. You'll see."

"Okay," I murmured. "Okay."

Devon gathered me up into his arms. His crisp, clean pine scent washed over me, and I let the blackness sweep me away.

Sunlight streaming in through the windows woke me up the next morning. I groaned and snuggled down deeper into the sheets, trying to block out the sunlight, but it was no use.

"Finally, cupcake," a familiar voice groused. "I was wondering if you were *ever* going to wake up."

I cracked my eyes open to find Oscar sitting in a pixie-size recliner on a table close to the bed I was lying on. A pixie-size table was also there, and Oscar was playing solitaire with a deck of miniature cards, while Tiny ambled around him, sniffing the cards to see if they were edible. The tortoise huffed, disappointed that they weren't.

Oscar put his cards down, flitted over, and landed on the bed beside me. "How are you feeling?"

"Better now," I said. "Much better."

He nodded, his face creasing with relief. I concentrated and realized that I did feel better. The stab wound in my side had been healed, and so had all the other cuts, scrapes, and bruises that I'd gotten during the latter part of my fight with Victor. Angelo and Felix had used their healing skills on me yet again and I felt perfectly fine.

Except for the bright blaze of magic in my body.

I could still feel Victor's power running through my veins, waiting to be unleashed, wanting to be used in some way. I'd thought it might burn out of me, the way monster magic did when you used it all up, but I felt the magic as strongly as I had last night. And I knew that if I concentrated, I could call it up, could call forth that lightning and use it however I wanted.

I shivered. The idea of having so much magic, so much power . . . it made me sick to my stomach, especially since it was Victor's magic, the blood magic he'd stolen from others. But it seemed as if it was mine to keep now. I didn't know how I felt about that, much less what I would actually do with the power, but I would worry about that later. Right now, I wanted to know what had happened while I'd been unconscious.

So I shoved a couple of pillows behind my back and sat up, my gaze flicking over the room. A bed, a nightstand, a cabinet full of medical supplies. I frowned, wondering if we were where I thought we were. "Are we back at the Sinclair mansion?"

"Yep, in one of the infirmary rooms," Oscar said. "After the battle last night, Claudia ordered that the injured be brought back here and that everyone else get started on the cleanup. I promised Devon I would watch over you until you woke up. He's been overseeing the guards and pixies who are going through the mansion, seeing to . . . everyone."

He bit his lip, took off his hat, and scuffed his black cowboy boots back and forth on the sheets. What he really meant was that the guards and pixies had been taking care of all the bodies of everyone who had been killed when the Draconis had attacked the mansion. He blinked a few times, holding back the tears in his eyes. Yeah. Me too.

Oscar cleared his throat. "Anyway, the Itos and Salazars have both come over to help as well. It's actually been . . . nice, knowing that we aren't at war with them anymore."

"And what about the Draconi guards?"

He shrugged. "Claudia has Deah overseeing them. The guards are going to remain in their quarters over at the Draconi compound for the time being, but it seems like most of them are willing to forget about Victor and what he had planned. Claudia, Hiroshi, and Roberto all plan to let the guards choose which Family they want to join. Or if they don't want to work for the Families at all anymore."

I nodded. I hadn't really thought about what would happen to all the Draconi guards, workers, and pixies, but it made sense that they would be able to decide what they wanted to do going forward. That was certainly more of a choice than Victor had ever given them about anything.

Since I was feeling better, I threw back the covers and went back to my own room, with Oscar flying through the air behind me, carrying Tiny in his arms. To my surprise, a new door had already been placed into the frame. My stomach twisted as I remembered the utter destruction of my room the last time I'd been in here, but I drew in a breath, turned the knob, and stepped inside.

Someone must have been working in here all night long because my room was already clean. All the ripped clothes, mattress stuffing, and other debris had been removed and replaced with new furniture, including a new bed made up with a black-and-white-striped comforter.

Somehow, Oscar's pixie house had even been patched back together and put on its usual table close to the patio doors. The ebony trailer was more rundown, rickety, and ramshackle than ever before and held together with glue and duct tape in more than one place, but it warmed my heart to see it sitting in its usual spot.

"Who did all this?" I asked.

"I did," a voice called out behind me.

I turned and Devon was there. He gave me a crooked grin and leaned against the doorframe. Dirt smudged his face and streaked his black T-shirt and khaki cargo pants, but I thought he had never looked more wonderful.

"As soon as he was sure that you were going to be okay, he came up here and started cleaning up your room," Oscar chimed in.

Tears stung my eyes, and a wave of love flooded my heart. Of course Devon had done all this. Because that's just the kind of great guy he was. I didn't know how I was going to repay him for this, but I would.

I ran over, threw myself into his arms, and hugged him tight. "Thank you," I whispered. "Thank you so much."

"I'd do anything for you, Lila," he whispered back.

I stood on my tiptoes and pressed my lips to his. Devon pulled me closer and I melted into him, both of us swaying up against the doorframe for support. I kissed him again, then again, then again, a dizzying rush of feeling roaring through my body, hotter and stronger than even the magic running through my veins—

"All right," Oscar groused, buzzing around our heads and breaking the spell. "That's enough of that. There's still work to be done around here, you know, so we might as well get started on it."

Devon and I broke apart, both of us grinning wide.

"To be continued later?" he asked.

"You'd better believe it."

Oscar snorted and rolled his eyes before flying across the room and dropping Tiny off in the corral, just like usual. There wasn't any grass for him to munch on yet, but Tiny nodded his green head and let out a snort of approval. He was glad to be back home.

And so was I.

After promising to meet me on the roof later tonight, Devon went back downstairs to check on the guards and pixies. I took a long, hot shower, while Oscar fished through what was left of my clothes to find me something to wear that Blake hadn't ripped to shreds.

An hour later, I was in my usual gray sneakers, gray cargo shorts, and a pale blue T-shirt. But instead of going to find Devon and the others, I went to the library, opened one of the balcony doors, and snuck off into the woods. It didn't take me long to reach the Sinclair Family cemetery and my mom's tombstone.

I stood in front of her marker. The sunlight streaming in through the trees made her name stand out like polished silver against the black stone.

"Well," I said. "I guess you know everything that happened last night. How it all went down. I hope you're proud of me. At the very least, Victor will never hurt anyone again. I just wish . . . I just wish that you were still here with me."

"She'll always be here with you, darling," a voice called out behind me.

I turned around, and Seleste and Claudia stepped through the open gate and into the cemetery. Claudia was wearing another white pantsuit, while Seleste was sporting a gauzy white dress and carrying a white wicker basket full of red roses, just as she had been the very first time I'd seen her at the Draconi Family cemetery.

"See?" Seleste said, giving Claudia a smug smile. "I told you she'd be out here."

Claudia shook her head, but there was a smile on her face too.

Seleste skipped over and hugged me. Then she dropped down on her knees and started humming while she arranged the red roses all over my mother's grave. Claudia walked over and the two of us watched her work in silence.

Victor had finally been defeated, but my mom was still gone, and I would always carry the hurt and pain of her loss with me. But for the first time, a sense of peace was mixed in with my emotions too. I'd kept my promises to my mom and Claudia. I'd avenged her death, and I'd kept my friends and Family safe from Victor.

And I knew what my mom would tell me if she was still here—that it was time for a new start, a new beginning, a new chapter in my life. One where I could focus on all the good things that I had, instead of all the things that had been taken from me.

I stayed quiet and still until Seleste had finished arranging the roses in a large star pattern. She got to her feet, standing beside me and Claudia, and the three of us stared down at my mom's tombstone.

"I still miss her," Seleste whispered. "She was my best friend."

Claudia reached out and squeezed her hand. "Mine too."

"Mine three," I added.

"But we still have each other," Seleste said. "And Deah and Devon and all the others."

"That we do." I nodded. "That we do."

I held out my arms, and Seleste and Claudia linked theirs through mine.

Together, arm in arm in arm, the three of us walked out of the shadowy cemetery and into the warm summer sun.

CHAPTER TWENTY-NINE

Claudia, Seleste, and I headed back to the Sinclair mansion. Claudia went to help Devon with the guards and workers, while Seleste skipped off to the kitchen, saying something about helping the pixies with dinner. I had no idea if Seleste could actually cook or not, but I watched her go with a smile on my face. Then I walked through the mansion, stopping and looking into every single room I passed.

All of the bodies had been removed, and much of the destruction from the attack had already been cleaned up. The broken glass, splintered furniture, and cracked doors had all been removed, but other, more gruesome things remained behind that were harder to clean up. More than one pixie hovered in midair, a rag clutched in his or her hand, scrubbing at the bloodstains on the floors, walls, and even the ceilings. Those would take far longer to get rid of, and I knew that I would always see them in my nightmares.

I pitched in and helped where I could, mostly by carrying bags of debris and ruined pieces of furniture outside to load up onto trucks to be taken down into the city to be disposed of.

Mo was standing outside, supervising that part of the process. He was dressed in another Hawaiian shirt, this one a vivid blue covered with white ocean waves. He had a clipboard in his hands and was scribbling down notes about the items that littered the lawn around him—tables with a few scratches gouged into them, chairs that had been banged up, and several mirrors that were missing small pieces out of their frames. Unlike everything else in the mansion, most of these items were still in one piece.

Mo waved me over. "Hey, kid," he rumbled, giving me a hug. "Glad to see that you're up and around again. You gave us all a big scare last night."

"What are you doing?" I asked.

He gave me a wicked grin and brandished his clipboard at me. "Getting some new inventory for the Razzle Dazzle. A little paint, a little polish, and all this stuff will be as good as new again. I've already got some folks from Ashland, Bigtime, and Cypress Mountain coming to see it. What does it look like I'm doing?"

I laughed. "It looks like you're collecting more junk to sell to the tourists at double the price of what it's actually worth."

"Would I do something like that?" he asked in an innocent voice.

I snorted. "Absolutely."

He winked at me. Mo went back to his inventory, such as it was, and I went back into the mansion. I helped the guards, workers, and pixies, but seeing all the ruined furnishings being carted off depressed me more than I thought it would. Besides, everyone kept staring and whispering about me. I hated being the center of attention, but that's exactly what I was right now and probably would be for some time to come.

I worked hard all day long and didn't go back up to my room until after eight that night. A small hammer and even smaller nails littered the ground outside Oscar's trailer, along with several honeybeer cans. Repairing his trailer must have worn out the pixie because he was leaning back in a chair on his front porch, his cowboy boots up on the railing and his black cowboy hat pulled down low on his head. He clutched a honeybeer can in his lap, and soft, steady snores rumbled out of his chest. Tiny was also taking a nap in his corral, upside down on his shell like usual. I didn't want to disturb them, so I slipped out of the patio doors, took hold of the drainpipe, and climbed up to the terrace.

Devon wasn't here yet; he was still down in the main part of the mansion, helping Claudia deal with everyone and everything that needed to be done to repair the structure. I was grateful for the peace and quiet, especially after all the stares and whispers that had followed me around all day long.

I put my arms down on the iron railing and stared out over the Midway. The view looked the same as always, but the neon lights somehow seemed more colorful and cheerful than ever before. Or maybe that was because I knew that the danger had passed.

For now, anyway.

Victor might be dead, but Nikolai Volkov was still out there, and no doubt he would start plotting to take over the void that the Draconis had left behind. But that was a problem for another day. And there would still be fights and skirmishes between all the Families, including the Sinclairs, Itos, and Salazars, as everyone tried to figure out how things would work in a town where Victor Draconi wasn't king anymore. But we *would* work it out. I knew we would.

Behind me, a door creaked open and footsteps sounded. I breathed in and the sharp, crisp scent of pine—Devon's scent—wafted over to me. In addition to acquiring Victor's lightning power, I also seemed to have enhanced senses now. All day long, I'd noticed that I could smell, hear, and even see better than I had before. I wondered just how much of Victor's magic—and how many Talents—I might possess now.

The thought of where they had come from still made me sick, but the magic didn't seem to be burning out of my body. I supposed I would just have to live with it like I did everything else. The important thing was not to be like Victor—and not to use this new power to hurt people the way he had.

Devon walked over, leaned his arms down on the railing as well, and stared out at the view with me.

"I thought I might find you up here," he said.

"I just needed some time to myself. Some peace and quiet to think about everything that's happened."

He nodded. "You missed dinner in the dining hall. The pixies made BLTs. Felix and I thought about sending out a search party when you didn't show up to get your bacon fix," he joked, trying to make me smile.

And I did, just a little, just for a few seconds. But then I turned and looked out over the Midway again, watching the lights wink on and off like stars cupped in the evergreen heart of the mountains. And I asked Devon something that had been bothering me all day long.

"Do you think it was all worth it? Everything we went through? All the fights and pain and heartache and loss?"

He sighed. "I don't know. We lost a lot of good people, a lot of close friends. I wish things had been different. I wish we could have stopped the very first fight at the restaurant before it ever got started. But Victor is gone now and he can't hurt any of us again. That's something, right?"

"I guess it is," I said. "I guess it will have to be."

We stared out at the view for a while longer, both of us lost in our own thoughts, memories, and aching regrets.

Finally, Devon turned to me and placed his hand on top of mine.

"You know, with everything that's been going on, we never really did get to have a proper first date," he murmured in a husky tone. "And before you say otherwise, sneaking over to the Draconi compound all those nights and stealing weapons doesn't count."

"Well, I think stealing weapons makes for an excellent first date myself." I arched my eyebrows. "Are you saying that you want to take me out, Sinclair?"

He flashed me a grin. "Always."

I looped my arms around his neck. "Why do we have to go anywhere when I have everything I want right here?"

He grinned again, and I stood on my tiptoes and pressed my lips to his.

The past would always be dark, always haunt us. But suddenly, the future was as bright as the two of us could make it.

A door slammed open, but Devon kept right on kissing me, and I did the same to him—at least until a voice called out behind us.

"See? I told you they would be up here."

The door slammed shut, and Devon and I finally broke apart to find Felix and Deah standing on the roof. Felix was shaking his head, but he was grinning, while Deah was looking around at everything. She eyed the punching bags dangling from the scaffolding like she wanted to slam her fists into them over and over again. I knew the feeling and how much she had to be hurting right now. Whatever else they had been, Victor and Blake had been her family and she still grieved for them.

I went over and gave her a hug. The motion seemed to startle Deah, but after a second, she hugged me back. We stayed like that for close to a minute before we finally broke apart.

"How are you holding up?" I asked.

She gave me a tight smile. "Fine. Although if someone else asks me that, I just might scream."

"Believe me, I know the feeling."

"I was showing Deah around the mansion," Felix said. "I told her that we'd find the two of you up here making out."

Devon slipped his arm around my waist and pulled me close. "Absolutely. The question is why aren't the two of you doing the same thing?"

"Yeah," I said. "What was it you said in the woods a few days ago about working your romantic A game from start to finish?"

Deah arched her eyebrows at Felix, and a hot crimson blush flooded his bronze skin.

"Um, well . . . you see . . ." His voice trailed off under her steady look and he gave her a sheepish grin.

She arched her eyebrows a little higher, then winked at him. "Well, just remember that you're not the only one around here with game."

Felix grinned and he slung his arm around her shoulders. "Oh, girl, you have no idea . . ."

And with that, he was off and running, talking a hundred words a minute about how great he thought Deah was, how much he loved her, how happy he was that she was going to be part of the Sinclair Family now. And he would have kept right on talking, all night long, if Deah hadn't let out an exasperated sigh, stood on her tiptoes, and kissed him.

She drew back and Felix just stared at her, his face soft and his dark eyes shining with all the feelings he had for her—feelings that were mirrored in Deah's gaze.

"Sorry about that," she said, turning back to me and

Devon. "But most of the time, that's the only way I can get him to shut up."

Devon laughed. "Not a problem. Believe me, we'll take what peace and quiet we can get around here."

Felix gave him a mock glare, but he slipped his arm around Deah's waist. Together, the four of us walked over to the railing and stared out into the night, just enjoying the fact that we'd won the fight that truly mattered.

CHAPTER THIRTY

"When you said that you wanted to finally go out on our first real date tonight, I didn't think you'd want to come *here*," Devon said.

He peered over the side of the Lochness Bridge. It was a week after my fight with Victor, and the bridge looked the same as it always did. No trace of the battle remained on the cobblestones, and the river rushed along like usual down below the span.

I laughed and kissed him. "Just give me a minute, okay? Then we'll go over to the Midway, stuff ourselves with junk food, sit on one of the park benches, and totally make out."

"I'll hold you to that," he murmured.

I grinned back at him. "I know you will."

Devon kissed me again, then walked over to the end of the bridge and climbed into the front of the SUV that we'd driven down the mountain. He shut the door, giving me the privacy he knew I needed.

I turned back toward the bridge. I dug three quarters out of my shorts pocket and laid the coins on the center stone to pay the toll like usual.

"You've done so much for me this summer," I said, hoping that the lochness was lurking in the water below and that the creature would hear and understand me. "I need you to do one more thing for me, if you will, please. It's the same thing you did for my mom, once upon a time."

I bent down and hefted several duffel bags onto the ledge, one after another, until they were all lined up in a row. A series of *clank-clanks* rang out as the swords, daggers, and other weapons shifted around inside the bags. Over the past few days, Devon and I had collected every single magic-filled black blade that I'd hidden in the library basement, as well as the few that the Draconi guards still had.

And now, I was going to get rid of them—every single one.

By now, everyone in all the Families knew about the black blades and what Victor had wanted to do with the weapons. There were simply too many of them, and they contained too much magic to store them at the Sinclair mansion. They would just make us a target all over again and I was sick of being in the line of fire. So this was the solution I'd come up with, and Claudia and the others had agreed. Besides, monsters had died to fill these blades with magic, so it felt right giving them back to the lochness.

"I want you to watch over these for me," I said. "This is the best, safest place I know, and I know that you won't let anyone steal them away from you. Will you do this for me? Please?"

A long, black tentacle rose up from the surface of the water and waved at me, as if telling me to go ahead. So one by one, I shoved the duffel bags off the ledge and into the river. They hit the surface with loud splashes and quickly sank below the waterline.

I stood there for the better part of three minutes, making sure the bags didn't surface. Once I was sure they were all gone, I turned to leave. The tentacle was on the bridge in front of me just the way it had been before when we'd been hiding under the bridge the night of the restaurant fight.

The tentacle reached out, and I carefully ran my fingers over the cool, wet, velvety surface of the lochness's skin. With my new, enhanced senses, I almost thought I could hear the creature sigh with pleasure down in the river below; then the tentacle moved away from me. It stopped long enough to scoop up my three quarters from the center stone, then slowly moved over the side of the bridge and sank back down into the water below.

I leaned over the ledge and waved at the creature a final time. Then I glanced back over my shoulder, looking in the direction of the apartment that I had shared with my mom four summers ago. This was the spot where it had all started that fateful day and it seemed fitting that this was where it was ending.

But it wasn't ending. Not really.

Because there were still dangers in Cloudburst Falls. Still mortals, magicks, and plenty of monsters, and I knew I would be in the thick of things, along with Devon, Felix, Deah, Oscar, and the rest of my friends. And that thought made me happier than anything had in a long, long time.

So I stuck my hands in the pockets of my cargo shorts and walked away whistling, knowing I'd done everything I'd set out to do.

Nothing that I hadn't done before.